I0662456

Many Sounds of Silence

The Seattle Sound Series
Book 4

Alexa Padgett

Many Sounds of Silence © 2016 by Alexa Padgett

Edited by Bev Katz Rosenbaum and Nicole Pomeroy
Cover Art by Sarah Hansen of Okay Creations

ISBN: 978-1-945090-13-4

For Madeleine

CHAPTER ONE
Clay

This was one of the last times I'd stand in this spot, ever.

Glancing around campus, inhaling the sharp tang of a late September morning, I reveled in it—that crackle of energy that always accompanied the first day of school. I'd looked forward to day one every year since kindergarten, when I finally got to join my brother at "big school." For the first time, nostalgia warred with excitement.

In nine months, I'd have my degrees in music theory and finance. I wasn't going to be caught, as my father had been, without an understanding of the business side of the music industry. That's what really mattered—more than talent or stage presence.

With my contacts in the music scene, Kai, Dane, and I were sitting in a mighty prime spot. Just where we wanted. Because next year, we were…My thoughts skidded to a halt. Why was that guy taking pictures?

We hadn't blown up big enough to warrant paps on campus. I quickly realized his camera wasn't pointed at me, but at the long, dark-red hair bobbing away from me. Yep, the photographer was snapping shots of that girl.

I tracked her as she walked across the Quad, near the fountain. Her hair glowed in the sunlight, whipping out behind her before sweeping forward across her face. She brushed it back with an absent-minded hand as she cast a furtive glance back at the photographer. She knew he was there, and if the tiny frown was any indication, she wasn't happy about his invasion of her privacy.

I totally got that.

She wore gray Toms and jeans, cuffs rolled up to show off a hint of slender calves and slim ankles. Her top was also gray, elbow-length. A kind of don't-notice-me outfit that blended into the crowd.

Except she didn't blend. Part of it was the way she held herself—tight, tense, waiting for the next blow. I knew that stance, because it was the one my mother held since she sat my brother Colten and I down to tell us our baby sister, Cassidy, had cancer.

The photographer was *still* taking pictures of her. Maybe she was a model or actress. I moved forward, trying to catch another glimpse of her face as a niggling feeling of recognition built. Her messenger bag's strap cut between her breasts, emphasizing them. She didn't look at anyone; she moved away from the photographer and toward one of the four buildings that housed classrooms on that side of campus.

Because she was alone, I assumed she was a freshman or a transfer student. Finally, I was close enough to see her profile. She didn't have the wide-eyed wonder of a first-timer, which made the transfer option more likely. I tracked her until a group of girls passed between us.

I blew out a breath, trying to push aside my annoyance and need. Annoyance *because of* the need.

I wanted to know her, tell her I understood her frustration. But that wasn't the worst of my ridiculousness. Already, I dreamed about the breathy way she'd say my name when I gripped her chin, tilted her lips up to meet mine.

A man stopped in front of her, and she stepped back when he touched her arm. Her body tensed, mirroring my own stiffening muscles. The pap moved in closer, the predator scenting blood.

Oh, fuck no. Before I realized it, I was once again moving across the open area.

I'd already pictured my fist in the guy's face when she brushed passed him. The photographer set aside his camera, clearly frustrated he didn't get a money shot.

A big group of students moved between me and the girl, laughing and joking, glad to be back on campus. If I went after her, the photographer would probably stick around. Craning my neck, I watched her open the door to Bagley Hall. The girl was into chemistry.

I smiled, feeling like a cat who was just given a bowl of cream, especially when the photographer packed up his equipment. Good riddance.

"You're that glad to see me, Clay?"

I glanced down at Bethany, quickly arranging my features. She was our version of Mel from *Flight of the Conchords* except Bethany was shorter, way clingier, and pretty much not someone I wanted to see. Ever. She reminded me of those pixies my little sister used to watch on TV. A bothersome one.

I spun about and started walking toward the Music Building. She fell in next to me. I tried hard not to sigh. And failed.

"What's that about?" she asked.

You. Not getting the hint. "Just tired."

"That's too bad. You should take better care of yourself."

I grunted. She kept trotting next to me.

"I missed you guys. I even stayed on campus, hoping you'd do some shows."

"Nope. We went home for a while. You know, to see family."
Which is what you should've done, too, I thought.

"I took a couple of classes. In fashion design? Oh, and my cousin came to visit. We went to a couple of gigs. Not as good as yours."

She batted her stubby eyelashes at me. Batted. Them.

I shied away. Whatever she was thinking wasn't going happen.

"Glad you got to spend some quality family time. So I have to go. I'm late."

"But it's 8:30. Next classes don't start until nine. We should grab a coffee. Catch up."

She put her small hand on my arm, and I suppressed the urge to shake her off. Bethany's expression collapsed into one of hurt. I gritted my teeth against the good manners so ingrained in me by my mother. There was only one woman I wanted touching me. The one with the beautiful hair and haunted expression.

"Meeting with my advisor."

"Then I'll see you at lunch?" Another hopeful, puppy-dog look.

I hoped not. "Got some stuff to take care of." A blatant lie I hated to give. No way I was eating on campus now. So much for first-day excitement "Bye."

I trotted into the music building and headed toward one of the empty practice rooms. Sure, Northern U wasn't Berklee School of Music, but turning down that spot worked out pretty well, because I was still getting an excellent education with state-of-the-art equipment and the chance to double major in finance. Meeting Dane and Kai that first week of school three years ago solidified the rightness of sticking close to home. My family had just gotten Cassidy's Hodgkin's diagnosis, and there was no way I could move to the East Coast and be so far away from my baby sister. I worried about her enough, and she was just fifteen minutes down the road. In fact,

I would've traded anything—including my band's successes—to make sure Cassidy regained her health.

Here was to hoping. I'd stop by this weekend, pick up one of my guitars, and get the scoop on Cassidy's latest PET scan.

My class didn't start until nine, and I hadn't brought my guitar. I decided to work on scales on one of the grand pianos in the basement of the Music Building, a place Bethany didn't enter. She'd been banned by the dean after she and Dane broke up.

I'd never understood his attraction. She was tiny, perky, more than willing to help out. But there was something about her I just didn't trust. Dane said she was fun in bed, willing to try anything, always open to his ideas. Which was a place I would *never* go. Bethany loved to flash those soulful eyes. Eyes that held sharp interest and dark secrets.

I *hated* secrets and lies. I'd lived with both from my peers and it was the fastest way out of my circle. Much as I wanted to kick Bethany out, I couldn't tell a girl who was barely tall enough to ride a rollercoaster to get out of my space.

I had, though, when she climbed naked into my bed after a party. Telling her to get out had been a no-brainer—but getting her to actually leave the room had been difficult. Still, I hadn't fought her territorial growling too hard, because the rest of the females on campus kept their distance. I liked the ability to walk around again without a mob of groupies following me—that had gotten old within weeks of playing our first gig our freshman year. As had the offers for just about anything sexual I could imagine. Not that I didn't like sex. With the right person, sex was fantastic.

I just wasn't interested in a long-term relationship. Nor was I interested in a one-night stand. Limited my choices.

Maybe I'd taken my celibacy too far, especially if I was panting after one glimpse of that mahogany hair and pert ass. I dropped my bag and shut the door. Setting the alarm on my phone, I sat down and began to play.

I'd worked through all the minor scales and had nearly finished one of my favorite Prokofiev's etudes when I realized who that girl was.

My fingers collapsed onto the keys. "Holy shit."

"I agree that was a really shitty ending."

I turned on the bench. "Kai." I fist bumped him. "Good seeing you, man."

"So what was that about? You were rocking that piece then you got this surprised look on your face and lost your concentration. I've never seen you do that before. Well, I don't see you play the piano often either."

"I saw Abigail Dorsey this morning. By the fountain. She walked into the science building."

My frown deepened. I hadn't liked that dude touching her. That bothered me more than the paparazzi. Kai raised his eyebrow. His arms were crossed and his dark T-shirt rode up his biceps, flashing his tattoos. One was some Celtic design. The one on the other side was Hebrew. He'd told me what they both meant right after he got them our freshman year, but I'd forgotten.

"And we care about some chick because?"

"She's Asher Smith's stepdaughter."

Kai dropped his hands to his sides and his eyes lit up. "Really? Think she can get me an autograph? Maybe a guitar lesson? That guy is amazing."

I shook my head and picked up my phone and bag. "You

don't play the guitar. You play the bass. And as the son of a rocker, I can tell you that's the last thing she's going to want. After you hitting on her, of course. She flattened a guy's ego this morning in under ten seconds."

"Aw, stop being a dick. I could learn to rip the chords, especially if a rock legend was teaching me."

"No, Kai. Don't do that. Actually, don't even talk to her. You'd just ask her for sex and then be mad when she turned you down."

"Didn't you see those pics of her? When she was at some school in Cali. Dude, she likes to party. Maybe Asher Smith brought her back to Seattle to get her to buckle down. He sure has since he met her mom. I'd be pissed if his music wasn't so amazing." Kai shook his head. "Maybe love can help with creativity. 'Cause the Supernaturals are hitting a second wave of awesome I've never seen before."

"Don't count on it."

The familiar flush of heat creeped over my skin at hearing the L-word. People went searching for it like it was the holy grail of youth and perfection. It wasn't. My parents loved each other, and it was hard work for both of them. I was glad they were still together. Most of the time, anyway.

"Asher's just hit his stride, found some creative juice in the tank. I'm surprised Abbi's here. I heard they didn't get along," I said, picking up my pack before turning off the lights, stepping out of the room, and shutting the door.

"Why are we talking about Asher Smith? Didn't he get married?" Dane asked as he strode toward us in the hall. He was shorter than me, thin, with a shaggy mop of blond hair. Both his eyebrows were pierced and he had a tattoo crawling up his neck.

7

Some Manga character I figured he'd hate when he was thirty.

My mom was old-fashioned. With a capital O. She'd made my brother and me promise not to get body art, and because my mom didn't ask for a lot, I was cool with her request.

"Saw your ex already," I said, letting my lip curl with disgust. "She was lying in wait for me. Expected a lunch invite. Because, you know, superfan."

Dane leaned his head back and closed his eyes. "We broke up over three years ago—we were still in our freshman year then. And she's more of a stalker than a superfan."

"Now she's got her sights set on Mr. Banjo-player here," Kai chuckled. "Thanks to Mumford and Sons and The Avett Brothers, the banjo is sexy. The new guitar and all that."

"If that was true, we would have traded you in for a cellist," I said without any heat.

Kai loved to tease me about the banjo, but when we'd started featuring it in our music, our songs—and following—took off. I could play it and the kick drum at the same time, a trick I'd practiced from the time I was seven when my dad let me start playing on his old set down in the basement.

"Bethany can look all she wants," I said. "From a distance. She just can't touch. And I wish she wouldn't talk to me. She's creepy."

"Dude, she's like a third your size," Dane said.

"That's part of the problem. We can't be from the same species."

"She claims to love you," Kai said.

My shoulders tensed and I glared at him. "Love and rock-and-roll don't mix. Like pickles and chocolate—two great tastes that, when put together, turn awful."

Kai snickered while Dane scratched his head, considering.

"Not buying that. Nessa's pretty awesome. Your parents are tight. Why don't you follow that example?"

"Clay thinks he saw Asher Smith's stepdaughter here," Kai said to ease my building tension.

I never spoke to anyone about my dad's affairs because that was the family line, and Kai and Dane assumed the long list of names linked to my father's were to sell more magazines and website clicks. But Kai also knew how sensitive I was about the topic. I shot him a glance of sarcastic thanks.

"I've seen her. She lives across from Ness and Jenna. From what they've seen so far, she seems fairly quiet and serious." Dane shrugged. "Maybe she pulled her shit together. Kinda would have to after those pics went live, right? I mean, she was a mess in those."

"Who cares?" Kai rolled his eyes. "Now's the time to live it up, baby. It's not like Asher's going to ride her about it. He did crazy shit when he was her age. Part of why he's my hero."

"I don't think she's a partier," Dane said. If Nessa told him that, he'd run with it.

This was another reason why I was against long-term relationships. Dane couldn't have his own thoughts anymore.

"I read an article about him—did you see it? Went live last week. He talked about how he was hurt and did lots of stupid stunts because the girl he wanted was with someone else. The girl turned out to be Abbi's mom. They're all settled in, playing family."

"She's hot," I said. "Abigail. Cool name, all old-fashioned. Probably why she's such a partier."

"Invite her to our show next week," Kai said. "Maybe she can talk Asher into coming."

I shook my head again. "If my folks find out she's here, they'll ask me to befriend her."

"Something crawled up your ass. So you have to be nice?" Kai asked. "It'll get you closer to Asher. And to Abigail."

"Nah, man, I don't want to use her like that." Mainly because I didn't want to get too close. My reaction to her—from a distance—had been electrifying. What if I actually met her? I could already see the headlines: Local Rocker Screwing School Party Girl. Both Go Up in Flames.

Nope. Not happening. Famous people couldn't stick it out. Look at Brangelina. If that paradise blew, then I didn't stand a chance at dating some chick with her own famous-people problems and hang-ups.

"It's like you have feelings," Kai mocked.

I shrugged. "I feel just fine. For the right people."

Kai snorted, thinking, no doubt, about my lack of dating the past year and a half.

"Hookups don't count."

"Yeah. All three of 'em last year. What are you up to, man-whore?" I responded with more rancor than any of us expected.

"Did you get Abbi's number?" Dane asked as he pushed between us.

Both Kai and I had some inches on him, but Dane was quick. Plus, he'd studied ten different kinds of martial arts growing up, so he knew all kinds of ways to break me into pieces, fast.

"You did that at least. Right?"

"I didn't get her number because I didn't talk to her. And you guys aren't going to bother her either. She's a hot mess." A beautiful, famous hot mess. "We don't need that shit in our orbit."

I glared at both of them until Dane threw his hands up in the air.

"I'm not dirty macking your girl. Got my own. Chill, dude."

"She's not my girl. Look, we've got to make this semester shine. We've been working hard for that contract. We're not screwing ourselves over because of some chick."

We entered the classroom. Each of us studied various aspects of music, and this was our only course together this year. I missed hanging out with Dane and Kai on campus more often, but I was glad to see the light at the end of this slog. Double majoring was a huge time commitment that kept me busier than either Kai or Dane. I'd gotten better at juggling, but there were still days when I questioned my commitment to so many courses.

"Whatever you say, bucko. But I can tell. You like her," Kai said.

"I don't," I said, scowling.

"Yet," Kai said. He stretched out in his seat, eyes wandering to the few girls already in their seats. Dismissing them, he turned back to me. "I've never seen you wound so tight about a chick before. And you didn't even talk to her."

"Yet." Dane smirked.

"Drop it. Both of you. I don't want to talk about her anymore."

The instructor came in, and I was glad for the interruption. But Kai had made a point, much as I hated to admit it. Something about Abigail had gotten to me. And I didn't like it—not one bit.

CHAPTER TWO
Abbi

"Good class today," Mr. Rippey told us. He smiled, a dimple winking from his left cheek.

A girl next to me sighed. Really? He was our *teacher*.

"Don't you think he's super hot?" she tittered. "I mean, he's so young and cute. I totally would become a scientist if most of the men looked like him."

I looked back at our TA. He was tall, fit, in his mid-twenties. He had twinkling dark eyes and curly dark hair. I shrugged, agreeing he was attractive in a rumpled professorial kind of way. He caught my eye and dipped his head in acknowledgment. I looked away, so not interested.

"I'm looking forward to those reports on Wednesday. Great first week of class. Enjoy your weekend."

I watched, disconnected from the commotion, as the students around me, laughing and talking, packed up their bags. Many were making plans for their weekends.

I wasn't. Never did.

Seth texted me last week to let me know he wasn't going to be on campus this year because he'd decide to extend his study abroad program in order to be closer to his Italian girlfriend, Ramona.

Seth was the son of one of Asher's band mates. We'd met nearly two years ago at a Supernatural's concert. He was funny and, more important, used to the less savory side of fame. He understood, to some degree, what it was like to be photographed and written about because of our parents' accomplishments.

I'd missed him last year while I was in Tech, and the lure of seeing Seth a few times a week was one of the reasons I'd enrolled at Northern. He'd promised to show me all his favorite spots on campus, and not seeing him was a blow—a big one.

At least I had Aunt Bri's standing Tuesday and Thursday lunch dates. I rolled my eyes. Yeah, I was really knocking it out of the park with this college lifestyle—my entire social life revolved around my classes and lunch dates with my aunt.

Part of the reason I shied away from making new connections was the paparazzi hung around like dirty gym socks. That, and some of the guys had propositioned me this past week, but after a few choice words, my fellow students left me alone. Mostly. The more persistent ones were a problem, but nowhere near the problem I'd had at Marin Tech. Its veterinary school was top-three in the nation, and there was no way I was going to turn down such an offer.

If only I had.

Much as I wanted to forget everything about my short year at what had been my dream school, I couldn't. The scandal followed me.

Coming home proved hard. Thanks to my stupidity, staying in northern California hadn't been a viable option, not with Steve there stirring the pot, just waiting to do something else that would shame me and get his name in the papers and all over social media. Double win for him, but definitely not for me.

I hated that gossip magazines and websites called him my ex-boyfriend. We hadn't dated long. Just a handful of times back in February and March. Still, he'd licked up the mentions, making a point of responding to each claim. Keeping his name, and

13

his band's name, in the news.

Asshole.

In just another couple of weeks, I'd lay the hell of last year to rest for good. I swallowed hard. Okay, so that was the best-case scenario, and I might not ever get beyond that night at Tech. At least I wouldn't have to live with the uncertainty much longer, and knowing was its own kind of closure. I hoped. I needed... something. Because I wasn't brave anymore. Hell, I couldn't look most people in the eye without psyching myself up for it.

I hadn't been willing to try another out-of-state school. My high school friends mostly stayed in Idaho; some moved to eastern Washington or Wyoming and were just starting their first year of college. I'd dismissed attending one of their schools before I finished my senior year. They'd begun to treat me differently once my mom started dating Asher, and I'd had to bail on most of the high school activities. Each time I explained I had to go to Seattle so my mom could help with her HBO miniseries, they said I was bragging. If I mentioned Mom and I were heading to San Fran for one of the Supernaturals' shows, I was trying to make my high school friends jealous.

So I quit hanging out with them long before we moved to Seattle, unable to endure the stilted envy that cropped up the summer between my junior and senior year. Losing my best friend Sally during that time was hard but probably for the best. When she quit talking to me, I'd agreed to transfer to a Seattle-area school for my senior year, which was really just a semester. Sally never bothered to say goodbye in those hectic weeks before we moved. In fact, the only person I saw before I left was Luke, my ex-boyfriend, who wanted to get back together...only because my mom was shacking up with a famous rock star. Um, his request met with a big fat *no way.*

Those last summer days in Rathdrum, bad as they felt, were so much better than the outright lies and vitriol Steve and his friends spewed.

"Hey, Abbi, want to grab a drink?" Jeff asked. He was a year or two older than me—as most of the students were. Even though I was classified as a sophomore, I was still eighteen, making me the youngest student in the program. He stood over six feet of mostly arms and knees. His glasses were always smudged. How could he see through the lenses?

He was probably nice, but I wasn't taking any chances.

"Sorry, can't," I said, keeping my face neutral. "You have fun."

"What about studying on Sunday?" he asked, voice rising in desperation.

"Busy with my family."

I didn't flash the smile that used to come so easily because that only encouraged attention. I settled for a small wave before I pulled on my messenger bag and trotted out of class.

I headed down the wide walkway, considering my options. I should go to the library. I needed to get a jumpstart on the biochem assignment Mr. Rippey just gave us. I wasn't confident I'd understood the material well enough, and because of Jeff's clinginess, I didn't stick around long enough to see if the other students were setting up study groups.

As usual, I crossed campus alone. The only time I didn't was when my aunt Briar was with me. I'd be embarrassed by my lack of friends if I wasn't thankful no one knew me well enough to hurt me. Again.

No matter how far my situation deteriorated, I couldn't blame my difficulties on Asher. He was awesome, and I was really lucky to have such a thoughtful father figure in my life. I just wished I could tease out the people who actually liked *me* from those who wanted something from me. Asher said it got easier. While I believed him, I was too busy trying to protect myself to suss out people's reasons for showing interest in me.

Being wanted, liked…that used to be easy. Until Sally refused to speak to me again. But now, a year later, she'd started texting me. Asking to meet up. To talk.

I'd considered doing so because I was lonely. But that made me an even bigger loser, and I just couldn't face Sally, letting her see what her defection had done to me.

Time to forget those golden days and focus on important details: enzymes and nucleic acids. Woo hoo. Exciting Friday night plans.

CHAPTER THREE
Clay

Footsteps pounded down the stairs. I braced myself at the bottom, legs spread and arms open. Cassidy hurled herself into my arms as she'd done every time I came home. She seemed even lighter than she had the last time I'd held her in my arms two weeks ago.

I rubbed her back, counting each of her vertebrae on the way down. I hated the physical manifestation of her illness. I squeezed my eyes shut, heart aching, as I held my baby sister for a long moment.

"Missed you, ladybug."

She wiggled free from my arms and set her fists on her little hips. "I told you not to call me that anymore. I'm fourteen. Do you want to embarrass me in front of my friends?"

"Course not, Cassidy. Just, you know, it's hard for big brothers to remember you're growing up." Sort of. I was beyond thankful she was home for her fifteenth birthday next week. Four years ago, Cassidy was healthy and even bubblier than she was now.

"How are you feeling?" I asked.

"You sound like Mom. All she did after our appointment yesterday was cry." Cassidy rolled her eyes.

Like me, Cassidy had inherited our mom's green eyes. But Cassidy's were darker than mine, more uniform in color, and looked way too large for her thin face. The second round of chemotherapy had been so hard on her, but her hair was finally growing back and she looked cute with the dark fluff swirling around her head. I was still trying to get used to the color—Cassidy used to have dirty-blond hair.

I opened my mouth, but the words wouldn't come. Clearing my throat, I tried again. "So that means the doctors were wrong and you're not in remission?"

Cassidy frowned at me. "It means I'm not dead yet, and I'd really like it if someone would remember that I have a life to live."

I swallowed down my follow-up question, knowing it would irritate her more. As soon as possible, I'd ask about the appointment. Right now, Cassidy needed normalcy.

"That you do, Cassie. How about we hit the pool?"

"Now you're talking! Be right back." Cassidy ran up the stairs.

Sometimes, like now, she seemed so unaffected by her illness, it was hard to remember just how touch-and-go her prognosis had been.

"Hey, honey," Mom said, sliding an arm around my waist.

"Cassidy said you cried after her appointment yesterday. Everything okay?"

Mom's eyes, so like Cassie's, filled with tears again. She'd aged a lot these past few years as Cassidy sank deeper into the disease. I bit the inside of my cheek, hating the secret I'd kept from her. Seeing her now, vulnerable, I knew I'd made the right decision. For her.

I hugged her tighter, wishing these past few years were different.

"The PET scan was clean."

"That's great." I grinned. Damn, that was the best news I'd heard in ages. "Excellent. So why the tears?"

Mom cleared her throat. "It's just…we didn't expect her to make it during the last round. I'm so happy."

I wrapped my arms around her again and let her cry. After a

moment, she patted my chest. "You're a good man, Clay. Thanks. I needed that. Your dad's trying, but…" She sighed, looking away. "Nearly losing Cassie changed him."

More than my mom knew. The anger swelled again. We'd all been to counseling while Cassie was sick, and Dr. Thomas suggested I talk to my dad about the situation. I'd been too hurt, then too angry to broach the subject.

With Mom and Dad stable and Cassie improving, it seemed like the wrong time to bring up Dad's affair. Correction. His last affair that I knew about. I didn't want to shatter my mom's happiness. She, like Cassie, deserved the best of everything. I bent and kissed her cheek.

"Anything for the prettiest lady I know."

Mom chuckled as she wiped away her tears. "You are such a flirt. Just like your father."

"Nah." Horror and frustration built in my throat, clinging there. If I didn't keep my feelings buried, my mom would notice. I looked away, pretending to be searching for Dad. "Where is he, by the way?"

"In the hot tub with Colten."

"Let's head that way, then."

"You go. I'm still too weepy to be much fun. I'll join you in a bit."

I gave her a final squeeze before heading out to the pool. It was indoors, taking up what would've been the basement if we'd had one. Seattle was really too cold for an outdoor pool most of the year, but Mom had insisted we put one in when Colten and I were young. We'd had too much energy for her to run off.

Once Dad finally figured out how to get and keep the money

he'd earned from his record label, he'd hired the workers as a gift to Mom, and the natatorium turned out to be the most-used room in the house.

My brother and Dad were there, leaning back and enjoying the hot bubbles.

"Clay. Glad you could come."

Dad smiled at me. I'd searched his eyes and smile for months to see if he looked different, acted differently. He didn't, and that led me to wonder how many times he'd cheated on my mom over the years. Had our pool been a gift to assuage his guilt?

I cleared my throat, forcing the word *asshole* back down.

"Sorry I'm late. Slept in. Cassidy told me the good news. I'm sure you're relieved."

A shadow crossed Dad's face. "Yeah, now Cassidy can enjoy being a girl again."

There was more to that statement, but I didn't push it. I wasn't sure I could handle another one of his secrets.

CHAPTER FOUR
Abbi

I shoved through the library doors, fumbling to turn down my iPod. I pulled the earbuds from my ears and headed up the stairs to the top floor. Few people liked to hike that far with all their books and the area was always deserted. Just the way I liked it.

I stopped at the top. A couple of guys—fraternity brothers, I guessed from their expensive jeans, tatty T-shirts, backward ball caps, and flip flops—lounged in the space. These guys used to be part of my scene. I was still officially a member of a sorority even though I hadn't heard from any of the girls since I left Tech nearly three months ago. I'd been told by the senior in charge of the group that I'd embarrassed the chapter. I'd barely managed to stifle my hysterical giggles.

So much for thinking I'd find new friends at Tech.

One of the guys smiled at me, all predatory. I turned back down the steps, taking them as quickly as I could.

"What's the hurry, sweetheart?" he asked.

"Just want to do some studying," I replied. I should've gone to my dorm. I had a single this year, so I could usually drown out the other girls' hallway conversations with my earbuds.

"Well, you can come right back up here and study my lips," the second guy said with a snicker.

"No, thanks. Not interested."

"You should be," the first guy said. "Neal can get you into all the great parties on campus."

I tried to ease around them, only to get caged between their looming bodies. My heart pounded against my ribs.

"I don't party. I'm sure you can find someone else who does, and who's grateful for the invite."

I gave Neal a pointed back-the-hell-off stare. He pressed in closer, too close. My heartbeat kicked up even faster.

"Pretty girl like you, you'd be the life of any party. Like you were last spring."

Neal grinned, so close his chest brushed mine. Even as I tried to ease back, the other guy pressed up tight against my back. Tears bit into the back of my nose. I slid down a step then another, but Neal was there again, catching my forearm and pulling me against his chest. No one else was up here, and I struggled in earnest now, fear taking over.

"Let me go," I cried.

"We aren't finished getting acquainted, sweetheart. I need a kiss to see if you're ready for my party tonight. Everyone knows you gave those away to the dicks at Tech."

He snickered, proud of his double entendre, and my face flamed. So much for thinking I was doing well, blending in. That the story had passed.

I opened my mouth to scream, but before I could, a big hand shoved Neal back. "She said back off."

I turned to see a third guy, taller than the other two. He had light green eyes and dark, wavy hair. His shoulders were broad and his biceps thick, just like my high school boyfriend, Luke. Instinctively, I edged closer to the new guy who used his body to nudge me out of Neal's grasp.

"Aw, c'mon. We were just having a little fun."

"She didn't seem to be enjoying it."

He glanced at me, his gaze cataloging each of my features

before checking out my arms and legs. My face warmed under his scrutiny, but it was a pleasant warmth, not the icky crawly feeling I normally got when guys looked at me now.

"You okay? They hurt you?"

I shook my head, still staring into his eyes. They were so unique. The outside was pale, almost celadon, but they darkened to a deep emerald. I'd never seen eyes like his.

"Get out of here. You guys better not make a habit of this. Because I will report you."

"Fuck off, Clay," Neal said. "Everyone knows she's a cock tease." But he turned to stomp back up the stairs. His friend followed behind.

I shivered, hugging my arms tighter to my chest.

"They really scared you," Clay said, his brow pulling down into creases of concern.

He had no idea, and it wasn't like I was going to tell him. That was even worse than the press I'd already lived through. He lifted his hand like he was going to touch me. When I flinched, he dropped his hand. Something shifted in his expression; he made some kind of decision, ending it with a subtle nod.

"Would you be willing to come with me? Just down this flight of stairs? You look like you need to sit down."

I nodded, thankful he hadn't touched me again. I wasn't sure I could cope with more manhandling. I knew I was overreacting, but I couldn't control my response. Just like I couldn't stand being touched by strangers since I woke up in Steve's bedroom last May.

Something about the way Neal looked at me, touched me, made me think he wouldn't have stopped. No matter what I said or did.

All because of those pictures. They were going to follow me, maybe forever. And thanks to those photos, no male in his right mind considered me relationship material.

I missed a step, and Clay cupped my elbow. His touch was light, careful, my undoing. My chin trembled and I swallowed hard, then again, trying to force the tears down.

For the first time in weeks, I wanted someone other than my family to touch me. He led me to a couch where a bunch of books was strewn about. He shoved a couple to the side and indicated I should sit. I slid my messenger bag off my shoulder and collapsed on the cushion, my head falling into my hands.

"I'm sorry," I gasped, embarrassment adding to my breathlessness. "I don't know why I'm this much of a mess."

"I'd cry if Neal touched me," Clay said. "And you're not doing that so it's a win."

He sat next to me, close enough for our thighs to touch. His nearness was comforting. In fact, I wanted to lean against him, have him put his arm around me, burrow into his warmth and smell.

That was an old Abbi reaction. I'd lost so much of me over these past few months. I wasn't sure I liked what was left.

His hand touched the back of my head, a subtle caress of my hair. I sighed and gave into the urge, letting my head fall against his shoulder. He stiffened, just for a moment, and I started to pull back. But he wrapped his arm around me, so I stayed tucked against him, soaking up his warmth, reveling in the feel of his shoulder under my head. A small shudder slid through me.

"I'll go back up there and punch Neal if it would make you feel better."

His voice was deep, sexy. I liked it almost as much as his eyes. I shook my head as I scrubbed my hand over my cold cheeks, wiping away the last remnants of this latest humiliation.

"No, don't do that. I don't want you to get in trouble. Especially because of me."

"Maybe it's for me. Neal's a douche."

I sat up and he let his hand drop from my arm.

"Thank you. For saving me. And for the, erm, hug."

Awkward. Why had I brought up our touching? Now he'd think I wanted to go further. Or that I was the tease Neal proclaimed me to be.

He smiled, making his eyes crinkle a little. Wow. That did things to my insides—happy things. I'd almost forgotten what those were. Didn't matter, though. There was no way I was acting on any of those feelings. I gripped my bag, legs tensing under me as I prepared to bolt.

"You're welcome. I'm Clay by the way."

"Abbi." I cleared my throat. "So, um, yeah, thanks. I should go. I'm interrupting your study time."

He touched my hand in a quick gesture. "Don't. Go, I mean. I've seen you around campus. You're in one of my brother's classes. He asked me to keep an eye on you."

My muscles stiffened further. "Oh?" I tried to keep my voice neutral, but I failed. I was close to tears again but for a totally different reason. I didn't want him to be like the other guys I'd met in the past few months.

"Not like that. He and I know what it's like to be noticed. He said you're always alone. Not smart for a woman."

He left off the *like you*. But we both knew it should be there.

Like I hadn't heard that and worse.

"Nice meeting you, Clay. See you around."

I started to push off the couch, pausing only when Clay touched my hand again. I looked at his hand engulfing mine. Raising my eyes slowly, I met his gaze. The interest was there—frank and sexual. I hated that look. So much. Like every male had a right to peel off my clothes because someone took pictures of me without my permission.

I blew out a breath and stood. "Look, don't take this the wrong way. You were super nice to save me, and I really, really appreciate it. But I don't want to flirt or go out or whatever."

"Okay."

He drew the word out, studying me. Well, I wasn't that easy to gauge, to pigeonhole.

"We'll study."

"Clay, you seem like a really nice guy."

"Because I am."

"But I had a terrible experience last year, and I don't want to get involved with anyone. I'm here to get my degree and get out."

My hands shook but the worst part was the lightheadedness, like I'd disconnected from reality. Those pictures. Bile rose, thick, into the back of my throat as I thought of Clay clicking on the images, sliding from one to the next. Seeing my flesh, thinking I wanted those men touching me.

I tried to steady my breath so I could leave. I wouldn't be able to walk if I didn't get my act together.

"Sit down, Abbi. You're all pale and wobbly."

For some reason, I sat, then leaned back into the couch, closing my eyes. I was tired. Sleep didn't come easily like it used to, back before my mom and Asher got serious.

"What *really* happened to you?"

The way he asked, I wanted to tell him. It was like he'd known me before, like he looked deep enough into me now to see the bits of me that were left.

How could he? We'd only just met, and I was already in his debt for saving me from the frat boys upstairs.

As much as I didn't want to blow apart this fragile new relationship, I'd learned that honesty wasn't just the best policy, it was the only policy I could live with. So I took a deep breath and turned my head, meeting his eyes.

"My stepdad is Asher Smith, lead singer for the Supernaturals. People get a little jealous of me because of that."

"Knew that. About who you were, I mean."

My mouth dropped open in shock. "And you want...what? Tickets to their next show?"

Clay smiled, his eyes dancing. "While that would be amazing, no. I told you, my brother asked me to keep an eye on you. He was worried about you being alone."

I blinked at him, unsure how to proceed. His hand hovered at the back of my head. When he took in my tensed features, he let it drop back with just a flash of disappointment.

"My dad's in a band, too," he said. Color tinted his cheeks.

Oh, wow.

"Really? Anyone I'd know? Does it bother you? The constant scrutiny?" I leaned forward. Now that I knew a little more about him, I craved answers.

"Pete Rippey."

I sat back, shocked. He did get it.

"Your dad's an awesome musician. Asher speaks highly of him."

Clay shrugged. "I like to think so. He can't improvise worth crap, though. Even after all these years."

That made me giggle. Any musician with that kind of experience could play the hell out of any piece of music, and we both knew it. Clay grinned back.

"You have a pretty laugh. Your whole face brightens. Bet you don't do it enough."

"Not so much now, no. I used to be a lot more open. I liked to have fun. But—" I shrugged, tired of being alone. Clay would understand this. "Some of Asher's limelight spilled onto me, especially after he asked my mom to marry him. I wasn't ready to handle the pressure."

I wasn't ready to handle the Steves of the world. Wasn't aware of the ways people could—and would—take advantage of me like that.

Clay absorbed my answer, and I knew he was thinking about the pictures. No, I wanted to tell him. I never did anything that crazy. Not on purpose, anyway. But I couldn't. Because the pictures showed I had.

"So you resent him for that?"

"No! I could never resent Asher. He's great. I mean, really great. I'd missed having a father around." I blew out a breath. "My dad died when I was twelve."

"What did he do?"

"He was a musician, too."

"Oh? Someone I'd know?"

I shrugged. "Doubt it. That's why my dad was bitter. He craved fame, but he couldn't play anymore by the time I was nine. He hated my mom's success—she's a writer. Anyway, after all that, having Asher in my life…it's the best. He always makes time for me, even when I know he's super busy. Which is pretty much always since their last two albums hit so big."

"My dad's like that, too."

Clay flashed a smile but it was strained. What had I said?

"My mom would kick his ass if he put his music first."

His brows furled, forming a thin line above his nose. He cleared his throat, eyes refocusing on me. I studied him for a moment. He had his own scars. A kid couldn't grow up with such a famous parent without a few.

"I really wouldn't know. My dad toured with his local band when I was young. He had to give up music, and he was pretty angry. He jumped out of a plane when I was twelve. It took both my mom and me a long time to forgive him for that."

Horror gushed through my chest as I realized what I'd said. My mom was going to be upset to see that story run again. I glanced down at my hands, now bunched tightly in my lap.

He reached up, brushing my hair from my cheek. "Don't worry, Abbi. I won't share your secrets with the world. Promise. It's part of the famous-kid code."

I laughed again, but it wasn't the easy one that used to come so naturally. I shook my head, needing to break the seriousness of the moment.

"I don't even know you, Clay."

I searched his face again, a strange feeling blooming deep in my chest. One I hadn't felt in a long time.

Hope.

CHAPTER FIVE
Clay

Her eyes were so blue. I'd never seen that shade of blue before—almost purple. They were shuttered, though.

One of the reasons the media started following Abbi Dorsey was because of her looks. Not many young women had the striking features she had. I studied her for a moment. No, striking was the wrong word. I'd read a series of works two years ago on beauty for a philosophy class I'd had to take. One of the authors suggested symmetry was necessary for true beauty.

Abbi's face was symmetrical, but it was also dramatic. Her nose was thin and well-proportioned between her sweeping cheekbones. Her browbone was smooth and rounded into her arched eyebrows. Her eyes were fringed in deep-brown lashes that darkened toward the long tips. But it was her mouth that I kept coming back to: her lower lip was plump, but the upper one was downright lush. I wanted to run my tongue over the seam, feel that first hot puff of breath as she opened for me.

People would always want to know more about such a beautiful face, especially once people found out she was related to one of the most famous musicians of our age. While the Supernaturals had been indie royalty for years, their last two albums—released just after Abbi had become part of Asher's sphere—catapulted the band into the stratosphere of elite international superstardom. Abbi had been pulled along for the ride, an interesting side note to her famous stepdad's new romance.

The first article I read about her, just after she'd moved to Seattle, talked about her volunteer work for a local animal shelter and how the board wanted her to do a series of ad campaigns to increase exposure for their nonprofit. Actually, the piece had been one of the board members whining that she wouldn't give more time and her face to the campaign.

She'd turned down the offer and what I had to guess were others since. There had to be. Abbi was more beautiful now, a year and a half after she was first photographed with Asher and her mother as a fresh-faced seventeen-year-old.

And thanks, in part, to that high level of scrutiny, she doled out tiny pieces of herself, each one only slightly greater than the last. The build was infinitesimal. Anything more would leave her open to attack.

The way she hesitated before she spoke told me someone had hurt her, deeply.

Not just her father, though his death was probably the start of her emotional upheaval. I got that, all of it. Being Pete Rippey's kid wasn't easy—journalists believed they had the right to take pictures and write stories about everything from the last book I purchased to the girl I took out to dinner.

All the scrutiny on my life meant I didn't get to do casual dating. Guarding my emotions came naturally now, something Abbi was still learning after just a couple of years in the limelight.

I cleared my throat, needing to focus on something besides her too-sad eyes. The world believed she was a party girl, but I'd gone back to study the pictures. Seen the glassy tint in her eyes. Like she was drunk. Or worse, drugged. Happened way more often than the college administrators thought, way more often than I wanted to think about.

And Abbi…she was one of those women men wanted to

brag about bagging. Being in those pictures was more about the guys than her, really, even though she'd been the one to suffer from them.

Which left me caught between wanting to run away as far and fast as I could from this lovely young woman, and sticking close to her side so no one hurt her again, ever. If only she weren't famous…

If she weren't, she wouldn't be scarred. That was certain.

She'd inched away from me again, clutching her messenger bag. Right. While I was thinking, I'd been staring, making her even more uncomfortable. "So. Studying. What did you come up here to do?"

"Biochem. I don't really understand the molecular formulae."

"My brother's the science brain of the family. I'm just reviewing some finance."

She blushed, her cheeks glowing a pretty shade of pink. "I'm still finishing my prereqs so I can get into veterinary school."

Not what I'd expected her to say. "Northern U doesn't have a pre-vet undergraduate degree. So why'd you transfer here?"

She slipped back into her shell, her eyes darkening and her cheekbones standing out more prominently. She was thinking about the pictures. I'd bet money on it.

The worst was the nearly nude one, where she was turned on her side, her face partially obscured by her hair surrounded by at least three men. That was the one every site and paper ran. But there were others of her barely dressed, unsteady, hair a tangled, matted mess, mascara dripping down her cheeks, walking out of a fraternity in the early hours of the morning, presumably the aftermath of that salacious pic.

No wonder concern poured in about the negative influence Asher had on his new stepdaughter. Anyone who knew anything about Abbi knew that wasn't who she was. And if she'd never been that party-hard girl, the attack she'd suffered would be even more devastating.

"I wanted to be closer to my mom and Asher. And Mason. Asher's son. He's totally rocking the double-digits."

She smiled, a fleeting but real one. So she loved her stepbrother. Good to know. She cleared her throat, her eyes drifting past mine.

"And my aunt got engaged. She asked me to help with the wedding plans."

"Sounds cool. Are you in the wedding?" I asked, still trying to puzzle through the growing mystery that was Abigail Dorsey. No wonder my brother asked me to look out for her. I'd been pissed when he'd asked, but after what I'd seen today, maybe...

"Yep," she smiled, eyes back to mine. "Mom, me and my other aunt. That's it."

"So when's the wedding?"

"January first. New Year, new life."

"So you needed to be close by to help out," I said, but something didn't feel right. On a hunch, I said, "Your aunt? Is she into music?"

Abbi wrinkled her nose. Dammit, I didn't want to find that so cute.

"No. She's going back to school to get a counseling degree to set up a program for cancer families. We have a set lunch date whenever she's on campus. This semester it's Tuesdays and Thursdays."

The music scene, like any other, was a small group when you

were enmeshed in it. They didn't have the same last name, but I knew the story. "Your aunt's marrying Hayden Crewe."

She nodded, her lips turning down at the corners.

"You don't like him?" I'd never met Hayden, but my dad said he was a good guy. Smart, stupid-talented on the piano. Difficult to get to know. Huh, that last part was kind of like Abbi.

"Hayden's wonderful," she enthused. "He taught me how to surf. That was so much fun."

That effervescence fit her—the natural skin she should be wearing. Not the cautious, guarded woman who I'd met first.

Abbi had had her share of disappointments, and I wanted to scoop her up, hold her tight against my chest until her pain passed. Which was stupid. Me even liking her was stupid. She was famous. No, infamous, notorious. Not the kind of press I wanted, mainly because I only wanted press about how awesome our music was.

"We'd hit the beach at sunrise just as the tide was turning," she said, smiling at the memory.

Abbi in a wetsuit. Hell, that lit me up fast. I shifted, trying to get more comfortable.

"But?"

"When we were surfing, there were, like, ten photographers snapping pictures of me falling off the board. Hayden, my aunt Briar, even Mom and Asher, are so calm about all the interest; just go about their lives like it's no big deal."

I grabbed her hand, unsurprised to find it shaking. The intensity of my desire when I'd pictured her in a wet, tight outfit fizzled. Sort of.

We sat there, thigh to thigh, my hand on top of hers. She

cleared her throat and extricated her hand.

"Is your major finance?"

"I'm also studying composition."

She slid back behind that shell she'd built around herself. Dammit, I already knew I didn't like that protective mechanism. It meant she had a reason to feel she needed it.

"English?" she asked, her voice hopeful.

"Music," I said, bracing myself for her interest.

The word deflated her, and we sat there, me in shock as her face froze. Fear filled her eyes followed by a slick blankness that had to have been practiced.

"I need to go," she said, picking up her bag.

I laid my hand on her thigh just above her knee. Her muscle clenched. Not an outright rejection but an instinctual need to run. I wasn't going to hurt her—hell, I'd just saved her from Charles and Neal.

Her eyes fell to my hand and her muscles tightened further, bright red flashing high on her cheeks. Her breath shattered. Mine followed suit as the thought flashed, hard and hot, through my mind.

The last man to touch her hurt her. Badly.

"I want to be your friend. Let me do that," I said, my voice low, like I was talking to the injured dog I'd picked up in front of our neighborhood when I was thirteen. Slurpy, Cassidy had named him, because of his penchant to lick. He was the best dog we'd ever had.

Finally, after countless painful heartbeats, Abbi raised those big blue eyes to mine. The pain in them rocked me back. The way she'd reacted to the frat guys, the way she held herself. Aw, fuck.

She looked like Slurpy had that first day, but his cuts and bruises were on the outside. Easier to repair and recover from.

"I can't," she choked out. "I just…Bye."

She stood, putting her messenger bag over her shoulder with trembling hands. But she walked with quick strides toward the exit. That walk, back straight, chin up, was so at odds with the woman she was now.

At the last moment, she stopped and looked back. Her face was in shadow but even from where I sat, I could feel her longing.

Her eyes, when she'd looked back, hadn't shuttered fast enough. The glimpse into her kept my butt on the couch. She turned away, hand gripping the banister as she sped down the stairs. I leaned forward, hands clasped between my knees and watched her disappear.

CHAPTER SIX
Abbi

I made it out of the building before the shaking overtook my ability to walk. I stumbled to the wall and leaned against it, gulping in air. My legs trembled harder than they did after I ran ten miles.

I tipped my face up to the late twilight, waiting for my heart to slow.

I didn't know what that was. When Clay touched me, I'd lit up faster than a sparkler. The need to get closer to him hadn't dissipated even now. My whole body ached for his touch, his smell, his warmth.

My reaction was beyond intense—like I'd cut off a piece of myself when I walked away. An important piece that would never regrow.

In the twenty minutes I'd talked to Clay Rippey, I'd been more at ease than I'd been with anyone in the past year. Even scarier was how hyperaware I was of his every movement.

I'd let him touch me. More, I'd craved the warmth from his hand seeping through my jeans to my skin. Like the addict I'd been accused of being, I already wanted another hit of Clay. My body urged me to run back up the steps and into his arms, screw the consequences. And there would be many.

Steve, for one. He'd release more pictures, stir up the gossip, something to get even with me for starting a new relationship that didn't include him.

I exhaled in sharp, painful bursts. Music composition. *Gawd.* I wanted to slam my head back against the bricks but I managed to refrain. How stupid was I going to be?

Clay was part of the very scene I *had* to escape. Steve had proven my inability to fit into his beautiful-and-famous-people world. I didn't understand the rules and I didn't know how to protect myself from the viciousness of the trolls who'd been more than happy to share those pictures. I was young, attractive, and for that—for just being—people hated me. Without even knowing me.

I'd lost so much of myself in such a short time. Much as I loved my family, I couldn't share what Mom's relationship had done to my life. Not when Asher was so kind and my mom was finally happy.

Mom and Asher fit. They didn't let the rest of the world affect their bubble. I wish I had that ability, but I didn't. Each critical word written about me hurt, a deep cut that wouldn't heal properly. I hadn't developed a thick enough skin to let the comments roll off. I wasn't sure I ever would.

I pushed off the wall. Grabbing my sunglasses from the pocket of my jacket, I shoved them up on my nose. They made my surroundings too dark, but I need the barrier from the rest of the world.

All I did these days was build barriers.

Walking toward my car, I firmed my resolve. I was here to learn, to reach my dream and become the best vet I could be. No guy, no drama, and no tabloid would take that from me.

"Abbi!"

I quickened my steps. I needed time to harden my decision into steely resolve.

Clay's feet slapped the pavement in an even, easy stride. My car was in the lot nearest me. Get in it, go home. Spend the weekend buried in my covers. Hiding was definitely the smart choice. If Clay looked at me again, I wasn't sure I'd be able to stay away.

"Abbi, please."

He was close, his breathing harsh from running. His voice lowered, the same yearning threaded through his words that slammed into my chest when he'd rescued me on the stairs.

I stopped, unable to deny either my attraction or his plea. Clay was moving so fast, he wasn't prepared for my abrupt halt. He caught my elbow and twirled me into his chest, still moving, until he landed, hard, in the grass near the edge of the path. He clasped me tight, keeping me hugged to his chest as he absorbed the impact.

"Not what I planned." He laughed and groaned all at once.

"I don't know," I giggled. "The twirl was pretty smooth."

His hands squeezed my waist a little. They were warm. Safe. Before I realized it, I'd relaxed into him with a sigh. He let his head drop back into the grass.

"Clay," I whispered, my muscles tensing for flight.

"Don't. Not yet."

His breathing regulated but I could still feel his heart slamming into his chest. I wanted to believe I did that to him, because I wanted him. God, I wanted Clay. So stupid. And wrong. My muscles tensed again, but he smoothed his hand down my back.

"Just listen for a minute," he said.

"Considering you're stronger and me struggling would only draw more attention, I guess you have my undivided attention."

I moved my messenger bag to the side, making sure it wasn't digging into either of us.

"Yeah, sorry. I didn't mean to make a scene. I couldn't let you leave. I tried."

He tipped his chin down and looked at me. I stacked my hands on his chest and propped my chin there, meeting his gaze. He lifted his left hand and brushed my long hair back, behind my shoulder.

"You have the most beautiful eyes. So guarded, a little sad, but bluer than anything I've ever seen."

"That's quite a line," I said, trying to make light of what he was doing to me. "I bet you write the lyrics to go with your compositions."

"Truth is, Abbi. Can't deny it."

He trailed his other hand up my back and I shivered. He cupped the back of my head, fingers splayed wide. I didn't know how he did that—made me burn and feel so safe.

He shouldn't. I shouldn't feel like this.

He hadn't even kissed me. He studied my eyes for another long moment. I waited, breathless, needing his lips on mine.

"Whatever happened at Tech," he started.

I scrambled up, my heart pitter-patting in my chest. Clay was just like all the other men I'd met. He was smoother, sure. But still just waiting for a chance to get into my pants or maybe get my side of the story. Last I'd heard, my version was worth a cool $100,000. Not many people would turn down that kind of money.

"Abbi, something bad happened there. To you. Didn't it?"

"Leave me alone," I said. The trembling worked its way from my voice back into my limbs. I searched for my sunglasses that had flown off when he pulled me into his arms.

I didn't see them. They were expensive; a gift from Asher when I finally came out of my room just in time for a trip to Australia where different journalists asked the same questions, unwilling to let the story die. Unwilling to give me any privacy or space.

I shouldn't have stopped. Dammit, I'd started to trust Clay. I wanted to believe in him. In a future untainted by those pictures.

"Just tell me so I can know."

"You've read what those sites say. I can tell. You know what the world thinks of me."

"I'd like you to tell me what really happened."

He kept his voice quiet, soothing. Like I was an injured animal.

I didn't have any friends, and I couldn't have a relationship with Clay. He'd hurt me if I let him. I opened my mouth, prepared to tell him off again.

"I want to know you, Abbi. Not just because my brother asked me to look out for you."

He sat up slowly, wincing, his eyes pleading. I shut my mouth, my chin beginning to tremble.

"No," I whispered, forcing my feet back. "I don't want any part of the tabloid lifestyle. So just leave me alone."

I bolted to my car. I didn't even bother to take off my messenger bag when I slid into my seat. My hands were shaking so hard, I struggled to shove the key into the ignition. My breath fractured with the need to leave, to get away. To ease the ache building in my chest. For a few minutes I'd been Abbi, just a girl talking to a friend. Sure, he was hot, but that hadn't been the best part.

I'd been *normal*. Until Clay reminded me of everything I'd lost. Tears ripped at my throat, burned through my nose. A sob built, choking me. But I clenched my teeth, holding it down.

I started the car. I fought the gearshift into reverse while trying to buckle my seat belt over the bulky leather bag.

I'd sworn off men for good reason. I couldn't forget that. Because I wouldn't survive another so-called romance.

CHAPTER SEVEN
Clay

I sat in the grass, my arms around my knees. My stomach hurt nearly as much as my ass. I'd screwed that up. Royally.

"Nice job there, lover boy," Kai snickered. He offered his hand, which I ignored. I watched Abbi's taillights until she turned the corner, out of sight.

"Clay! Are you okay?"

Kai rolled his eyes, and I groaned. *Of course* she'd be here. I'd swear she'd implanted a homing device in me somewhere.

"Fine, Bethany."

"I was worried about you," her eyes were so big in her triangle face.

"I'm good."

"Great!" She was so chirpy. And tiny. Like the baby bird my little sister had tried to save after it fell out of its nest. I'd never been able to muster much sympathy for that creature. In fact, my family laughed at how grossed out I'd been when it made noises.

"Don't you have somewhere to be?" Kai asked, his irritation obvious in both tone and the set of his mouth.

"I'd planned to hang out with you guys," she said.

We were about the same height while I was on the ground. She put her hand on my forearm, rubbing back and forth.

"You wanna go do something? I mean, it's Friday so we could, like, hit a bar. Play some pool?"

I yanked my arm back.

"Can't. We've got plans." I dipped my head toward Kai.

"Yeah," he said. He stuck out his hand for me. This time, I let him haul me to my feet, wincing at the pain in my tailbone.

"You sure you're okay?" Bethany put her hand on my arm again. I glared as I shook her off. "That girl was totally in your way."

"I'm fine," I gritted. I bent to gather my stuff. Abbi's sunglasses were tangled in my bag. I picked them up, staring at them for a moment, before pocketing them.

"That was one hell of a fall. Or save. Either way, I'm not trying it." Kai grinned.

"Not recommended."

"So that's Abigail Dorsey?" Kai asked, falling into step next to me as I started walking toward my car.

I grunted.

"She's even better looking in person," Kai said, tapping his chin. "I mean, smoking."

I shook my head, still reeling from my realization. I'd have to call Colt to see if he'd come to the same conclusion.

"Are you, like, seeing her?" Bethany's voice was high. Well, higher than usual.

Crap. I hadn't realized she was following us. Who did that?

I groaned as I stopped walking and turned around to look at her. I didn't want to be an asshole, but there was no way I was going to encourage her.

"No," I told Bethany. "But I like her."

I tucked my lips into my mouth, wondering if I'd said too much. Bethany's shoulders slumped, her expression sliding from shock to hurt. Time to leave.

"Kai and I need to head out."

Kai started walking first. I followed, annoyed his shoulders shaking.

"Well, bye," Bethany called.

I threw my hand up in a bit of a wave but kept moving.

"I can't believe you told her you liked Abbi," Kai said, chuckling.

"She wasn't taking any of the subtle hints most people get. You know, like me walking in the other direction whenever I see her."

I scowled. My ass hurt, I'd upset Abbi, and I was tired of running into Bethany every time I tried to walk across campus. Much as I didn't want to, I'd have to ask my dad for advice on how to deal with Bethany's rabid desire to make us a couple.

"Yeah, Bethany's tenacious and I don't mean that in a good way. She's gonna think you're interested in Abigail."

"I might be," I said, surprising myself.

Kai stopped walking. "I get that; she's gorgeous."

"That's not why," I said.

"So why then? Why mow her down?"

"I didn't handle that well," I said.

"Lucky for you, there weren't many people out here to see it. 'Cause otherwise—day-um, that would've made some great social media footage."

My step hitched. Would Bethany be that mean? I looked over my shoulder. Nah, she didn't have her phone out. Plus, irritating as she was, Bethany wanted me to like her. Posting my lame-ass exploits on the Net wouldn't make that happen.

"You're uncaring, Kai." My back loosened up finally, and I was able to walk without a limp. "And you better not post anything about Abbi. I mean it."

45

"Dude, I'm not going to do anything to her. Scout's honor."

Kai held up two fingers. The wrong two. I shoved his hand away from my face. "You're such a friend."

"That's right, buck-a-roo. If you buy me a beer, I won't even mention your crash-and-burn to Dane."

"Not sure I care if you do or don't."

Kai gaped at me, but I shrugged and kept walking. "I'm going to keep an eye on her. Colt asked me to, and Charles and Neal were hassling her in the library tonight."

"What's that got to do with you?"

I shrugged. "I don't know. But there's more to her story than we know. I have a terrible feeling it's bad and that those pictures of Abbi aren't the worst of it. Do you know who posted those?"

"I have no idea. Why would I?"

"She looked at me the way Cassidy did once she got her diagnosis."

Kai put his hand on my arm to pull me to a stop. His normally laughing eyes were serious when he faced me.

"You can't fix people or their problems. I mean, look at Cassidy. That's not something you can simply will away."

I crossed my arms over my chest. I didn't like to talk about Cassidy. Kai studied my expression, pressing his advantage.

"I'm officially worried, man. You're talking about dating the girl with the most downloaded pic of the decade."

"I'm not going to date her."

"But you've thought about it. You don't do relationships."

I didn't. Because I didn't believe they'd last. Or, they'd twist around into something ugly, like my parents' marriage. I didn't want that either. Easier to be single, remain unattached and uninterested.

I clapped him on the back. "Nothing for you to worry about because there's nothing there between us." Such a liar. "Let's get that beer."

CHAPTER EIGHT
Abbi

I pulled over a couple of blocks from campus and removed my bag to buckle up properly. I also needed the time to calm down.

I shouldn't have run from Clay like that. I dropped my head against the steering wheel. I hadn't wanted him to see me cry, but that wasn't a good reason to leave the guy mid conversation not once but twice. My cheeks burned.

I hated that he'd seen those pictures. Once Steve opened the floodgates with the first picture of me at the fraternity house, hundreds of pictures of me hit my social media accounts. I'd had no clue so many people snapped shots of me. I had no control of what I looked like, where I was, what I was doing in those pictures. They'd been taken and posted without my knowledge or consent.

Most of them were boring: me studying at the library, walking to my dorm after class. But some, like the pictures from that night at the fraternity house, were provocative and hinted at the reputation I'd been given. *Slut.* I shuddered, hating the word. And the people who threw it around had no idea of its power, the way it cut, deep.

I could sue Steve for starting the social media storm that had slandered my character and destroyed my ability to go back to Tech this year. I might even win. I'd thought about it, mainly because I didn't want him to get away with bullying me for not wanting to continue a relationship with him.

And I really didn't like that people thought I was the bored party girl willing to do anything for the next thrill.

But if I did press charges, I'd have to relive those months at

Marin Tech. Each time anyone even hinted at that night and the weeks that followed, my mom had to stifle a panic attack. I wasn't going to be the reason she had another one. I'd made myself that promise back when we still lived in Rathdrum and I'd pulled up to our house to see an ambulance in our driveway. She hadn't been hurt too badly, but it was my actions—not answering my phone—that caused the problems in the first place.

I set my bag into the passenger seat and rebuckled my seat belt. I tapped my fingers on the steering wheel. Two choices: go back to my lonely dorm and mope until bedtime or go home and play video games with Mason for a couple of hours.

Like there was a choice. I was and always would be a social creature. That's why Clay's offer to be friends was so tempting.

I snorted. I didn't want to be his friend. No, my hormones wanted a lot more action than I'd seen tonight, splayed all over Clay's impressive chest. Which anyone could've photographed. I cringed.

I couldn't be near him again. I forgot all the reasons why I needed to stay private. Hidden would be better. I refused to let some guy, even one as kind and sexy as Clay, be the reason I was ripped apart by the media again. There wasn't enough of me left to withstand another round.

Pulling into the driveway, I wasn't surprised to see my Aunt Briar's car parked out front. The absolute best part of my life was the closeness of my family. Even Briar's fiancé, Hayden, was more than willing to step up when the pictures broke last spring. He'd whisked Aunt Bri and me off to Sydney for a vacation.

I'd needed that time to finish licking my wounds. But Hayden insisted I get out, not let the weight of the story grind me under.

Because, as he put it, it wouldn't blow. Briar concurred, and I figured she knew what she was talking about considering her love affair with Hayden was such a media frenzy from the beginning.

Within the first five minutes of her very first lesson, Briar proved to be a terrible surfer, much to Hayden's supreme disappointment. But the time alone meant Hayden and I bonded over the rip curl.

I'd been thankful for my family's support, but I needed to handle this story my way. I wasn't sure what that was yet because I didn't have all the information I needed. And I wouldn't have that for another couple of weeks. The longer I waited, the harder pressing charges would be. I wasn't sure I could handle something so personal playing out so publicly. I stood on the porch for a long moment, forcing the fears back down where they belonged. I had my family, and they were happy. I'd be strong for them.

I smiled as I opened the door. Laughter spilled from the back of the house; my mom was an amazing cook, and people always congregated around to watch and smell her newest creations.

"Hey guys," I called.

"Abbi!" Mason slammed into me, arms wrapping tightly around my middle. He'd turned ten a few months ago, and he was growing like a weed. Soon he'd be taller than me, which would be weird.

"Good to see you, too, bud," I laughed, hugging him back. The top of his head came to my shoulder now.

Briar and Hayden stepped forward, concern building in their eyes. "What?"

"Your eyes are red and puffy and you're covered in grass stains," Aunt Bri said. "What the hell happened, Abigail?"

"I had a bit of a run-in with a guy. I'm fine because he took the brunt of the fall," I said. Glancing down at the left knee of my jeans, I winced. "I'm pretty sure he's going to be bruised for a few days."

"I hope this rolling in the grass isn't a new college hobby," Asher said as he gave me a side hug. I returned it, leaning my head against his shoulder.

In so many ways, he was the only father I'd ever had. Hearing Clay articulate some of the comments I'd heard about my relationship with Asher pissed me off. Asher loved me, just as he loved Mason.

"Your mom's going to have something to say about using euphemisms."

"Puh-lease." I had to roll my eyes as they expected. "I don't roll anywhere. With anyone."

"We know that," Asher said, his face whitening just as it had when I'd come home and had to tell them about the pictures hitting every media outlet. Yeah, they'd been that bad, but I'd refused to let anyone make a statement. I'd told them the stories didn't deserve any attention. Definitely not a denial.

"Hey, Abs." Mom pulled me into a hug, and I wound my arms around her tightly, burying my nose into her long hair. She always made me feel safe and loved. "You went rolling through the grass with a guy, huh? I hope he was worth those stains."

"Doesn't matter. It's not going anywhere."

Briar raised her eyebrow. "Hayden, you and Asher can handle the salad." She gripped my wrist in her right hand, my mom's in her left, and tugged us toward the stairs.

"Turn off the stove," Mom called over her shoulder.

Once we were up the stairs, Briar led us into my room and shut the door. I glanced around, still trying to get used to the fact I didn't live here anymore.

"Spill it, Abigail," Aunt Briar demanded.

"What?"

"The guy. Did he hurt you?"

I shook my head. "Not at all. He saved me." I explained the situation at the library, about the guys crowding me, grabbing me. Mom's eyes dimmed, and her hands were clasped tight in her lap.

"Oh, Abbi. I'm so sorry, honey."

"This has nothing to do with you or Asher, Mom. It was a couple of guys taking things way too far."

Mom didn't look convinced. I hated that I was the reason for her distress so I rushed on.

"So then Clay and I talked for a while. I wanted to come here. He ran out to ask me something, ended up going too fast and plowed into me instead. He caught me before I fell, making sure he took the impact."

I smiled a little, thinking of his face when he realized what had happened.

"So it's like that," Aunt Bri said.

"What?" I moved toward the window seat, needing space.

"You like him."

I shrugged, careful to keep my face turned toward the window this time. "He's nice." But he'd recognized me from the photos. I'd bet anything he believed what he'd read about me. Why wouldn't he?

If I'd put out a statement refuting those pictures, maybe, then maybe, Clay would have seen the real me, not the assumed slutty version.

"Sounds like," Mom said. "Is he as cute as Luke?"

"Way better. More mature, bigger," I said. I sealed my lips together.

I turned back in time to see Mom and Aunt Bri exchanging a look.

"Why didn't you bring him to dinner?"

"Because we aren't really friends. I mean, I just met him."

Mom stood from the bed and walked toward me. She smoothed my hair back from my forehead. I'd liked Clay touching my hair more. Much more. I shivered and clutched my arms to my chest as I relived the feel of his large hand cupping the back of my head.

"You've kept so much to yourself. It's not like you. I know you were upset about the drugs and you should be, especially since those boys took pictures…"

Mom hadn't brought it up once I'd made it clear I wasn't talking about it. Even with her.

"You're different. Harder. Untrusting. I'm worried about you, Abbi. I don't expect you to tell me everything, but I realize there's more to the story than you've wanted to say. If it's because you're worried we'll be upset—"

"Everything's good. I'm making smart decisions that won't hurt any of us."

"You're hurting yourself by blocking others from your life, Abs," Aunt Bri said. "You're a vibrant young woman. A year ago, I would've said vivacious. You, especially, need those human connections."

"Not with this guy. Not now."

"Why's that?" Mom stepped back and studied me.

"Because he's Pete Rippey's son. Can you imagine the field day the media would have with that story? I moved from a small-time, relatively untalented musician to Clay Rippey. I can already see the headlines about me trying to up my chances of fame with my own rock star in the making. No thanks. I've had more than enough time in tabloids already."

Again, Mom and Briar exchanged a look. Mom was nibbling the corner of her lip like she did when she was worried.

"Can we eat? Whatever you made smells ah-mazing."

Mom continued to stand there, looking unsure. I hated that I'd broken her happiness yet again. Much as I wanted to, I couldn't change the past. I smiled, gripped her hand, gave it a little squeeze before stepping back.

"What did he want to ask you?" Aunt Briar probed.

"I don't know. We started talking about something else."

"Hmm," Aunt Briar said. Mom was tugging on the ends of her hair.

"I bet Mason's starving."

"Always," Mom said, but her tone made it clear she wanted to push for more information.

I opened the door and headed down the hall. Mom and Aunt Briar trailed behind me.

"What did you say his name is again?"

"Clay," I said. Just saying his name made something warm unfurl in my chest. He'd been nice in spite of my reputation. I smiled at Asher and Hayden, who wore matching expressions of relief when we entered the kitchen.

"I turned off the stove, and I didn't let Hayden touch anything," Asher said.

He snagged his glass of beer and headed to the other side of the counter. The safer side. The only one of them that could do more than microwave and boil water was my mom. It's part of why they all hung out so much. Aunt Bri said Hayden was even more inept in the kitchen than she was.

"Watch it, Yank. I set the table," Hayden added, pulling my aunt into his arms and kissing the top of her head. I turned away, aching for what I'd never have—that kind of easy love was hard-won, I knew, but also so deep, nothing could rip it apart. I despaired at ever finding something close, even a pale comparison, of that love for myself.

"Can we eat? I'm starving," Mason cried.

"Who's Clay?" Asher asked. He tried to keep his need to protect me safely curled inside, but I knew he wanted to take on all my detractors, same as he would for my mom. I loved him even more for it—and for keeping his mouth shut, trusting me to make my own decisions.

"Abbi's new friend," Mom said.

I narrowed my eyes and she busied herself with serving her paella.

"He's Pete Rippey's son," Aunt Bri chimed in.

Asher set his beer back onto the counter, eyebrow raised. "Really? I ran into Pete last week at the studio."

My stomach slid sideways. Clay had said he'd been asked to look out for me. "Did you tell him I was at Northern?"

"Yeah," Asher said. "But then we got to talking about the cancer charity event."

"Pete's been great," Aunt Briar said. "He's one of the names that helped bring in tons of support, I'll add. Great family."

"What?" I asked. "They're going to attend the cancer counseling gala?"

The awful concern that Pete had asked Clay to look out for me rippled into panicked certainty, making my skin chill. What if Clay went to the event? The panic popped and warmth built in its place, filling me up. I'd get to see him again. Talk to him.

"You haven't been on the Internet much," Mom said, her eyes narrowing. "The Rippeys are one of the biggest donors for Briar's counseling program."

"I try to avoid going online as much as possible."

I turned away, filling the water pitcher at the fridge. That seemed like a safe distance from my mom's too-knowing eyes.

"You having him play, love?" Hayden asked.

"And not you? No way," Aunt Bri said. "This isn't a concert, just a charity gala. Pete's wife, Maryanne, called me almost a year ago when I first started talking to the hospital executives about my counseling program."

"I didn't realize the Rippeys were such big donors until I talked to Pete," Asher said.

"Oh, they've been amazing," Aunt Briar said. "Their little girl has Hodgkin lymphoma. Maryanne said their family needed tons of counseling to get through all the fallout. Not just for the disease, but I hear that a lot. They're lucky—they can afford to get everyone back to healthy mental space. That's why they've decided to back the program."

"Wait," I said. "Their daughter has Hodgkin's disease?"

"Sad story. They found out when she was eleven. She's still fighting it."

"Shit," Asher said, shaking his head. His hand fell on Mason's shoulder, curled into Mason's shirt. Asher's baby daughter died before she turned one, and even I caught glimpses of his grief when he looked at Mason or me.

"Still?" I asked, my voice swinging higher. "So she's still alive?"

Mom said losing someone wasn't something you ever got over. It was something you learned to live with.

I hoped I would never find out. Well, besides my dad. And I'd feel worse about it, but he'd always been sick, talking to me about his imminent death from the time I was old enough to understand.

Clay hadn't mentioned his little sister when I talked about my dad. My stomach churned. How bad off was she?

"Do you know how she's doing?" Hayden asked.

He'd lost his mom to cancer last year. In fact, that was how he and Aunt Briar met. They'd been visiting the same hospice center.

Aunt Bri shook her head. "They were hoping for news soon. At least, that's what Maryanne said last I spoke with her. It was really touch-and-go for a while, but Maryanne said Cassidy was at home again. That sounded promising. Can you ask Clay, Abbi?"

I shrugged. "I only met him today. We didn't really get that far into our personal lives. And until he tells me about her, seems like an invasion of his privacy."

"You're right," Mom said. "But it wouldn't hurt to let him know we're all thinking about her. All of them."

I shoved my hands into my pockets and rocked back on my heels. It might hurt. I liked Clay. More, I was attracted to him. To ask about his sister left me open to more questions about me—and Clay had already shown a distinct interest in that night at the frat house.

"So Pete's son is at Northern?" Hayden asked, clearly trying to steer the conversation back to more positive territory.

"Abs?" Aunt Bri asked.

"Both of them, yeah. But I'm talking about Clay. He helped me at the library tonight. We don't have classes together or anything. It's not like I'll see him around much. His older brother teaches my biochem class. I can ask him next week. Our lab's not until Tuesday and it's weird talking to the TA about personal stuff."

I glared at Aunt Bri. Her big mouth. This time Mom and Asher had one of those wordless conversations.

"Stop it," I snapped. "You don't need to worry about me. Clay's nice and maybe we'll hang out again." I forced myself to shrug like I wasn't that interested. Before anyone could ask me anything else, I picked up two plates and carried them to the table. "Sit by me, Mason. I want to hear about your week."

He scrambled into the chair next to me, words pouring out of his mouth. I nodded, not really paying attention. I nibbled at the paella. I'm sure it was delicious but I no longer had much of an appetite.

Instead, I was picturing Clay's green eyes. I'd liked how they'd warmed up as we talked. He really did understand, not just about the fame but the fear of losing someone important. He'd know all about that helpless anger I didn't know what to do with when I couldn't change the outcome.

I shouldn't have run. Next time, I'd apologize.

If there was a next time.

I bit my lip, moving the rice around my plate. I'd have to make sure there was a next time.

———◆———

"Are you Abigail Dorsey?"

I turned toward the high-pitched voice. The girl speaking wasn't even five feet. Her gamin's face was pinched tight, and her hands were balled into fists. Whatever this was, I could tell it wasn't going to end well. Especially since she'd accosted me the moment I walked into my dorm at 8:30 on a Saturday morning.

"I am. And you are?"

"Bethany."

She didn't offer her hand or her last name. Definitely bad.

I walked across the empty lobby to a set of couches and sat on the one closest to the exit. She settled onto the very edge of the one opposite me.

"I'll be quick. Stay away from Clay Rippey. He's mine."

Well, that wasn't what I'd expected.

"Um…" I wasn't sure how to respond. Clay and I hadn't discussed his relationship status, but I'd thought he wanted to kiss me in the quad. I'd sprawled on his chest and he'd held me there.

Shame flooded my cheeks. No wonder this girl was here, to stake her claim. I'd acted exactly like she'd expect me to based on those photos.

"Look, I know about your behavior at Marin Tech. I'm sure it'll be harder for you if those pictures see another spike, so just leave Clay alone. Otherwise, I will make sure they're all over campus."

I stood slowly, my body shaking. Steve's betrayal had devastated me, but this…no, I would not be emotionally trampled again.

"You need to leave. Now."

"I mean it, Abigail. If I see you two together, I'm going to destroy your rep—"

I laughed. I couldn't help it. She was angry, and I knew she meant every word, but, really, there wasn't anything left to my reputation.

"Clay's my *friend*. Our parents are in the same industry. I'm going to see him at a charity event next weekend. Threatening me isn't going to change that. In fact, it'd make the whole situation worse. Because we both have to go. And we'll talk. The press will take pictures. They'll speculate. Social media will froth at how I'm not good enough for him. It's what always happens."

I wasn't sure that was true, and I was talking with a bravado I didn't feel. But if I didn't stand up for myself now, Bethany wouldn't stop harassing me.

"You think he likes you for you?" Bethany hissed. Her cute pixie face twisted with disgust. "Please! Clay wants his women focused on him. You, you're not even close to what Clay deserves. So even if he seems interested, it'll fade. Especially if he sees *those* pictures."

I shook my head, frustration and shame battling with surprise. All of which fell away when I realized exactly what Bethany had said. Steve had intimated he had more graphic pictures— ones worse than the ones that were already released. I hadn't stuck around long enough to find out what he planned to do with them.

"Clay knows what really happened." Okay, not entirely true, but he would know, because I'd tell him. Soon. Nerves jangled in my belly. I sucked in a deep breath, forcing away the doubt and shame. "Just like my family does. I won't be bullied again. You don't want to go there, Bethany, or you will hear from my lawyer. Now, seriously, you need to leave."

"Yes, you do."

I turned to see two girls who lived in the room across from me standing just behind my back. I didn't know their names, but I appreciated their support.

"Stop trying to build yourself up into something you're not, Bethany," the taller blonde one said. "You're not Clay's girlfriend and you don't have any claim to him at all. Everyone knows Clay kicked you out of his room last year when you tried throwing yourself at him. I'm sure there are pictures of you, naked, doing a *real* walk of shame. Because Clay didn't want you."

Bethany's fists clenched tighter, and her face turned so white I worried she'd faint. Just when I was about to step forward to catch her elbow, her cheeks flushed a deep crimson.

"Watch it, Jenna. I don't see you in a relationship with Kai even though everyone on campus has watched you pant after him. You, too, Nessa. You're nothing special."

The dark-haired girl strolled up next to me, smirking. "Oh but I am. I've got Dane wrapped all over this." She indicated her generous figure. "Clearly he loves real women. Just like Clay's into Abbi because she has a great personality to go with all that gorgeousness. Which is why we like her."

Even I heard the subtext there. I'd managed to land square in the in middle of another hornets' nest. Some luck I was having.

Bethany opened her mouth, then snapped it shut. She wheeled around and slammed out the door.

The girls high-fived. "Oh, damn," Nessa said, chuckling.

"That felt really good."

She stuck out her hand. "I'm Nessa. This is Jenna."

"Abbi. And thanks." I backed away. Nice as the girls were, I didn't think they'd helped me to, well, help me so much as to tell off Bethany. "She was waiting for me when I came in."

"She's been territorial about Clay since we started last year. It's about time someone put her in her place, and I'm so glad it was me." Nessa scrunched her shoulders and beamed.

"Okay then."

"Anyone on Bethany's shit list is someone we gotta know," Jenna said. She eyed me up and down. "You a runner?"

I nodded, surprised by the sudden change in topic.

"Thought so. You've got the legs. We're about to hit the track. Want to join us?" Jenna asked.

I nibbled my lip, considering. These girls had definitely heard what Bethany said. I was pretty sure they knew who I was. Knew what was posted about me. Did I want to open myself up to another round of jealousy and drama?

"Um, no. But thanks."

Jenna touched my shoulder. "Is it because of what Bethany said? You don't need to worry. We don't believe her. She lies all the time."

"If you're dating Clay, then we'll be spending lots of time together," Nessa said. "Dane, my boyfriend, is the guitarist in their band."

"Got it," I said. "But Clay and I aren't dating. We barely know each other." I shrugged. "Maybe he'd say we're friends."

"He's definitely mentioned you, especially last night after Neal and Charles cornered you on the stairs," Nessa said.

"Which was no *bueno*," Jenna said with a scowl.

"Let's drop your stuff up in your room," Nessa said.

I already had on a pair of yoga capris and a sports bra and tee. I'd planned to hit a treadmill at the gym, but I preferred running on a track. Could I really go with girls I didn't know?

"I'm not sure. I just stopped by to pick up my iPod. I'm actually driving to Portland this afternoon. To meet a friend who goes to school there."

After my family interrogation, I'd fled to my room where I'd let Sally finagle me into talking to her. I picked at my cuticle, wondering again if reopening any kind of relationship with Sally was a good idea. Probably not, but her last text had caught my attention.

I have information for you. About Steve and Marin Tech. I want to help.

"Oh, come on, you look primed for a workout. Don't tell me that wasn't your original plan. We'll come up to your dorm with you," Jenna said. "I've been dying to see inside your room since you moved in."

I stumbled and Nessa caught my arm, linking hers through mine. "Don't mind her. She's just hoping you keep a life-sized cut-out of your stepdad in there. Which would be super creepy. So you better not because I'll revoke my offer of friendship."

I shook my head, still uncertain how to take these ladies. They were a powerful duo, these two. "Come on in," I said. "I'm really boring."

"We noticed," Jenna sighed. "We were hoping you were more like the Internet stories. We need more excitement here. At least a steady stream of hot guys." Nessa nudged Jenna with her elbow.

"What?"

Nessa glared, and Jenna turned her horrified face toward mine.

"Oh, God! I didn't mean the slut part." She covered her mouth with her hand. "I am so making this worse."

I sighed as I sat my bag on my chair and weighed my options. Bethany said she had access to the unreleased pictures—the ones I was terrified existed. But now that she'd confirmed they did indeed exist, no amount of wishful thinking would keep them out of the public eye forever.

I took a deep breath and met Nessa's eyes then Jenna's. They may seem nice now, but they'd turn tail and run as soon as those pictures got out. And why wouldn't they? Being near me meant being tainted by my party-girl brush.

"I've never made a habit of sleeping around. I'm not much of a partier, never was. I mean, I like to have fun. I just," I shrugged, thinking about how to phrase this next part without seeming bitchy or self-absorbed. "I thought Steve liked me." I huffed and tipped my head back. "But he just wanted me to ride Asher's coattails to fame. I knew he was embarrassed when I didn't invite Asher to his concert. He'd told everyone Asher would be there." I swallowed. "Then the pictures came out."

I waited, not looking at any of them. I startled when an arm fell over my shoulder.

"Man, that's…He was your boyfriend?" Nessa asked.

"Not really. We hadn't gone out long enough for him to be my boyfriend."

There was more I wanted to say, but I was too scared. I picked at my cuticle again, sighing when I drew blood. Jenna handed me a tissue.

"So you think he posted the pics to get even?" Jenna asked.

"I don't know. I left as soon as I could. We didn't talk again."

"But Bethany said something about more pictures," Nessa said. "We heard her."

"Why didn't you report him?" Jenna asked. "I mean, you didn't want your picture taken."

"I don't really have any way to get him in trouble for taking the pictures," I said, trying to walk a difficult line of being truthful and still protecting myself from their defection. Or, worse, betrayal. "It's more if I could prove something illegal happened."

"That's horse shit," Nessa growled.

I was surprised by how angry she looked.

"He's slut shaming you. To get even for you not doing what he wanted."

"Oh, it's worse than that." I swallowed down the rest of the truth. Soon. I'd know for sure soon. Silence built. I pulled at another of my cuticles, wishing I still bit my nails.

"So here's the deal: We like concerts and would love to meet your stepdad and uncles. But we're going to be your friends even if you don't introduce us," Jenna said. "And, yes, of course, we'd be happy to come with you to Oregon."

I dropped my hands to my sides and stared at her, mouth agape. "You—you don't have to do that." I didn't want her to do that. Did I?

"You don't understand. Telling Bethany off was the *best* thing to happen all year. I've hated that girl since she tried to sleep with Dane again—the night after our first date, I'll add—last year," Nessa said. "He swears up and down she climbed in his bedroom window."

Yet another reason to steer clear of Clay, then. I couldn't deal with another jealousy-crazed person in my life.

"Wait. Don't they have a concert tonight?" Jenna asked.

Nessa bit her lip, clearly torn. "I told Dane I'd be there, but this is important, too. I mean, I want us to hang out, Abbi."

Jenna snapped her fingers. "I'll go with Abracadabra here and you can still have your nasty night with Daney-boy. Win-win, losers."

I tucked in my bottom lip, not sure if I should laugh or call the local substance abuse center. Nessa raised her eyebrows and shrugged, letting me know this was fairly normal. At least for Jenna.

Oblivious to my wordless communication with her friend, Jenna continued, "It must suck to have your whole life scrutinized like that. I mean, everyone has a right to go out and have fun without worrying about their activities flashing all over social media. I never realized how great it was to have a bank manager for a mom before."

I swallowed down the lump of tears gathering in my throat. I wanted to tell them I hadn't been drinking that night. But that walked a dangerously thin line where I had to admit to the rest of the story.

"It's why Clay and I won't be more than friends. I hate the spotlight. And, really, I get it if you don't want to hang out with me either."

Jenna narrowed her eyes. "Not a good reason to give up Clay Rippey, but I see your point." She tipped her head, then shook it, causing the blond hair to shimmer in the dim light of my room. "No, I don't. Abbi, he's a great guy. And being friends with you isn't going to be that much different than being friends with the guys. I mean, we're already well-known on campus because we hang out with them so often." She shrugged.

"But you'll get lumped in with my wild-girl lifestyle," I said.

Nessa spread her hands. "I can see all the super wild here. Now, stop worrying. The boys can use some new interest. I mean, they're in a band. They like the attention the media gives them."

"Now, since you're the reason Bethany showed up this morning, you're buying breakfast after our run," Nessa said with a smile. "And Jenna here can pack away some food. So expect a really large bill. Consider it our initiation to our gang."

———

The trip to Portland was entertaining thanks to Jenna's antics. She kept fast-forwarding songs so she could just sing the chorus.

"It's the best part. You know you wanna do it all the time."

I chuckled.

"What's your favorite song?" she asked.

My mom's was Asher's "Sweet Solace." Asher's was "Moonshine Eyes," which he'd written for my mother nearly twenty years ago. Hayden's and Briar's was "Between Breaths," the song he'd written for her about their meeting in Seattle last year.

"I don't have one."

"Why not? Everyone has a favorite song. Mine's 'The Monster' by Eminem."

"Not one of Clay's band's songs? They're called Lummi Nation, right?" I'd Googled him last night and spent too long drooling over his beautiful face.

She shook her head as she fiddled with her phone. "No. Kai sings about how fleeting love is." She shot me a look I didn't know how to interpret. "But that could be Clay's influence. He's almost a monk. Weird for a popular, talented twenty-two-year-old."

Not touching that one. Not going near it. "Why Eminem then? Doesn't he do the same thing?"

Jenna scrunched her nose. "Yeah. But I really connected with the second verse. Plus, Rihanna can belt out a song."

We were quiet for the duration of the next couple of songs. "So why do we care about driving all the way to Portland again?" Jenna asked, not bothering to cover her huge yawn.

"Because Sally—the girl I'm going to meet—said she had information about the pictures at Marin Tech."

"And she would know this how?"

I gripped the wheel tighter. "I don't know."

"So we hate this girl who has information about the slime ball who took pictures of you. The enemy of our enemy. Totally Old Testament. Got it."

I worried the skin on my thumb as I puzzled out Jenna's logic. "Yeah, kinda. And I don't hate Sally," I said with a sigh. "She was my friend—my best friend starting in third grade."

"Betrayal's a bitch. I know. I've practiced it."

I glanced over, my eyes wide.

Jenna waved me off. "With my high school boyfriend. He thinks I cheated on him. Which would never happen, but he never bothered to listen so…that's a no-go zone." She slid down in her seat, frowning. Well, there was a story there. "Tell me more about this Sally chick. I need to be prepared."

I slid my damp hands along the top of the steering wheel. "I haven't talked to her in over a year. She started texting and calling, even emailing me, a few months ago. A couple weeks after the pictures hit. Said she needed to talk to me."

"Hmmm. Maybe she's realized being your friend is better for her social standing. I mean, I got donuts out of the deal." Jenna patted her stomach.

The laugh caught me by surprise as much as it did Jenna. "Thanks for coming with me."

"You already said that, like sixty times. I'm gonna nap. Running makes me tired. Actually, that's not true. Being around people makes me tired. It's not personal, Abbi. 'Kay?"

With that, Jenna rolled her head toward the window. Within five minutes, a soft, snuffling snore filled the small space. I clicked the music back on, trying to ignore the building tension forming in my shoulders.

An hour later, Jenna stretched with a groan. "I need a soda."

I put on my blinker and eased my car off the next exit before pulling into the lot of a convenience store. I parked and we both hopped out, taking the opportunity to go to the bathroom then buying the largest caffeinated beverage in the store. Jenna also bought a whole plastic bag of junk food to tide her over until lunch, which was in another hour and a half.

"Want me to drive?" she asked around a mouthful of cookies.

"I'm good. But I'd love for you to talk to me."

"Anything in particular?"

I shook my head.

"That's a lot of pressure," Jenna sighed. "I'm nowhere near as interesting as Nessa. Or as good in new social situations. Um…" She dragged out the sound. "So some more history on our target might be good."

"Sally's at Lewis & Clark." I took a long sip of my chai. "A freshman. I should've been one, too, but I had enough credits to graduate a semester early."

"So you're a super nerd?" Jenna asked. "That's awesome."

I chewed the inside of my lip. "Yeah, I guess so. But my friends from high school would point to my track trophies or my cheerleading days."

"You were a cheerleader?" Jenna giggled. "That's so messed up when I think about you now. You're studious. Just waiting to slide on a pair of wire-rim frames. I bet you'll look perky, all bespectacled."

"Well, I needed to refocus on what was important—what I could control."

Jenna shook her head as she stared out the window, her open package of cookies forgotten. "Because of what Steve did to you? I mean, I know social shaming is kinda the rage, but this isn't for entertainment. You never found out why?"

"No."

"He really hurt you," Jenna said, her voice soft.

"He really did."

"I get that," she muttered.

We sat in silence until I put on my blinker to take the 308. I followed my GPS to a green-roofed house on NE 25th Street. The concrete walk was pitted and cracked, but the house itself had freshly painted beige siding and the flower beds were full of tulips.

"Let's do this," Jenna muttered, her mouth set in a firm line as she shoved opened the door.

She sucked in a huge gulp of air as we headed to the door.

She seemed nervous, but that was odd. I was the one putting myself out there, admitting just how bad the situation with Steve had gotten.

"You know, you're prettier in person." The voice was feminine, soft—kind. A middle-aged woman with dark hair streaked with gray stepped forward. Her brown eyes were serious behind chunky red frames. She was dressed casually but had that bearing of someone used to commanding a large group.

"I'm sorry, I don't know you."

"I'm Jean Menson. Sally's aunt."

"Oh. Hi. I'm Abbi Dorsey and this is my friend, Jenna."

She smiled. Jenna shuffled from one foot to another, ending up behind me.

"I know who you are, dear. I've kept a close eye on that story as it came out. I know your mom through my sister. Sally's mom." She glanced away. "I hope it's okay that I had Sally contact you. She needs to talk to you. For both your sakes."

A moment later Sally stepped onto the porch. She didn't look much like she had all our lives. She was thinner and her hair was whacked off in some short pseudo pixie cut. But the weirdest part was her dropped gaze.

"Hi, Abbi." Her voice was the same but her brown eyes wouldn't meet mine. "I'm glad you came. I thought it would be better to meet here rather than on campus. Do you want to come in and sit?"

I shook my head. Jenna crossed her arms and leaned closer. Like she was my bodyguard. Sally glanced at her aunt, who nodded before stepping up onto the porch. The front door shut behind her with a soft click.

"Fair enough. First, I need to tell you how sorry I am for the way I treated you." Her eyes filled with tears and her chin quivered. She met my eyes briefly before glancing away again. "I was so jealous of your new life. I quit seeing you as my friend."

The pain was still there, but this was a fresh slice, deep in my chest. "I know. I lived it, too."

"I was wrong. Um, maybe you want to know what I found out?" Sally thrust a folder at me. It was filled with loose pages.

"There was a chat room. It was all about hating you." Sally swallowed hard. "It…I started it."

I didn't know what to say. The idea that my once–best friend could do that hurt so much.

"I met Steve there. Online. After you broke up with him."

"We never really dated," I said, folding my arms around my waist.

"Yeah, I figured that out. He was really mad at you. He was also in major financial trouble because he'd booked that concert venue with his dad's money. Money he took without permission. When the venue didn't sell well, he was out a lot of cash, and the band wouldn't help out with the cost."

"So he decided to sell pictures of me," I said, my lips numb.

Sally shook her head, wiping away tears. "No. He was just really mad at you, trash-talking, calling you names. I'm the one who suggested he sell pictures of you."

"What is wrong with you?" Jenna demanded. Her eyes blazed. "Those pictures on the Internet? They'll *always* be out there."

"I know," Sally's shoulder slumped and her tears came more quickly. "I'm really sorry, Abbi. I'll help you if I can. I mean that. I'll do an interview, write whatever you want. I didn't know Steve got his band involved until the pictures went live."

I clutched the folder tighter to my chest, my fingers digging into the paper, wrinkling whatever was within. "That doesn't make you any less culpable."

Sally wiped her nose on her sleeve before wrapping her arms around her middle. "I know. I made some really bad choices. I've seen how it hurt you. Hurt your mom. She's talked to my mom, and that's when I got it. What I'd been part of." She blew out a breath and met my gaze. "You won all those track competitions, were the best cheerleader. The best dancer. Just *the best*. All golden and perfect. I was jealous of you then and that was before your mom fell in love with a huge rock star. It—it just seemed like everything was handed to you. And Steve…he fed my envy as much as I fed his."

There wasn't more for me to say. "Bye, Sally."

"Wait! I talked to my aunt about it. I've closed the chat room. I also told the police what I knew. But they said you'd have to file a formal complaint to do more."

"Oh, like that's going to help her," Jenna said. "That's public record. The media will look into it and see what you did. What Steve did. Abbi's going to have to relive that again because you were *jealous*." Jenna hissed the last words, her eyes narrowed, her cheeks full of color.

My chest felt tight, my heart flitting faster than a hummingbird's wings. Everyone would know what they did to me. What I couldn't remember them doing to me.

"Do you…do you think you can forgive me?"

Shocked, I glanced up into Sally's tired brown eyes. Her aunt was right. Sally was different. Seemingly chastised. But I wasn't sure I believed her.

"Those pictures of me…like Jenna said, they're always going to be out there. Always. I had to change schools just to get away from the nightmare. They'll crop up in twenty years, and I'll have to explain them to Mason's kids or something. That's what you gave back to me after all those years of friendship." My jaw felt hard, my heart thudded slow and cold in my chest. I liked this better than hurting.

"Abbi, my parents are so mad at me. My dad said if I got jail time, he wouldn't bail me out."

Sally's eyes filled with tears. Her father was the sheriff in Rathdrum, where'd we'd grown up. Ralph was also one of the nicest men I'd ever met. Affable, my mom said. Rhonda, Sally's mom, was one of her closest friends.

"Did your parents tell my mom what you did?" I asked.

"Not yet. I needed to talk to you first."

I nodded once. "I'll talk to my mom. Tell your parents that." I looked her up and down, feeling…nothing. The anger and hurt were there, I was sure of it.

"Okay. I get that you're mad."

"*Of course* she's mad," Jenna's tone was scathing. "You betrayed her. In the worst possible way."

Mrs. Menson stepped out onto the porch, her gaze focused on the three of us. I lifted my hand and waved to her. She nodded back. Sally studied my face, but she must not have liked what she saw, because she turned and trudged up the steps. She stopped there and turned back. "All I can say is I'm sorry, Abbi."

———◆———

"That was really uncomfortable," Jenna said, hopping from foot to foot like a toddler needing to pee. "Come on. I need to get out of here before I beat her up. That girl has it coming to her. I'll drive and you can read."

I handed her my car keys and settled into the passenger seat. I opened the folder, shocked by the number of people who'd been part of the chat room. Over one hundred, all of whom I'd known. Some were girls who'd wanted to date Luke back in high school; some were from neighboring high schools who'd claimed I'd cheated at my track competitions. Some were from my sorority at Tech. That explained why none of them had kept in touch since I left.

"What does it say?" Jenna asked, glancing at the pages while we idled at a red light.

"Mean stuff. How I'm not that wonderful or interesting and I'm using Asher's fame to make myself into someone important." The comment that burned the most was the assertion I wasn't smart enough to get into Tech without Asher's name. "Oh! Bethany was one of the last members who joined the hate-Abbi-club chatroom. Maybe that's how she found out about the pictures."

"No surprise there. She hates Nessa, too. Not because Nessa ever did anything to her, really. Well, not until this morning. She hates Nes simply because Dane liked her. Same with you. Because of Clay."

"But I didn't do anything to any of these people," I said. "Including Bethany."

"Doesn't matter. You have something they want. Fame, first place at a competition, a cute guy interested in you. That's why envy's one of the seven deadly sins. It corrupts people's judgment.

Some saint said envy was sadness for someone else's good. Seems like that's Sally to a T. Bethany, too."

I studied Jenna. Her hands were in perfect position on the steering wheel, her fingers white from gripping the molded plastic so hard. She was much deeper, more sensitive than her original impression.

I really liked this girl. Stupid though it was, I trusted her to be my friend. A real one that I shared my secrets and pain with. Well, not all of myself. Not yet.

"I guess I'm glad Sally stepped forward," I said. But my heart ached. Part of me had always hoped we'd make up and be the friends we'd once been. I dreaded telling my mom about Sally's role in my scandal. She and Sally's mom had been close for years.

"Oh, God," I whispered.

"What?" Jenna yelled. Her body jerked.

"Just—just pictures. Of me."

"Worse than the ones on the Net?" Jenna glanced over, eyes wide. "Holy fuck. Abbi, those are horrible."

Tears burned my eyes, and I tried to swallow down the lump. They were. They were worse than I'd imagined.

I closed the file, my hand shaking.

"What are you going to do with that?" Jenna asked.

"I don't know."

"Hiding hasn't worked," Jenna pointed out, her voice gentle but threaded with steel. I sat up straighter, gripping the edge of the folder. "And those…they'll find a way into the wrong hands. Onto the Internet."

"I don't want to hurt my family. These pictures would do that."

"Then you're going to live afraid one of those'll come out,"

Jenna said. "Fear eats at you. Makes you different and never in a good way."

She spoke from experience. I should ask what she meant by that but right now, I couldn't think at all. I kept seeing those images. Those horrible images of me. Naked. Exposed. On a bed that multiple men surrounded.

"Were you unconscious?" Jenna asked. She sounded as choked up as I was.

"Yes."

"Abbi, I'm going to ask you something because I've wondered even before I met you. The way you look in those photos…I've seen girls look like that at parties. Were you drugged?"

Nausea crashed over me as I wondered if I was going back to the weeks where I shivered and vomited in the shower every single morning.

"Yes," I whispered, head bowed with the humiliation Sally, Steve, Bethany wanted me to feel.

Those pictures had been taken for one reason and one reason only—to shame me into silence.

"That's the illegal bit you mentioned before," Jenna said.

"I don't know, Jenna. I just don't know if I'm ready for another round of intense scrutiny." I wasn't sure I had the right to ask my family to go through that again.

I wasn't sure I could live any sort of life at all, always fearful, waiting, if I didn't.

CHAPTER NINE
Clay

Dane patted my back when I came into the kitchen to get some coffee, his eyes filled with amusement.

"Heard about your trip to crazy town last night from Kai."

I grunted, wanting my eyes to focus.

"Just so you know, Nessa wanted to bring Abbi to the concert tonight."

"Wait—they met?"

Dane nodded, his mouth pinched with displeasure. "This morning. They bonded over a Bethany experience."

I stiffened, disgusted just at the mention of Bethany's name. "Do I even want to know? Everything okay?"

"Yeah. Nessa told Bethany off. She said Abbi's really nice, by the way. She and Jenna just left for Portland. They won't be back till late."

"Abbi didn't want to come to our show?"

"Not how I heard it. Nessa said Abbi was meeting someone down there. Jenna decided to go with her. You know she doesn't like crowds."

I grunted, slamming back another gulp of my coffee. Probably some dude Abbi knew. I didn't want her talking to other men. I didn't want her doing other men. I scrubbed my palm over my face.

"They're meeting one of Abbi's old friends from high school. Apparently, she wasn't very nice to Abbi, so Jenna said she'd tag along for moral support."

A girl. Relief eased the tightness building in my chest. "For the best. She's a distraction I don't need."

"Tackling her probably wasn't your smartest decision. Especially if you want in her pants."

He had no idea. Last night's restlessness was punctuated by dreams of Abbi in my arms and what I'd like to do to her once I got her there again. The 3:00 a.m. cold shower hadn't done much to ease my aching balls, but it had wakened me enough so I didn't fall back asleep until well after five.

I never lost sleep or obsessed over girls. That was my brother Colt's deal. Until now, I'd never dated anyone seriously, something my dad worried over when I was in high school. So much so he'd decided to take me for a father-son fishing trip. Looking back, I was sure my mom had asked him to. My dad, for all his ability when it came to playing music, tended to be oblivious to the little things like my life. Which was just fine with me.

We went on a weekend toward the end of my junior year, and I'd spent most of the time considering which of my many options to take to prom. I'd ticked through the list, bored out of my mind, as I waited for a fish to bite. My dad had a beer—something I'd gotten drunk on the weekend before and now couldn't stand the smell of—but I had to make due with a hot can of cola.

Dad had cleared his throat. "So your mom thinks you're gay."

I'd just taken a sip of my drink and managed to inhale it up into my nasal passage. The bubbles stung.

"What? Shit. That hurt."

"Sorry. I should've waited. But I just wanted to let you know that's cool. We love you, Clay. If you're into dudes and that makes you happy, then go for it."

"I'm not into dudes," I'd managed to wheeze. My nose had

hurt so much, I thought for sure it had to be bleeding. Coke in your nose was not cool.

"It's fine. In case you were worried."

"I'm not worried because I'm not gay. I like girls."

While that conversation was embarrassing and the epitome of unproductive, my dad had tried.

Now, six years later, I wished I had the same conviction in my family and the same naïve belief that all girls wanted me for was me. Both were patently false and caused lots of heartache, which was why I didn't like my continuing obsession with Abigail Dorsey. I wanted her to the point I was thinking about her and what I'd like to do to her both waking and in my dreams.

Sure, she was beautiful and smart—the two prerequisites for grabbing my attention. But the vulnerability she exuded made me want to curl her up tight in my lap, hugging her there until she was ready to stand up again on her own. That desire to nurture and protect just wasn't my style.

———◆———

I headed to my parents for my weekly check-in on Cassidy. When I arrived, Mom sent me down to the pool area. "Cassie's still sleeping. Go be loud out there so she can rest."

My parents had a big house—I doubted me talking to my mom in the kitchen would be an issue, but one more look at her face, her tired eyes, and I understood she needed some more time to collect herself. I wondered if my dad had done something to upset her.

I loved my father, I really did. He taught me how to play

multiple instruments and took me on stupid fishing trips when he could fit them in. But his treatment of my mother, the parent who'd raised and loved me when he wasn't around, pissed me off. Maybe I'd get lucky and he'd be recording. Nope, he was lounging in the hot tub next to Colt.

"Dad." I nodded in his direction. "Colt." I shook his hand and ruffled his damp hair. "Good to see you."

"Hey, bro. If you'd called me back, I would've driven out with you."

Colten was older than me by twenty months. He'd finished his bachelor's of science and was now in his last year of his master's program. While we were both at Northern, we rarely ran into each other.

"Sorry. Last night didn't go the way I hoped and I overslept."

Colten raised an eyebrow. Of the three of us, he looked the most like our father with his piercing dark eyes and black hair. He even had Dad's mannerisms, like the way he tilted his head when he was giving you his full attention.

Colt was the least musically-inclined of any of us. He lived for chemistry, specifically, biochem, which Abbi had talked about yesterday. While I hadn't been interested enough to learn all the details, I'd heard my brother spout enough on the topic to have a basic sense of what she'd been talking about.

"Girl trouble?" Colt asked with a smirk. He'd been in a serious relationship for the past couple of years, even mentioned he was starting to think long-term, which made my stomach ache and my palms sweat. If my parents, who'd known each other long before my dad's rise to stardom couldn't cut it, the odds were against Colt and me, who had always been media darlings, finding something lasting.

"No. I'd have to be dating a girl for there to be trouble."

"Ah," Dad said. "Why don't you join us? I want to hear about the girl who shot down the mighty Clay Rippey."

Ignoring him flitted through my mind for a second, but I'd come here as much to get his take on the situation as to see Cassie and my mom. I kicked off my shoes and pulled off my T-shirt. Stepping into the water, I waited to get accustomed to the heat before I sank down fully into the warm water, leaning back against the rim of the hot tub.

Cassidy tumbled through the door, dropped her towel onto one of the benches before jumping into the pool. Dad smiled, his eyes filled with pleasure. He was as relieved as the rest of us were to see Cassidy's energy so high.

"Don't wear yourself out too much, Cassie," Dad said. "You're still building up your strength."

She swam to the edge and glared at us. "I know my limits."

"Of course you do, sweetie. I know you want to come to the gala next weekend, and I want you to feel well enough for that."

"Dad! That's a whole week away. I'm going. I told Briar I'd write a speech. She was excited."

"Briar?" I asked. No way she could be talking about Abbi's aunt.

"Briar Moore," Cassidy sighed, long and drawn out like she did whenever she enjoyed knowing something I didn't. "Engaged to Hayden Crewe. She's opened a counseling center at the hospital to help families of cancer and terminally ill patients."

"When and what is this event?" Colt asked. Like me, Colt took all things related to Cassidy's illness seriously.

"It's a charity gala," Dad said.

I raised an eyebrow. Dad hated those events.

"Your mom called Briar to tell her our story and ask what we could do to help out. It's a great idea."

"So is Asher Smith and his family going to be there?" I asked.

Dad pulled his eyes from Cassidy to focus on me. "Yeah. I ran into him last week. He and his wife were one of the first donors to the project. Her first husband died from an auto-immune disease." He paused, eyes narrowing on mine. "You seem really interested."

"What do you know about his stepdaughter?"

I directed the question at Dad, but Colt answered.

"Abbi? You been looking out for her like I asked?"

"I ran into her at the library last night. She was getting hassled by a couple frat guys."

"Figured that was going to happen," Colt sighed. "She's a pretty girl, always alone. Bothers me to see her so isolated."

"Asher said she was at Northern. And that she was really messed up by what had happened last year," Dad said. "I don't understand these boys' desire to drug a woman."

"You know more about it?" I asked.

"Careful, Clay," Colt said. "Sounds like you're interested, and Abbi's naked skin has been flashed all over the Internet. That's a lot to handle."

My dad must have realized I was pissed because he cleared his throat.

"Remember that time you were 'engaged' to Leah Bradford?"

Colt rolled his eyes. "Yeah, from a picture of us holding hands. I was seventeen."

"Or how about that time I was cheating on your mother with three women at the same time."

Colt snorted, but I had to bite back a retort pointing out that wasn't too far from the truth. Anger surged, hot and vicious, into my chest. I focused on Cassidy's splashing.

"Okay, I hear you," Colt said. "From what I can tell about Abbi during class, she's smart, and she's a hard worker." He glanced at me. "And she's rebuffed every guy that's asked her out."

"How many guys are we talking about?" I asked.

"Pretty much all of 'em. Not often chemistry nerds have such a hot girl hanging around."

I ground my teeth together.

"She's got you tied up in knots," Dad said. He kept an eye on Cassidy but smiled at me. "Your mother did the same thing to me. Damn, I was a mess."

Didn't last, though, did it, Dad?

"I asked a couple of questions about the girl, and you think I'm moving toward something serious." I let some of my contempt seep into my voice. I couldn't challenge Dad without hurting my mom, but that didn't mean he couldn't know I was angry.

He met my gaze, his troubled. This wasn't the first time we'd gone a round or two since that day he'd cut out at the hospital, leaving my mom alone to deal with Cassie's fading body. For all I knew, he thought I was holding a grudge about that. Maybe I would have if he hadn't walked up to that woman in the hotel lobby.

"The way you asked the questions and the look in your eye when you heard about the competition…yeah, I think you're serious, Clay."

I folded my arms over my chest. "I don't want to like her, but I do."

"Then you'll be glad to know I have extra tickets for you and your brother to come next week. If you'd like one."

Cassidy pulled herself out of the pool and we all turned to look at her. Her short hair was slicked to her head. Her hipbones protruded sharply, and her arms were thin—too thin—but her eyes were bright and her smile was infectious as she climbed into the hot tub.

"That was fun. I've missed swimming." She yawned.

Dad pulled her close, his eyes soft. "It's good to see you playing again, kiddo. Just don't overdo it."

"No problem. So you're talking about Abbi Dorsey? Briar mentioned her. She seems upset that Abbi wouldn't put out a statement about those pictures."

I started. Sure, my sister was in her teens, but she was so small. I wasn't used to her being part of these types of conversations.

Dad nodded, his eyes taking on a thoughtful gleam. "Asher said the same thing. It's obvious he cares about her. There's gotta be more to that story than we know."

Cassie yawned again. "The press are such jerks. 'Member the story they wrote about me?"

Dad kissed the top of her head. "I'm glad you're here, Cassie-girl."

But Cassidy wasn't paying him any attention, she was looking at me. "You better be nice to her, Clay."

I shifted on the bench. "I was nice to her."

Cassidy snorted. "I bet you dismissed her like you do with

anyone you don't think is worth your time. I hate that brush-off thing."

"I was nice, Cassidy."

She glared at me. "See that you stay that way. I heard what Dad said about her being drugged, and I saw some of those pictures. She didn't get a choice to be there."

Hearing my baby sister state that made the entire situation Abbi had endured even more obscene. If Cassidy was drugged and photographed...I wouldn't know what I would do. Had Abbi been assaulted without her consent? Without even her knowledge? My hands fisted.

"Abbi needs a friend. If you guys were her friends, she wouldn't be so alone." Cassidy's eyes filled with tears. "That's the worst part."

I reached over and squeezed her fingers. "We're friends, ladybug, but I'll make sure I look after her. Like I do you."

"Good," she sighed. She pressed her cheek into Dad's chest. In the next second, her soft snore rose over the roar of the bubbles.

"I didn't know she still did that," Colt said.

"She doesn't usually. Not unless she's really tired." Dad stood up, cradling Cassidy in his arms.

"Oh, good. Just in time," Dad said as Mom walked into the room, carrying a thick stack of beach towels. "Spread out a towel for her, will you, Maryanne?"

Mom hurried to do his bidding. The two of them fussed over Cassidy, making sure she was dry and bundled in towels.

"So, Abbi Dorsey," Colt said.

"I helped her out last night. We got to talking. She's different from what I expected."

"Focused, smart and very, very wary?"

"Yeah. Man, you should have seen the way Charles and Neal were talking to her. It was disgusting."

"I bet she liked you coming to her rescue," he chuckled.

"She was shaking." Both Colt and I frowned, his deepening when I said, "Reminded me of Cassie."

"That's why I asked you to keep an eye on her." Colt's eyes were serious. "I've overheard some conversation. Since there's a nearly naked pic of her online, it's like guys no longer see her as a person. Doesn't matter that she's not coherent in it. She's nude and, thus, an object. I've yet to see a girl talk to her."

I ran my hands through my hair. "That bad?" I asked.

Colt narrowed his eyes. "Worse. I like her, by the way."

My shoulders tensed and I probably looked pissed because Colt shook his head, his lips curved up in a devilish grin.

"Not like that. I mean, she's pretty and she's smart, but she's also at least six years younger than me. And I've got my own girl."

"Good."

"I'm worried about her."

I hopped out of the hot tub and wrapped a towel around my waist, and Colt did the same. "Well, I promised Cassie I'd be her friend, and she's hooked in with Jenna and Nessa now apparently. I'd watch out for her, but she shot me down. Ran away like a rabbit sprinting from a greyhound."

Colt grinned. "Count me in for next week, Dad," he yelled. "It's going to be fun watching Clay lose his mind over this girl."

"What girl?" Mom asked.

Colt laughed as he walked back toward the stairs.

CHAPTER TEN
Abbi

"What are you going to wear to the gala tomorrow night?" Mom asked.

I'd come home because I needed to get away from my growing attraction to Clay. Not that I'd seen him much this week, but Nessa and Jenna talked about him and the other guys in the band. That's why I knew they had a show again tonight at a well-known bar. Pretty much a weekly occurrence from what I'd been able to discern.

I considered going for about three seconds but I just couldn't see Clay. Each time his name was mentioned, my body warmed and my heart beat faster. I hated the reaction because I was powerless to stop it.

He'd stopped by before my first class last Tuesday to return my sunglasses. I'd forced myself to look him in the eye. Mortification swept through me as I did so. What if he could see how much I reacted to him?

"Hey, Abbi. Just wanted to return these." He held out my sunglasses in his palm.

"Thank you." I smiled, pleasure blooming in my chest. "I was worried they'd flown into the fountain. Nessa, Jenna, and I ran by there Saturday."

"I heard you met Nes. She's awesome."

"We went for a run and had breakfast together. Both she and Jenna are really nice."

I slid the aviators out of his hand, and Clay grinned. I cleared my throat, needing a second to get my focus back on our conversation.

"Asher gave them to me just before I left for Sydney. I hated to think I was so careless." I pulled my lips into my mouth. I had to stop babbling.

"Not you. Me. I hit you pretty hard."

"A spectacular sack," I said, smiling. "How's the bruised butt?"

He threw his head back and laughed. "Bruised," he admitted. "Like my ego. Could use some TLC."

I'd stepped back, fighting the building need to touch him. "Okay. Thanks again." I raised the glasses, almost as if they could shield me from his immense sexual pull. "See you around."

The attention that short exchange had drawn was unreal. I'd pushed past at least fifteen people, all of whom wanted to know why rock god Clay Rippey had spoken to me. I'd hurried to class, head down and heart pounding.

Mom's words pulled me back to the present, and I glanced over. She settled on my bed, just as she had since I was twelve—about six months before my dad died. It was part of our wind-down ritual. Whenever I was home, she came into my room for at least half an hour to talk over our days.

"Something I already have," I said, shrugging. I couldn't care less about how I looked. Maybe if I wore something really ugly, the media would ignore me.

"I can take you shopping for a new dress in the morning. It'd be fun."

I fell back onto the pillow next to her. "Maybe I shouldn't go tomorrow."

"What? Why? Because Clay might be there?"

"I'm more worried about the media. I don't want to date,

Mom. I just want to be left alone."

"Abbi." Mom sighed, turning to face me on the bed. "I know you're hurt, maybe even scared. And what that boy did, what all of them did, was so deeply wrong. But I don't want to talk about them. I want to talk about you. How to make you happy."

"Sally gave me a folder. It's full of people who hate me," I said, my voice quiet.

Mom sat up, her eyes searching my face. "Why didn't you tell me?"

"Because I just found out the details. Well, I got it from her last week. I asked her not to tell you yet. You can't be mad at Rhonda and Ralph. This is all on Sally." I pulled out the folder—minus the pictures, which were now stowed away in another safe place—and glanced at it. Finally, I handed it over. "She admitted to suggesting Steve take the pictures to get back at me."

"For?"

I shrugged. "Everything."

"That's not much of an answer, Abbi."

"For being a better runner and cheerleader."

"Because of Asher," Mom's voice was quiet.

"That was one of her reasons. But it's ridiculous. He can't help being famous. You know I love Asher."

Mom looked down at her folded hands. "I'm so sorry my relationship has hurt you."

I sat next to her, put my arm around her. "Oh, no, Mom. No. It didn't. You didn't. If Sally's like that…well, she's not a true friend."

Mom took my hand and squeezed my fingers. "Did she have anything to do with those pictures, Abbi? I mean, did she help set them up? Put the drugs in your drink?"

"She says no. Just suggested it to Steve as a way he could make money off of me. To pay off his debt to the concert venue." I picked at my cuticle. "I think that's probably true."

"You didn't tell me you talked to Sally," Mom said.

"I didn't plan on it, but she was insistent. I went down to Portland last Saturday. With Jenna. Sally wanted me to forgive her."

"And will you?"

"I don't know. She went way too far."

"She did." Mom paused. "I'm struggling with her part in this, but at least she's given you some help to start an investigation. Asher and I'd like to do that. For you."

"I don't know. What if it's worse? Getting Sally in trouble— hashing it all out again." I swallowed hard, thinking about those pictures. My stomach rolled, and I took a slow, steadying breath.

"What do you want then?" Mom said, nodding to the folder.

I walked to the window, hugging my elbows. "Honestly? I just want it to go away. But…this girl at school—her name is Bethany—she's part of that hate-Abbi club. She seems to know about other pictures. They're worse, I guess." I knew they were, but I couldn't stand telling my mother that. "She said she'd leak them if I hung out with Clay."

Mom wrapped her arm around my waist and leaned her head against mine. For a long moment, we stayed like that, me hurting and confused, my mom doing her best to soak all the negativity up and away from me.

"I won't tell you how to live your life, Abigail," she said, her voice muffled with suppressed tears. "But consider talking to Briar. She spent years investigating cases not that different from this one, making sure the bad guys were exposed."

I winced at the word. "It's not that bad, really. I mean, it's just some pictures taken too far." I looked down at my hands, hating the lie.

"Abigail, if there's more you need to tell me, I'm here. Your family will help you. All of us. Any way we can."

"I know that. I just…" I blew out a breath. "I need a chance to figure this out. What I want. Who I am now." What those pictures I didn't want to share intimated Steve and his friends had done to me, *taken* from me.

Mom settled back on the bed. "I won't push more about it."

"But?"

"You're young. You need to go out, have fun. Live."

I ran my finger on the edge of one of the throw pillows. "It's not just what Steve did. Everyone at Tech believed his representation of me." I struggled to swallow. Keeping secrets from my mother was hard. Harder because this one was eating at me. "They all wanted to believe that about me."

Mom's fingers wrapped around my hand, stilling my tugging. "Which we both know isn't true. So does the rest of your family and anyone who actually knows you. People say mean things, do cruel things. You can't let them win. Sally and Steve—this girl, Bethany—they want your happiness. Right now, they own it. Don't let them keep it."

"I don't want to feed the rumor mill. It's so hurtful, Mom. I don't have anything to fall back on talent-wise, even academic-wise. Each of their words rip me to shreds."

"You can't avoid that. You're lovely and related to famous, rich people. Others, even people you care about like Sally, are going to get jealous and act stupid. The best thing you can do is live your life and say a big 'fuck you' to the haters."

I giggled. My mom wasn't much for cursing, and vulgarity from her always sounded funny. Mom propped herself against the headboard. "Remember when I teased you about the pill?" she asked.

I rolled my eyes. "Like I'd forget."

"Well, I think you should consider it."

I wrinkled my nose. "Don't take this the wrong way, but I really don't want to talk to you about this."

"Since you've become a hermit without a friend your own age, you don't have anyone else to talk to, honey. Whether you choose to see Clay or not, there will be other men you're going to want to date. And sex, the right kind, is about building a connection. Deepening a relationship. You need that in your life."

"Says the romance writer."

Mom smiled. "Exactly. I'm an expert."

I chewed on my lip, considering how much to tell her. Mom and I had always been close, but her marriage to Asher had changed our relationship. Not her, she was still an amazing woman, a fabulous listener. But as the situation at Tech got worse, I'd closed off.

"This is so not the way I thought our conversation would go. Aren't you supposed to ask about my classes, what I plan to do this weekend?"

"You're getting straight A's and you're going to the charity event with us tomorrow. Sunday, you'll go back to your dorm where you'll hole up, studying until your classes on Monday. You need a social life, Abigail. This is killing you slowly, and I hate it."

"I have Jenna and Nessa. They drag me out."

"To run and get a bite to eat, which is good. But you were born to interact with others. You crave social situations, as much as I panic at the mere thought of them."

"I don't like the comments, the looks."

"The best thing you can do to make the speculation go away once and for all is to be seen with a man. Let the rumor mill make up all kinds of ridiculous stories about your affair. Clay seems like a great candidate. From what Asher's said, his dad's a nice man. Briar likes Clay's mom. You like Clay. Total win."

She paused, letting her argument sink in. "And think how great it'll feel to know your horrible excuse for an ex-boyfriend is reading about your hot new boyfriend."

I giggled again. "That's not exactly right."

"Give me my fantasy, please."

"I didn't know you had it in you, Mom."

Mom smiled, her gray eyes alight with mischief, but the corner of her mouth held sadness as she smoothed my hair back.

"I've lived through enough now to know when to pick my battles. I think your happiness is a battle worth winning."

CHAPTER ELEVEN
Clay

Suits weren't comfortable. While I was glad Mom kept some nice clothes for us here at their house, I detested the ties she picked out. I wasn't a power-tie kind of dude. Correction, I wasn't a formal attire dude. I scowled at the knot I couldn't get right.

"Clay!" Dad yelled. "We need to go. Now."

I grabbed my wallet, shoving it and my phone into my pockets. Snagging the cufflinks Cassidy gave me for Christmas last year, I stuffed them into the buttonholes as I headed down the stairs.

"I'm ready."

"Looking good, handsome," Cassidy said. "It's the cufflinks. They tie everything together."

"You know it. Thanks for buying them for me."

I grinned, barely resisting the urge to ruffle her hair. Not that it was long enough to mess up, but I knew the gesture would offend her grown-up sensibilities.

Cassidy twirled, showing off her chiffon dress. "What do you think?"

"Oh, we're trading compliments?"

"You're so mean."

Cassidy stomped toward the front door. I intercepted her. My heart twisted at the tears in her eyes.

"You look pretty, ladybug. Really pretty. I'm so glad you're my date."

Colt shoved me out of the way. "Get your own date. I'm taking Cassidy. We've got dancing plans."

"You've got Kara," I said, shoving him out of the way.

"She's not coming. Went home for the weekend."

I turned, needing to see his eyes now that I'd heard that note in his voice.

"Everything okay?" I asked.

Colt's face tightened, his eyes shadowed. "I don't know."

"Fight later. Get in the car now." Mom swept by us, pulling me along with her.

Colt shook his head and raised his eyebrows. No, I wouldn't say anything. He relaxed, but his face was still drawn.

"I don't think we've ever been on time to one of these things." Mom sighed.

I helped her into the front seat.

"You look great."

She beamed at me, happier than I'd seen her in years. Her short, light-brown hair flipped out, swinging around her jaw.

"She does, doesn't she?" Dad said. He turned her head to kiss her.

I rolled my eyes at the soft connection of lips and climbed into the backseat of the SUV. Cassidy took up her normal spot in the middle while Colten slammed his door.

Dad hated limos and preferred to drive himself. That was one of the things I had to appreciate about my dad—he refused to let others dictate his life.

"Buckle up," Mom said. She turned to look us over. "You're a good-looking crew."

I smiled at her, and she winked.

Normally, I wasn't much for hobnobbing with Seattle's rich and fast set. Not that everyone going tonight was fast. But they'd all be wealthy.

Maybe because I'd grown up with all the material trappings of success, I craved simpler moments. Sure, I liked performing. I was good at it, too. I'd learned to play the piano, guitar, banjo, drums, and even the tuba during a crazy stint in the marching band my freshman year of high school. That's what happened when you were the son of one of an era's top-ten best drummers.

Dad had been surprised I hadn't taken the most glamorous role as lead guitarist. He'd pointed out I had the looks and flirting capabilities necessary to carry a band. But I wasn't in music to be the face of a group and didn't crave that attention. Kai was better in that role than I'd ever be, something Dad grudgingly agreed with when he came to one of our more recent shows.

Arriving at the hotel, I helped Mom from the Tahoe while Dad tossed the keys to the valet. Colt offered Cassidy his elbow and the two of them marched past the cameras. I handed Mom off to Dad and followed my siblings into the ballroom. We knew the drill. Our folks would find us once they'd completed their media duties.

"So what'll it be to drink, ladybug?" I asked as we made our way into the crowd.

"My name is Cassidy." My sister glared. "And I want sparkling water."

I nodded and raised my brow to Colt, who called out, "Beer."

"Everything cool?" I asked.

He shook his head, the tip of his nose turning red. "Not now. Not here."

Well, damn. I rested my hand on his shoulder before trotting off to the bar, pretending I wasn't looking for Abbi. Returning to Colten and Cassidy, we wandered through the space until we found a table to place our drinks on.

"You want to sit for a few minutes?" I asked Cassidy as Colt was pulled off into a conversation with some scientist he'd met a few months before.

"I need to talk to Briar. She asked me to give a speech. I need to know when I'm up."

"I don't know her, but we should be able to pick her out of the crowd."

After a few minutes of circling the room, we still hadn't found Briar. I took Cassidy back to the table, worried she'd already overdone it for the night. But her cheeks were rosy and her eyes bright.

"Quite a turnout," Mom said, settling her wrap and bag next to Cassidy's chair. "I'm glad. Briar's idea is such a good one."

"We looked for her. Cassidy wanted to know when she was giving her speech."

Mom frowned a little, trying to gauge Cassidy's endurance.

"Clay."

Goosebumps rippled across my skin at Abbi's voice. That had never happened before, and my reaction pissed me off. She was just a girl. One I should really steer clear of. I turned slowly, gritting my teeth.

I wasn't ready for the vision of Abbi Dorsey all dressed up. I'd thought she looked good in rolled up jeans—because she did—but tonight, she was stunning.

Her long, reddish hair was pulled up in a simple twist at the base of her neck, showing off the long line of her throat and those elegant cheekbones. Her makeup was minimal, her lip gloss natural, emphasizing the plumpness of those lips. The dress was simple with one shoulder strap that fell in an elegant line to the top of her high-heeled sandals. The soft lilac color enhanced the luster of Abbi's Seattle pallor and brightened her amazing eyes.

"Hi. You look really pretty," Cassidy said.

Cassidy had stepped into what was becoming an awkward silence as I continued to drink in the sight of Abbi. I wanted to study the small grouping of freckles I'd just noticed at the base of her neck.

Abbi shot Cassidy that unguarded smile I'd already come to crave.

"So do you. I love the color of your dress. Matches your eyes."

Cassidy preened. "We got it from Nordstrom this morning. Where's yours from?"

Abbi looked down, confusion puckering her brow. "I have no idea. My mom picked it out. So, I'm Abbi, by the way. And I'm assuming you're Cassidy." She held out her hand to the younger girl, who shook it with enthusiasm.

"Uh. Sorry," I said, finally finding my voice. "So, yeah, that's Cassidy. And my mom, Maryanne. You know my brother Colten. My dad's talking to Cassidy's oncologist back there." I tipped my chin.

"Pleasure to meet you," Abbi said to my mom, her eyes as hesitant as her voice.

"You, too, Abbi. I heard Clay ran into you last week."

Abbi glanced at me, a smile tugging at her lips. "Bowled me over, more like."

"I did teach him manners, regardless of what you saw."

Abbi laughed, a bright sound that seemed to sparkle. She really needed to do that more often. "I'm sure you did."

This easygoing Abbi was someone I liked more than the guarded woman I'd met a week ago. She tipped her head back so she could look up into my face. I leaned closer, ignoring my own warning. Abbi stilled, her smile dimming.

"I wish you would've come to our concert last Saturday. Or last night. I know Nessa invited you."

"Concerts aren't really my thing. Not that I doubt your greatness. I'm sure you are. Great, I mean."

Her teeth sunk deep into her lower lip and her eyes darted from mine. I resisted the urge to smirk.

"So Aunt Bri wanted to know if you still planned to give a speech," Abbi said, directing her attention toward Cassidy. "I'm the advance guard while she and my mom work out some details with the hotel staff."

"Is there a problem?" Mom asked, looking around.

"Oof." Abbi lurched, nearly falling into me. I placed my hands on her hips to steady her just as another set of arms wrapped around her from the back.

A freckle-faced boy peeked out from behind her, smiling wide.

"Sorry about the terror. His name," Abbi said, extricating herself from both sets of our arms, "is Mason. My brother."

He smiled wider, and I was sure it was because she left off the "step" part of their relationship.

"Hi," Mason said. He stuck out his hand toward me. "You're the Clay guy, right? The one Aunt Bri and Dahlia were talking about?"

Abbi's cheeks flamed, and I chuckled. "My name is Clay, anyway. Nice to meet you, Mason."

"My dad said your dad plays drums," Mason said, plopping

into the chair next to mine. "I like the drums, but I play saxophone in the school band. It's okay."

"Abbi, come over here and tell me more about tonight's agenda," my mom said. Abbi glanced at me and Mason, the color in her cheeks still bright, before wending her way around the table to sit on my mom's other side.

"She likes you," Mason said, his voice low. "So don't hurt her feelings. Or I'll have to kick your butt."

I didn't doubt for a minute this scrawny kid meant what he said. He might be young, but he'd grown up in the music community. He knew, as I did, just how hard the media churn was on relationships.

"I like Abbi, too. I don't intend to hurt her."

Mason nodded, his freckled face set in solemn lines. "That's good. I'm not supposed to know about what her last boyfriend did. All because Abbi didn't ask my dad to come to his concert."

"Wait. Her ex wanted her to have Asher come play at some gig?"

"Yeah. But not for my dad, for the guy's band. They're crap. That's why no one bought tickets."

"Huh."

Mason shrugged. "Least, that's what I wasn't supposed to hear and know. But I know he took pictures of her. Abbi cried a lot, and now she's scared all the time. I don't like her like this. She used to be really fun."

I held up my hands, my mind spinning with thoughts. "So how do you know this?"

Mason shifted, his eyes darting around. "That's not the point. You just need to know you're the first person Abbi's mentioned in months. Don't make her sad again."

"I'll do my best."

"Good. 'Cause I worry about her. She needs real friends, not like that girl who set up the photos."

CHAPTER TWELVE
Abbi

All during the dinner, my eyes drifted back to Clay. Mason wouldn't tell me what they'd talked about, but I'd felt Clay's gaze more than once—like he was pondering an equation and I wasn't the right answer. I wasn't hungry, not with my stomach so knotted up with wanting and not wanting to want Clay.

When Cassidy jumped from her chair, Clay half stood before his brother pulled him back down. I'd noticed that about him—that protective streak. A little shiver slid across my skin. What would he think if he found out why those pictures of me existed?

A camera flashed in front of my face and I blinked, a frown and a headache building. Mom's hand came down on my knee, squeezing gently. "Just ignore him. Not a big deal."

I tried, pretending I didn't feel the next two flashes as I focused on Cassidy.

"I was almost eleven when I found out I had Hodgkin's," she said. "Too young to really understand what the doctors were talking about but old enough to realize I must be really sick if both my parents were upset enough to cry."

She paused to look around the room, her presence seemed to grow. This young woman understood how to work a room, how to hold court. Warmth bloomed in my chest along with pride.

"Cancer doesn't affect a certain group of people. It hurts all of us, no matter our age, our number of friends, the size of our house or anything else we might have. Cancer reminds us, especially the kids at the hospital, that we're the same. That we're sick and have to fight for each day, sometimes each breath.

"One of my friends came from a very wealthy family who didn't like to visit her. Another's parents worked four jobs between them to try to cover the bare minimum of her chemo costs, but they found time every day—*every day*—to visit Camille. And guess what? Camille's in remission. She had a reason to fight. So did I." Cassidy paused, letting the words sink in. She looked out at the crowd.

"Camille and I, we're so lucky to know we have another chance at life. But even that's not always easy. I didn't expect to be here, and I've had to relearn how to be friends with normal kids. How to go to school and let comments about my lack of hair and skinniness role off my back. I did that with help from my therapist, who's as much a part of my team as my oncologist." She smiled, a small dimple forming on her right cheek as she waved at someone in the back of the room. The audience laughed.

"So here I am." She lifted her arms from the podium, holding them outright. "Against the odds." She looked down for a moment, her eyes somber when she raised them back to the elegantly dressed people just beyond her podium. "Many of you are here to do some charity work, and that's great. But some of you"—her gaze settled on me— "know about loss and pain."

I sucked in a breath.

"You know what can happen when things don't go the way you want them to." She broke eye contact, moving on to someone else. I sat, frozen, her words magnified in my ears.

"For those of you who've been there, the question is, what do you plan to do with your life? How much is a second chance worth to you?"

My eyes were damp, and I clapped hard, proud of the petite

girl in a taffeta dress with patches of scalp showing through the black fuzz. I was humbled that this child had been through so much, faced death, and I was the one cowering back behind the scenes, letting go of my chance at a full life.

I met Clay's eyes as his sister returned to their table. I wasn't sure I'd ever be as brave as Cassidy Rippey. I'd mulled over my mom's words most of the night, hating that Steve had won. Bethany's threats were just as bad. With her, I was setting a precedent of letting her shame me. But only if I continued to let them.

I took a deep breath, stared down at my hands. Sometimes choices really were that simple. I *wouldn't* let them.

The countdown was almost unbearable. Just ten more days, and I'd know enough to move forward with the plans I'd been considering. It was time. I needed to make my stand, take back my life.

Later, after the last speech by Aunt Briar thanking everyone for attending, the music kicked in. Asher pulled me out of my seat against my protests.

"Dance with Mom," I suggested, trying to slide my hand from his.

"Trust me, Abbi. Dance with me."

"Fine." I sighed, glancing nervously at the cameras now pointed in my direction.

Dancing with Asher was fun. He knew how to waltz, telling me his mom made him take lessons when he was in middle school. I was laughing so hard at his story about stepping on some poor girl's feet all night that I didn't see Clay until he was right behind Asher. I stopped laughing but managed not to miss the next series of steps.

"If you don't mind, I'd like to dance with Abbi," Clay said.

Asher stopped as the song ended and raised his eyebrow, waiting for me to make the decision. I gave a tiny nod, my eyes still trained on Clay.

"I'll get your mom out on the floor. She should be willing now that she's finished her glass of wine."

Clay pulled me into his arms. Immediately, I felt safe. I dropped my gaze, trying to keep a reasonable distance between us.

"Thank you for saying yes. Would've been pretty embarrassing to be turned down in front of all the cameras. And your stepdad." Clay swung me into a wide turn. We both smiled for the myriad flashes before slowly working our way into the middle of the half-filled dance floor.

"Who put you up to it?" I asked.

"Why would you think that?"

I looked up at him, waiting.

"Fine. Cassidy. She likes you. She wants us to be friends."

"It that something you want?" I asked, my voice catching.

He met my eyes, looked into them deeply. "Yes. I do."

"Your sister's amazing," I said, trying to break the seriousness of the moment.

Clay nodded, his eyes darting back to Cassidy, who was laughing at Colten's attempts to lead the foxtrot. "The best of us, to be sure."

"Your mom's nice, too."

"She told you something embarrassing about me, didn't she?"

I laughed and shook my head. This conversation was nice—normal, even. "No. We just went over the schedule and then she asked me about my classes."

"Good. She likes you, too. No reason to freak out."

When my foot slid, Clay brought me a little closer—not enough to touch his front but enough for the heat from his body to seep into mine. It was heady. Luscious. He smelled woodsy and male. I wanted to lay my head on his shoulder but managed to resist.

"Mmm. Not sure there's any reason to be scared. Is there?"

"Of me? No." He squeezed my fingers a little tighter. "I'd never hurt you, Abbi."

"I appreciate the sentiment, but things happen."

We swung around the floor, the silence warm between us.

"I want to ask you something, but I'm afraid you'll get upset. And I like hearing your laugh too much for that," Clay said.

I tipped my head back and smiled at him. "Ask away."

He squeezed my waist a little tighter. "I like seeing you happy."

"I forgot how much I liked to dance."

"You're very good at it." He smiled at me. "Makes me look good, too. So thanks." He winked. "Why did you run away from me?" He asked, his voice low so it didn't carry past us.

I swallowed, trying to get moisture back into my dry mouth. He held my hand even as it began to tremble. "I don't want to talk about that."

"You know, Abbi, I think you lied to me." His voice was soft, not accusing.

The song ended but Clay held on, pulling me even closer.

"I don't lie, Clay. I hate liars." I pressed my lips into a tight, thin line, wishing I could take back the vehemence of the words.

"Liars like Steve?" he asked, his voice nearly as gentle as his eyes.

But his grip on my waist and hand was firm, a reminder that

he was here with me. What he didn't know was how much I needed that reminder as I started to slide back into that night.

"Abbi. Stay with me."

I blinked and forced air into my empty lungs. Cassidy would be brave enough to tell the whole truth. The words trembled on my lips, the shame just behind them.

"You can tell me. Anything."

"I don't remember," I whispered.

His brow furled. "Remember what?"

"That night. I went to a party with a girl who was supposed to be my friend. We were in the same sorority. We hung out in the front room for a while. She left me, and I remember walking across campus."

"By yourself?" Clay growled.

I forced my eyes back to his. "Yes."

"And then—"

"I don't know," I said, the guilt and shame eating at me. "I don't know what happened."

"But there are pictures of you coming out of the fraternity house in the morning."

I smiled, but it was without any humor. My face felt tight, my lips stiff. I wanted to leave, to run and never stop. But Cassidy, a teenage girl who'd come to tonight's event in a much younger girl's dress with barely enough hair on her head to not be considered bald, stood up and told me to live.

I pressed my shaking palm tighter to Clay's, drawing strength from his touch. I pushed my shoulders back and met his troubled gaze.

"I walked out of Steve's bedroom. Once I found my dress and

underwear."

Clay's curse was vicious but low.

The song ended. One I hadn't even heard. Hayden appeared next to me and offered his hand. "The perfect song to dance to with my surfing mate." He winked at me, then turned to Clay. "Smile. The media has had you two engaged and broken up in the last ten minutes."

Clay patted Hayden's shoulder before he bent down and kissed my cheek. Just a social touch, but I gasped, my body tingling with his proximity. Even though I knew spending time with him would mean more media, more attention.

"We'll finish our conversation soon," he whispered into my ear. "That's a promise."

He walked over to Cassidy, playfully shoving Colten out of the way.

"Your mum was worried you were upset, and Asher's stuck talking to some executive director of a treatment facility," Hayden said. "So I get to play knight-errant. I make quite a dashing one, eh?"

I nodded, my mind still on the conversation I'd had with Clay.

"Asher and I talked to Pete while you danced with his son."

I moaned. Hayden chuckled, flashing that dimple Aunt Briar liked to run her finger over. "None of that now. He's a musician. We're musicians."

"And you were talking licks and rhythm all night," I said. Hayden spun me before bringing me back into the circle of his arms.

"You're a bloody good dancer, Abbi. This is way easier than dancing with Briar. She tries to lead."

I tried to stifle a laugh and ended up snorting. "Oh my god. She does, too."

"Took one helluva bloke to handle that lady. Fair dinkum."

"It's a good thing Americans don't actually understand half of what you say, Hayden. I have a feeling you're insulting us."

He grinned again. "Never your gorgeous aunt, love. Nor the rest of your family. So. Pete. He says Clay's got his head on straight, for all that he's a hormonal male." Hayden spun me in a circle before completing a serious of complex footwork. I followed effortlessly, relishing the opportunity to show off twelve years of lessons.

"Don't all men have raging hormones?" I asked, slightly out of breath.

"Too right." His gaze was stern. "And don't you forget it."

Hayden spun me around the dance floor a few more times before I partnered with Asher again, then with Mason. By the time I'd finished my dances, Clay and his family were gone. I tried not to feel disappointment, the slick slide of worry at what I'd admitted, but failed.

"He left you this," Mom said, handing me a folded napkin. "He and I talked for a little while. I like him a lot, Abbi."

So did I. That was the problem.

Abbi—

Cassidy was tired, so we slipped out early.

I enjoyed our dance.

We should do it again sometime. Soon.

I'll be in touch. I have a promise to keep.

Clay

"You look dreamy," Mom said.

I glanced up at her, noting the hope in her eyes.

"He's nice, Mom. But we're *not* dating."

"The way you looked at him," she said, her voice soft. "I haven't seen that look in too long."

"I don't know what you're talking about."

"Just let yourself feel, Abbi."

I wanted to. I wanted the rush of falling in love. I wanted the romance with long kisses and moonlit talks. I wanted…what I couldn't have. Not yet anyway. Not until I cleared up the mess that was my life. Prying open my fist, I smoothed the napkin then folded it back and slid it into my small, beaded purse.

Mom sighed. My attempt to protect her from disappointment had failed.

CHAPTER THIRTEEN
Clay

I'd tossed and turned most of the night, much to my frustration. Finishing my conversation with Abbi, holding her close to my body, took precedence.

"Hey, Clay." That voice was like nails on a chalkboard. But worse.

It was my fault. I'd come to the campus coffee shop, hoping the walk would help me wake up. It didn't, but now I had to deal with the fallout.

"Bethany."

"Your picture's in the paper."

I didn't say anything because there was nothing to say, really. The charity gala was big news all across the state, but also nationally and internationally, thanks to the presence of my dad, Asher, Hayden and a few others, and Briar's press connections.

"I've never seen you in a suit before."

And she never would in person if I had my way.

"Was that girl your date?"

My brow furled as I tried to suss out what she was asking me. The only girl I was with last night was my sister.

"Must not have been too memorable," Bethany said. A small, smile turned up her lips. "Did your family make you dance with her?"

Anger bit into my throat, my frown getting fiercer. They had. All of them, but I wasn't going to tell Bethany that. Point of fact, I'd enjoyed my time with Abbi.

"I mean, I know her stepdad's famous and all, but really,

she's not even *that* pretty. You could do so much better. With a nice girl."

My anger, which had abated slightly as Bethany continued to talk, slammed back into my chest.

"You mean my very good friend Abbi? We've had this conversation, Bethany. I like spending time with her. She's amazing."

"Thanks." Abbi's hand cupped my shoulder, and I reached up to squeeze her fingers. Bethany's eyes stayed there, burning, at our entwined hands.

"You're not bad yourself," Abbi said, humor lacing her voice.

"You should have told me you were coming here today," I said, tipping my chin back so I could see her better. "I would have bought you a mocha. I do have a promise to keep."

Abbi was dressed in a flowing linen skirt and a dark jean jacket. Her hair was pulled into a thick braid that trailed over her shoulder, the end dangling saucily a couple of inches above her right breast.

She looked good. Casual and comfortable. I wished I could add well-loved to my growing list of adjectives.

The idea of anyone else touching her, as she'd inferred last night, made my hand tighten around her fingers enough for her to wince. I let go, running my palm up and down her hand to ease some of the sting.

"You ready?" I asked her.

She cocked an eyebrow, her gaze darting to Bethany. I stood and pulled her closer to my side, reveling in her warm curves and the heady herbal scent of her hair.

"We can work through our thing," I continued, eyes begging.

"That's why I stopped by," she answered. "To see if now was a good time."

I gathered my papers, cramming them back into my binder. I cringed, knowing I'd have to rewrite my notes now that they were a wrinkled mess. Sucked to be so meticulous about my work, but I wasn't changing now.

I shouldered my bag and reslung an arm around Abbi's shoulders. She stiffened, her back bowing at my touch before she relaxed. I glanced down at her but her face was turned in profile, her eyes downcast.

"See you, Bethany," I said, pulling Abbi toward the exit.

"Bye," she said, her small voice dejected.

I pulled Abbi closer, giving her a proper hug. "Thank you for coming over. We're totally even on the rescuing now."

"I don't think so," Abbi said. She laughed but it was strained. Because I was holding her? No, she melted closer as we walked. "That girl wasn't going to hurt you, just undress you with her eyes."

"That was more than enough," I shuddered. "I need another shower."

She peeked over her shoulder. "She's still looking at us. Like she wants to kill me."

"Whatcha got there?"

"Green tea," Abbi said.

"You don't like chocolate?"

She wrinkled her nose and shook her head. "Not in coffee."

Interesting. I'd assumed, like Jenna and Nessa, she liked mochas. Yet another quirk of Abbi's personality. I glanced around the gray-washed late morning. It was Sunday, so few students were out yet.

"Where to?"

Abbi shrugged. "I was going to the library, but I needed some caffeine first. They didn't have any tea at the student center."

"Not much in the way of caffeine in there," I teased.

"There's enough." Abbi glanced behind her shoulder. "She's following us. Has she always been like this?" Abbi asked, tilting her head back.

I stopped in the middle of the empty sidewalk and ran my thumb along the smooth, soft curve of her cheek. I leaned in closer, wanting more of Abbi.

"For the last year or so. Before that, she was pretty focused on Dane."

"That's Nessa's boyfriend?"

I nodded. I waited until Bethany walked around us, shoulders hunched and arms wrapped around her waist. The look she shot Abbi was vicious. Instinctively, I stepped closer, protecting Abbi with my bulk. I kept my eyes trained on Bethany's slight figure until she disappeared through a set of doors.

"She's gone," I said. "I watched her walk toward the fashion building."

"What's her deal?" Abbi asked before she took a sip of her drink. She winced. "Hot," she murmured.

I chuckled. "Bethany's actually a fifth-year senior. A year older than me. She took off a semester a year ago. Some people said she had a nervous breakdown when Dane refused to hook up with her again. He was dating Nes, and we all know that's got the potential to go somewhere good. Even Dane will tell you Bethany was a mistake. One I'm not willing to make."

"She really likes you. She's more than ready to defend your honor."

Abbi smirked but I could see the vulnerability there behind the grin.

I pulled her in closer, unable to resist the urge of brushing a kiss next to her ear. Heat zinged from my lips straight down to my groin. "I heard about your run-in with her. I won't let that happen again."

"It's just something I'll have to deal with."

"No. I'll deal with it," I said. "I like you. I want to spend time with you. I can't say the same about Bethany."

She glanced up at me from under her lashes, a tiny smile tugging at her lips.

"I'm glad to hear that. Because, you know, according to the Seattle Times, we're the newest 'it' couple. If that pronouncement had been made with anyone other than you, I'd be hyperventilating in my bathroom. But, you, Clay, you're a charmer who makes me dance like a professional and forget my plans to keep my mouth shut and stay far away from anyone's camera lens."

"You're perfect, Abbi. Don't let anyone tell you different." The words were ones I'd said to Cassidy more than once, but I knew with Abbi they meant more. Betrayed, hurting, scared—somehow Abbi was still the most amazing woman I'd ever seen.

"Let's talk."

She narrowed her eyes. "About what?"

"You. Us. Our it-ness. How we want to play that. Mainly, why you're so sad and hurt."

"Clay, I—I told you more than I've told anyone else. And I'm just not ready to bare my soul."

"I would never ask that of you, Abbi. Just tell me…were you aware those pictures were being taken?"

She'd glanced away, which gave me a better view of her neck and the pulse beating there. "No," she said, her voice stronger than a whisper but still too quiet.

"And did you choose to go with those guys? The ones in the shot with you on the bed?"

Her throat worked as she swallowed down some emotion. Eventually, she shook her head just a little bit.

"Don't you see, Abbi? They stole your ability to trust. Not just others but yourself. Your judgment."

She stood frozen, unable to confirm or deny anything further, but her eyes…Those big, blue eyes were shattered. And damn me if I wasn't a sucker for needy females.

I pressed a kiss to her temple but pulled back quickly, needing to distance myself from her soft, fragrant hair. Even though my touch was platonic, my dick was more interested in continuing this in a not-so-friendly fashion. Or an overly friendly fashion. It wasn't picky.

"Mason told me I better play nice with you."

"He's become very protective," she murmured. A frown wedged its way across her smooth brow. "Do you think he knows about the pictures of me?"

Much as I didn't want to be the one to tell her, I nodded. She swallowed, her eyes dropping as she turned her face from mine.

"So. Our awesome new relationship," I said with a wink.

"I don't expect anything from you."

Her soft voice, the unhesitating way she said it, pissed me off. She *should* expect something from me.

"Too bad," I said, keeping my tone cheery though I wasn't sure what the hell I was doing. I didn't want a relationship, any relationship, but especially with a woman who'd spent more time in the gossip rags this past year than I had. Not the direction I wanted to send my band, but there was no way I was letting Abbi fight this fight alone. "I danced with you not once but twice and now we're an item. So. Let's go hang out."

I slung my arm back over her shoulders, pressing a quick peck to her opened mouth. Much as I wanted to deepen the kiss, to feel how soft she was, how sweet she tasted, I wouldn't. Not with what Abbi and Mason had told me last night.

I'd been wrong to judge her before knowing her, and it pissed me off that I had. More, that I'd been so wrong.

I ignored the looks we got from the people we passed, doing my best to keep Abbi laughing at my stories about Kai and Dane. No, being friends with Abbi wouldn't be easy.

I wanted her. Bad. The longer I spent in her company, the more my need grew. But, right now, she needed a friend and a protector. And I'd let myself be elected both.

CHAPTER FOURTEEN
Abbi

"So we have a problem," Nessa said as she entered my room the next morning.

I'd already become used to her comings and goings in the past couple of weeks, and I was beyond glad to have someone popping into my life again. She was like my own personal Kramer, barging in without bothering to knock.

Her droll humor was its own kind of charming, and I loved her insights into the other students on campus. But Nessa wasn't smiling at the moment. Her shoulders were back, her neck tense and her mouth set in a flat, determined line.

I stuffed my last book into my messenger bag. "What's wrong? Didn't you stay with Dane last night? Did he roll on you in your sleep?"

Nessa threw herself onto my bed. "I did. That's why I know we have a problem. But don't worry. Jenna and I have already started sorting it out."

Dread bubbled up in my chest. From the look she was throwing my way, half pity half anger, I knew I was the problem.

"Clay walked me back here from the coffee shop, and I didn't even leave my dorm room yesterday afternoon. What could I have possibly done?"

"You didn't do anything. Bethany did." Nessa's mouth twisted as if she'd stepped in a steaming pile of dog shit. "She's the epitome of mean girl. It's uber concentrated because she's so small."

"She talked about me, didn't she?"

"Oh, yeah. She's run her mouth all over campus."

119

"I knew seeing Clay yesterday was a bad idea. All he did was walk me back here. I only went over to talk to him in the first place because he looked so unhappy."

"You didn't do anything wrong, Abbi."

"What, exactly, did Bethany do?"

"Remember Charles and Neal? They didn't like you turning them down. So Bethany gave them photos of you."

The reverberations in my head hurt. I sank back to my bed. "The ones already out there?" I asked.

Nessa shook her head. "New ones."

"Worse ones?"

Nessa took a deep breath. "There are two of them. You're topless and sandwiched between two guys, both of whom are minimally clothed. Before you ask, it's definitely you."

I pressed my finger to my temple, willing some memory from that night to bubble up. Nothing. But I had seen those photos. They'd been in the folder Sally gave me. Along with a few worse ones. Ones I really didn't want leaked. I blinked back the burning sensation. I would not cry.

"I don't…I didn't. It's all over campus?" I whispered.

"Something like that. But, like I said, Jenna and I have you covered."

"You can't fix this for me, Nessa." I bit the skin next to my thumbnail.

"I can't, true. But I can make it safer and easier for you to move around campus. I'm walking you to breakfast and your first class with Jenna. She should be here in a minute."

"Right here, yo."

Jenna slammed into the room wearing a pair of skinny jeans,

120

Chuck Taylors and a gray hoodie. Her hair was in a high pony-tail, showing off her pearl earrings. How she could pull that look off was beyond me. Jenna poked Nessa with her finger and then sat on the edge of my bed.

"You should've waited for me." Jenna pouted.

"You don't have to do this," I said. "I don't want to drag you down into my mess."

"We like your murky, stinking cesspool of a life," Jenna said. Nessa glared. "What? She knows I'm joking."

"What Jenna, the only woman without any type of filter between mouth and brain, is trying to say is you're our friend. We bonded over our six-mile-runs and donuts. And Bethany-hating. No one can take that back."

"My thighs are killing me this morning," Jenna moaned. "If I'm going to hurt, I need more of that greasy sugar bread. You rock the distance running, Abbi. If you weren't nice and didn't feed my addiction, I'd hate you."

I shook my head. "It's going to be bad out there." I sat in my chair, head in my hands. "Maybe I should just unenroll from the university. Get an online degree or something."

"No way," Jenna yelped. "Since I don't get regular, hot sex like *someone* we know, you're the purveyor of my greatest pleasures in life right now."

I swallowed down regret. "But my reputation will spill over onto you."

Nessa stood and stretched. She looked relaxed, languorous even. "Good. Dane will like the added spice this brings to our relationship."

"It's not spice," I yelled, close to tears. "It's horrible! The touching, the innuendo. Everyone staring, whispering."

I looked away, my throat working furiously.

"What that guy did to you was wrong, Abbi," Jenna said, putting her hand on my shoulder. "And *no on*e is going to touch you. We won't let them."

"What Bethany's trying to do here is just as bad," Nessa said. "And we're not letting her get away with shaming you. I really hate that pixie-stick. More so now for doing this to you."

"We're your friends. We're sticking. And…" Jenna ducked out the door, returning a moment later with a bat. One of those metal ones the baseball players used to warm up. "I borrowed this from one of the baseball players. See? No touchy." She gripped the middle and waggled it at us.

"Borrowed?" Nessa asked.

"Fine. I stole it. Whatever. It's awesome. I look totally bad ass."

Nessa shook her head. "Why didn't I think of protection?"

"You two are crazy," I said, trying to stifle a giggle. "Thank you. Thank you so much for this."

Nessa threw her arm over my shoulder. "You're just figuring that out? Let's go. I'm starving. You owe me my morning donuts."

———◆———

Jenna took a swing at some frat boy before we made it to the student union for breakfast. The bat did deter most people from getting too close, but one still yelled inappropriate comments.

"That's not even possible," Nessa said, under her breath, glaring at the lanky guy with long hair. "Where do they come up with this shit?"

"How did you survive this at Tech?"

"This isn't bad." I couldn't begin to tell them about the time two guys cornered me at the end of the hall, one with his hand up my shirt and the other grabbing my bottom. Until the incident here at the library the other day, that was one of the worst experiences I'd had on any campus, punctuated by my professor yanking one of the guys off by his collar.

Shame bloomed across my skin. I knew all guys weren't bad. Clay, for one, had been kind. He'd treated me like I was worth more than my sex parts.

"I got what you need!" Another guy yelled, sending his friends into hysterical laughter.

"It's like they forget you're an actual person," Jenna mumbled. "What is this?"

"It's going to get worse," I whispered. "When I don't agree to screw at least one of them, someone will get insulted. That ups the abuse."

"If nothing else, you and I can be lovers," Jenna said. She looked me up and down, her gaze critical. "You're hot, Dorsey. We'd make a very photogenic couple." She winked.

We walked into the dining hall, and silence slowly descended and heads swiveled in our direction.

"Chin up," Nessa said, glaring at a table full of young women who were clearly whispering about me. "You have nothing to be ashamed of, Abbi. Oh, good. Here are Dane and Kai."

She stepped forward and wrapped the shorter guy with flaxen hair in a hug. He bent down and kissed her with more exuberance than necessary. Jenna tipped her chin at the taller, tatted guy ambling toward us, his hands shoved deep in the pockets of his ratty jeans.

"Kai," she said.

"Jen," he replied, a cynical smirk pulling at his lips. "And you're the infamous Abbi Dorsey. This shit's crazy."

"You have no idea."

He turned to glare at some big, linebacker type who was making crude gestures and yelling "you know you want it!"

"I know it isn't right," Kai said.

Dane wrapped his arm around Nessa's waist. They were cute, standing together. Nessa, all curvy and glamorous, Dane, spare and broody.

"I'll get the ladies breakfast," Dane said, acting impervious to the stares and the catcalling. As performers, maybe this didn't bother them much. "Get them settled at a table, Kai. And don't you dare leave them alone."

A pang hit me low in my stomach. I didn't want to want that type of protectiveness but a large part of me yearned for it. I wished I had someone willing to take on the world for me. I didn't, and I was to blame. I'd shut down my family's attempts, and I didn't have anyone else who wanted to get involved.

Clay said he'd be my fake society boyfriend, but he wasn't here. He'd sent his friends while distancing himself. That hurt. Deeply.

But I had Nessa and Jenna, who was once again tapping her metal bat into her open palm. Kai glanced at her, and his eyes widened at the bat.

"I'll get the food," Kai said, eyes sliding from Jenna's continued tapping. "Everyone want coffee? Abbi, do you eat the same fried crap as the rest of them?"

"Toast is great," I said.

"Enjoy your time with Nes," Kai said, spinning on his heel before stalking into the line.

"This way, Abbi," Dane said, arms out to shepherd us toward a corner booth.

"Where's Clay?" Jenna asked.

Yeah, I wanted to know that, too.

"He should be here," Jenna said, scowling at the other diners. "Staking his claim."

"He's helping Cassidy with some school project. But he knows, and he'll be back this afternoon." Dane looked at me, eyes serious. "You're not allowed to walk around by yourself. Clay was adamant. Nes, Jenna, and I will get you to your two classes today, but then it'd probably be best if you holed up in your dorm room."

"I'm going home after my last class," I said.

Much as I wanted to avoid this, I needed to get the other pictures Sally had given me. With the newest stirring of this story, I doubted they'd stay hidden. Mom had been on my case to talk to Aunt Briar, and now was the time to make that happen.

"You gonna fight back this time?" Jenna asked, gaze still scanning the room.

Cassidy's words from Saturday came back to me. *For those of you who've been there, the question is, what do you plan to do with your life? How much is a second chance worth to you?*

I couldn't live like this, and I couldn't ask my friends to do so either.

"Yes. I'm going to own it, and I'm going to work it my way," I said. I took the coffee Kai handed me with a grateful smile.

"Really?" Jenna asked, her eyes wide.

I spread my hands out to include all the people still staring at me. "Do I really have a choice?"

The rest of the table fell silent as they, too, glanced around. This was sooner than I wanted. Much as I wanted to cry against the unfairness of it all, I kept my cool as I sipped the coffee, hating the thick, bitter taste as it hit my tongue.

"I think it'll be better if I stay at my mom's tonight. That way you don't have to babysit me."

"'Cause it's so hard," Jenna said, rolling her eyes. "What with your snappy comebacks and hilarious stories of famous people. Kai, you know I don't like bear claws. What the hell?"

"That's for me, sweetness," Kai said, his voice sardonic. "I got you the nasty jelly-filled thing you like."

Jenna stuck out her tongue and Kai rolled his eyes, but a smile tugged at the corners of his mouth. They were cute but in a sibling kind of way. Interesting, considering Bethany had made that comment about Jenna panting after Kai.

I'd have to get the story later. Right now, I needed to do damage control.

The four of them walked me to my class, ensuring the professor was in the room before leaving me.

"Had to get a posse for your pussy, huh?"

It was the same big dude from the dining hall. His features were blunted, his neck nonexistent. I'd never seen him in here before. Could be because I hadn't paid attention, or it could be he hadn't bothered to come to class until now.

I settled into my chair, face flaming. The professor, a small man with grizzled hair and thick white eyebrows looked up, his eyes catching mine. I shook my head a little.

"Just because you're a rock star's stepdaughter doesn't make you that special," the guy's friend said.

"You are hot," the first guy said. "I'd do you. Once."

I slammed my hand on the table before the professor could react. While it stung, I was too focused on my newest attackers to care.

"Well, I won't *do* you. You take some social media pictures as truth without even bothering to ask what or why. I'm not just a rock star's stepdaughter. I'm Abigail Dorsey, a woman with a 4.0 GPA and the hours sitting at my desk, studying, to prove it."

I paused, sucked in a deep, full breath and looked the guy dead in the eye.

"I chose not to answer those allegations last spring because I didn't want to further hurt my family. But you know what? By not doing so, I hurt every other woman who's been treated like crap, both in the media and by thugs like you. You cannot objectify me without my consent again." I looked him up and down, a sneer peeling up the corner of my mouth.

"As you so kindly pointed out, I have a rock star stepdad who's been urging me to use my voice and tell people the truth. Well, here it is: I was drugged and photos were taken of me against my will in an effort to shame me into keeping me quiet. I won't be quiet, and I will *not* take another insult from anyone without a response. From my lawyer."

The silence that filled the room was thick. My face drained of color, my head buzzed from lightheadedness. Would the professor kick me out?

Then someone began clapping. A girl with dark red ringlets stood up and wolf whistled. Her friend shoved her chair back and did the same. Within seconds, every girl in the room was standing, clapping and cheering.

The professor waited for the room to quiet down before he asked, "Any further comment, Mr. Olson, Mr. Fein?"

The two guys ducked their heads, cheeks a dusky red.

"Good." The professor smiled at all of us. "And just to be clear, I believe women have a right to own their bodies, minds, sexuality, property, and whatever the hell else they want, because they are just as capable and smart as their male counterparts. But for the rest of this class, we're focusing on calculus."

I sat in my chair, sweating and shaking but lighter than I'd been in months, maybe years. I couldn't believe I'd snapped. I really couldn't believe how good I felt taking control of my life.

Granted, this wasn't over. I was ready for the next step; after this class, I was going home and picking up those pictures. Steve didn't think I'd pursue the photos. Neither did Bethany. She expected me to hide as the media crucified me. Because I had before.

But this time I wasn't going to back down.

CHAPTER FIFTEEN
Clay

Without an actual crime or evidence, there wasn't much the campus security staff could do. The whole innocent-until-proven-guilty bullshit had saved more than one of my father's rabid fans from jail time.

Sure, Jan Silver, the victim's advocate, made a copy of my complaint and stuck it in Abbi's growing file, along with a letter from her calculus professor about the incident this morning. But the campus security team wasn't interested in increasing security, not for Abbi nor for any of the other women on campus. Nessa, Jenna, and I got the "we have a budget" talk.

"What if something does happen?" Jenna asked, clearly as frustrated as I was. "She's high profile. If she's raped, then you're going to look like assholes who don't know your way out of a paper sack. Because I'm going to make sure I tell everyone I know about this conversation."

Nessa put her hand on Jenna's arm and even I sat back, unsettled by Jenna's outburst. Not that I wasn't thinking the same thing, but this felt…personal.

The woman across the desk scowled, throwing her black hipster frames onto her desk. Yeah, not as much fun working with victims as you thought it would be. Because this shit is real, not a scripted TV show.

"So you say. But without more than a he-said-she-said, I can't do anything. We'll keep an ear out. Her calculus professor, Dr. Callen, let us know about the remarks made in class today." She flicked the edge of the folder. "They're in here. We're building a case, but whom would we even charge? There's rumor, innuendo. No crime. What do you expect?"

"You to do your job," I replied. "Like you're supposed to. Did you talk to Bethany Reynolds?"

"About what, exactly?" Jan asked, annoyance lacing her words.

"Accosting Abigail Dorsey in her dormitory. Giving the pictures to Charles and Neal. Starting the rumors. Making this an unsafe environment for her. The list is pretty long," Nessa said.

"And I advocate for victims. Ms. Dorsey isn't a victim yet."

"I'm going to remember the *yet* part of that statement," Nessa said, standing up. "Come on. This is a waste of time."

I looked at the woman across the desk. She was about Colten's age. Already, she'd been roughened by the system. Lines were developing around her mouth and her eyes were both sad and angry.

"You could do something here. Something worthwhile that would help not just Abbi but a lot of young women on this campus. I have a sister. I'd want to know she was safe walking to class, hell, even going to a party. That starts with the school's attitude. And right now, yours sucks."

Jan Silver's eyes rested on my back as I walked out. She didn't bother to call me back because we both knew she wouldn't do anything until it was too late.

I stood near the door to the chemistry class my brother said she had at 8:30 a.m. every Tuesday. Nessa, Dane and even Kai stuck close to Abbi yesterday while I was helping Cassidy with her school presentation. After finishing that late morning, I'd needed time to meet with campus police.

Abbi stayed at her mom's place last night, which was a smart move. The situation wasn't calming down even after Abbi gave a freaking soliloquy that ended up online. What didn't these days?

We'd monitored social media and so far, it was flying under the national radar. I didn't expect that to continue. Not when the headlines last spring and summer had sold so many click-throughs. And wasn't that what this was all about? A shame fest that someone else profited from.

If anyone was going to take on the world for Abbi, it was me. I was the other half of the "it" couple the media pronounced us to be. And I'd told Abbi I'd take care of Bethany. Some help I'd been.

I'd positioned myself to see the entire quad. Jenna and Nessa stopped at the doorway to the building, tilting their heads in acknowledgment to my presence. I raised my chin back, but my eyes never strayed far from Abbi as she made slow progress up the steps.

Her head was bowed and her shoulders folded in as if the weight of the world were pressing on her. In a way, it was. We all knew the fallout from this story could be huge. And ugly.

I stepped forward, and her head popped up, her eyes filled with fear but also with fire. Good. She was going to fight.

She slowed down when she saw me, her chest rising and falling in rapid succession. She stopped a good ten feet from me, uncertainty written across her face.

"I hoped you'd be here, but I wasn't sure." I wanted to touch her, do something to help her. "I'm sorry yesterday was so shitty."

She shrugged. "I still have to go to class. I'm here to learn. To get a degree."

She looked pale, a bit unsteady, but her jaw was set in a

determined line. I'd missed looking into those eyes. I wasn't used to wanting to hear a voice, listen to concerns, dreams. When I'd asked Colt about that on our way home from the gala he'd rolled his eyes at me. That was his you're-an-idiot face.

"So you feel like that with Kara?" I asked him.

"Yeah. That's why I wanted to marry her. I don't even look at other women." Colt's face fell. "But she doesn't feel the same way. She's seeing someone else, keeping us casual."

"She dumped you and hooked up with someone else?"

"Pretty much," Colt said, eyes never leaving mom's seat in front of him.

My eyes had flickered to my parents as I shifted Cassidy's sleeping form more fully into my arms. My shoulders bunched into such hard muscles, my head started to pound. While I'd never felt strongly enough about a woman to want the commitment, I'd believed in the power of devotion once. Until I'd seen how easy it was to betray.

"Clay? What's wrong?" Abbi' stepped closer, her long, slender fingers resting on my forearm. Despite her worries, she was comforting me.

We both looked down at our flesh, the heat building, growing, wrapping us together in a cocoon of mutual desire.

What this woman did to me. I'd never felt need like I did with her. And damn if that didn't scare me. Lust alone, I could handle. But this was more.

This was what Colt had described. I wasn't ready for this intensity, for a commitment. Especially with someone like Abbi, who'd always garner attention whether she wanted it or not. Even now, she burned bright enough to turn people's heads, to lure more paps onto campus.

I stepped back, putting some space between our bodies. Immediately, I missed her. My hand twitched, wanting to wrap around her waist and tuck her into my side.

"I'm fine. Just thinking about something else."

"Is Cassidy okay?" Abbi's concern washed over me, forming cracks in my much-needed self-control.

"She's great. I went to her school yesterday and played the guitar while she rapped a poem." I smiled. "She was good. Very Anna Kendrick."

Abbi smiled, but her eyes were more guarded. Shit. I'd hurt her.

The unhappiness clawed at my gut. I didn't know what to do with my jumbled emotions. She was dealing with too much, had already dealt with more than her fair share. But at the same time, I didn't want to take advantage of her emotional needs.

I offered her my hand. She hesitated for a moment before she raised her arm and placed her palm in mine. The pulse in her neck pounded and her nostrils quivered. Good. I affected her like she affected me.

"I'll pick you up after your lab. My brother told me when it was."

Consternation fluttered across her face. "I'm not a charity case. I don't want you to go to any trouble on my account."

"I never thought you were. Look, Bethany's actions…that's my fault. She wouldn't have bothered you if I wasn't interested."

Her face paled, her eyes seeming to grow and darken. "What do you mean exactly?"

Her voice was low, but she was steady. I let my hand drop back to my side.

"We're already linked in the media. That's also my fault. I asked you to dance. For now, I'm the other half of your 'it,' and I'm not letting you walk through this alone."

Her skin paled so much I caught the faintest outline of freckles on her nose. I wanted to kiss them, nip at her jaw. I wanted to feel her writhe under me.

"Clay, you don't understand."

"Oh, I get it. And it pisses me off that someone's preying on you. I'm sticking by you. So are Nessa, Jenna, and the guys."

She wrapped her hands around her elbows, hugging herself. "I'm so thankful for you all. For the support. It's making me rethink my stance on what happened before."

She didn't say it, but I could guess the words rolling through her head based on the look in her eyes: *I hoped people here would like me. I hoped here would be different.*

When she looked like that, trying so hard to be brave in the face of a terrible situation, she reminded me of my little sister. I might not like all Abbi's choices, especially her decision to cut people out of her life, but she was doing her best.

"So you need to go to class. I'll be here afterward. And Abbi, for the record, I don't mind that the media's paired us up. At all."

She pulled her hand back slowly. Would she sneak out the back door while I waited at the front? Her next words, spoken even more quietly, were a surprise. "I really appreciate your help. Again. Seems like you're always saving me."

"Once we figure this out, you won't need saving again. You're more than capable of taking care of yourself." I leaned in, enjoying our mingled breaths. "I heard about your throw down in calculus yesterday. Watched it on YouTube last night."

134

Dull red built across her cheeks, and her mouth twisted. "Not my best moment."

"I don't know. Seemed pretty good to me. See you in a couple of hours."

With a wink, I turned and walked away.

"Clay." Her soft voice drifted over me, almost like a caress.

I glanced back over my shoulder.

"For what it's worth, I wish I'd come to your concert. Either one." She stepped close enough for me to smell her shampoo. Lavender, maybe. I liked it; I liked her minimal makeup and her cautious eyes. Much as I wanted her to be just a friend, she wasn't. Not like Nes or Jenna.

"Next time," I said. "I'll pick you up."

She blinked, nibbling her upper lip. I gently tugged it from between her straight, white teeth. Unable to stop myself, I ran my thumb over it and then her lower one and nearly groaned at the soft, lush feel of her skin under mine. "Wait for me."

———◆———

Like always, Bethany found me.

"Hi, Clay."

Did she really expect me not to know? I swept the area one more time, looking for Jenna and Nes. Well, I wasn't letting this opportunity go. I rearranged my scowl and turned to face her.

"Ah, just the woman I was looking for."

Bethany, always the eager puppy, might as well have wagged her tail when she looked up at me.

"You were?" She grabbed my arm, but I shook off her pale

fingers.

"You and I need to talk about what you did yesterday."

She stepped back, finally hearing the anger I wasn't trying to hide.

"You seem upset," she said, eying the path near us.

I nearly snorted. She was going to see me more than a little upset.

"We've never been together, Bethany. We never will be. Ever. Is that clear enough for you?"

She shook her head, looking up at me with those huge eyes. Like I'd kicked her. Which made me angrier.

"I thought we were meeting at the fountain," Nessa panted. Jenna was behind her. "Good thing Jenna spotted you. What did we miss?"

"Nessa told me about your visit to the dorm two weeks ago. I've talked to a victim advocate and the campus police about that and the comments you made to Charles and Neal. Nessa and Jenna did, too. In case you were wondering, Charles and Neal were more than happy to rat you out."

Bethany's face was scrunched up in consternation and more than a little bewilderment.

"What, why? I'm not allowed to talk to my friends?"

"Neal didn't seem to think you're as friendly as you do. Neal's roommate heard your conversation on Sunday. His older sister committed suicide in high school after her classmates posted pictures of her in the gym changing room. He told the campus police about your conversation, handing over the pictures to Charles and Neal. They squealed immediately."

"Those stories you told people about Abbi. Did you ever think what would happen if they were lies?" Jenna asked.

Bethany's eyes filled with fire and her back stiffened.

"They're not. My cousin was there, saw the whole thing first-hand. Abbi's an attention-seeking slut."

"No, it's hearsay," I growled. "Which is why I'm telling you to stop. This is your one warning. Slander isn't something you can wiggle out from under. I'll make sure it sticks."

"She didn't deny the allegations," Bethany said. She shuffled her feet, her voice losing some of her confidence.

"She didn't have to," Nessa said. "Anyone who knows Abbi at all knows those posts were lies."

"We've been friends for years, Clay," Bethany said. "I can't believe you'd throw that away on a-a—"

"Here's the deal," I said. My instincts about this girl had been right. "We aren't friends. I get to decide who to spend my time with. It's never been nor is it ever going to be you. I suggest you start cleaning up the mess you made. Otherwise, you'll hear from my lawyer."

"But…"

I turned away. I cupped Nessa and Jenna's elbows so they'd have to walk with me.

"Aw, Clay. That was just getting fun," Nessa complained.

"Did you record it?" I asked.

"Yep," Jenna said, pulling out her phone. Nessa did the same, showing me the clip.

"Good. Thanks for talking to the campus police with me," I said. I opened the door to the union, holding it so they could enter first. "And for leaving the bat in your dorm room."

"I like that bat," Jenna said with a grin. "I think I'm going to keep it around. You know, as an accessory. It looks good with my Chucks."

"Bethany needed to come down a long way," Nessa grumbled. "Who does that shit?"

"I wanna threaten Bethany again," Jenna said. She leaped ahead and whooped.

"We didn't threaten," I chuckled. "We explained the situation."

"Whatever," Nessa yawned. "I had to get up at six to get Abbi to her class on time yesterday and then at seven thirty today. Dane isn't happy. We missed two days of wake-up sex."

"Don't need to hear about that," I sighed. Only because now I was once again thinking of Abbi, naked and flushed from sleep. Definitely not helping.

"So buy me the biggest, chocolatiest coffee you can find. It's a poor substitute, but it'll have to do."

"But then we're going back to see Jan Silver with your recordings."

Jenna saluted while Nessa looked thoughtful.

"I hope Abbi's grateful for how much trouble we've gone to on her behalf. Two mornings in a row, and I am not a morning person."

"We aren't telling her," I reminded them. "She has enough going on without us adding to it."

Nessa looked up at me, her mouth pulled into a thin line. "That's a really bad idea. She's not going to like us going behind her back."

I'd worry about that later. Right now, I needed to make sure she was safe.

CHAPTER SIXTEEN
Abbi

I finished shoving my last book into my bag when someone sidled up to me. I whirled, surprised to see my instructor standing there. "Mr. Rippey."

"Hey, Abbi. Sorry we didn't get to talk more at the gala. I had a hot date." He smiled.

My throat tightened. I did not need more speculation about the Rippeys and me.

"Cassidy's speech was amazing," I said, stepping back a little. "I'm sure you're all very proud of her."

"We are. And she is. My brother's stopping by in a minute to walk you to your next class. I just wanted you to know the faculty's aware of the situation, and we're here to help."

"Oh, okay," I said. I didn't bite my lip like I wanted. Instead, I squared my shoulders and lifted my chin. "I appreciate the concern, but I don't want to be a burden."

He leaned in, not so much into my personal space, but almost. I scooted back quickly, feeling like a hermit crab skittering across the inhospitable sand, looking for shelter. His eyes, similar to Clay's, opened wider. He searched my eyes before I managed to drop my gaze.

"Be careful out there, Abbi."

I picked up my bag and slid it over my shoulder.

"Thank you, Mr. Rippey. Is that all?"

He stepped farther back and I looked around, noting the interested looks and even some whispers from some of the girls trailing from the class. Did people think he was propositioning me? Fabulous.

I wanted to shut my eyes and pound my head against the desk, but I couldn't. Not with everyone watching me.

He seemed to realize the curious stares at the same time. He dropped his head a little, looking both sheepish and frustrated. Yeah, this is what it was like to be me—the focus of speculation and the expectation of the salacious.

I turned on my heel and headed for the exit.

"Wait for Clay."

I ignored his call and headed out of the lab, pulling my short corduroy jacket closer around my body.

"We had an understanding."

I jumped and let out a squeal.

"Whoa, there, Abbi," Clay said. "No need to freak."

"You scared me," I managed.

Clay chuckled. "Got that. Now, let me calm you down." He waited until the last few students straggled past us. His brother saluted us as he headed the other direction, up the stairs to his office.

Clay cupped my elbow and led me from the building. Rain fell in a light mist, turning the world around us hazy and soft. Clay must have been holding an umbrella because he opened it as we stepped outside.

I moved closer to him when water spilled onto my shoulder. He slid his arm around my waist, and while I stiffened at the familiarity, I didn't pull away. He felt too warm and solid. He smelled like rain and pine trees. I leaned closer still. Clay chuckled.

"If I knew you liked to snuggle, I would've waited for rain before I tried talking to you."

"Oh. Sorry." My cheeks flamed. "I was smelling you." My

face heated further. I lifted a cold hand to press to my cheek. He laughed harder.

"Do I meet your approval?"

"You know you smell good."

"Most people need to be told these things."

"Stop teasing me."

"But it's so easy."

He glanced down at me, his fingers tightening at my waist, halting me. He waited until I lifted my eyes. All those white teeth flashed.

"You smell great. Almost as good as you look."

"Thank you."

"Want to get lunch?"

I did. I *so* did even if it meant braving the stares and whispered comments. Which was why I shouldn't. I shook my head. "I'm meeting my aunt."

He stopped walking. Turning, he focused on me. We stood there for a moment as he battled something, his eyes never leaving mine. With a sigh of resignation, he brushed my hair away from my face.

I couldn't help the small sound that slipped out. He smiled again, broader, more predatory. My insides burned hotter than my cheeks.

"Give me your phone."

Not what I was expecting him to say. I handed it over. He typed into it. After pressing a few more buttons, he handed it back.

"You have my number, and I texted my phone, so now I have yours."

"Oh."

"You could try to sound enthusiastic. It's not like I hand my number out very often. At least not my private one."

"Thank you," I said, tucking my phone back into my jacket pocket.

"You should put a lock on yours. Doesn't it have fingerprint recognition?"

"Probably. It's one of those new ones."

"Use it. If anyone wanted to get your personal information, like your list of contacts or emails, and that of the people you contact, they can. Doesn't mean you should make it easy for them."

He pulled my phone out of my pocket and showed me how to change the settings. After a few minutes, my phone was locked down, only responding to my fingerprint or special passcode.

"Thanks," I said, nonplussed.

"C'mon, Abbi, don't sound like that. This is your identity, your life. I want you safe."

I nodded, understanding his point even as I hated yet another tiny piece of independence taken from me. I'd lost my dignity, and I didn't want to lose my freedom as well.

He rubbed the back of his neck as I shoved my new Fort Knox-safe phone back into my pocket. His sigh was heavy.

"Text me the rest of your schedule. I'll meet you when you get back to campus and walk you to your dorm. If you want to go out to the library or the union, text me. I'm at your disposal all day." He winked.

Heat built in my chest, but it was from shame.

"Clay, I hate that you've been pulled into my problems. It's not fair to ask, and I don't want you to—"

"We've already been through this. Nessa and Jenna are walking you to class again in the morning. But I'd love to spend time with you this afternoon. Maybe you can come to my place? We can study. Get some dinner. Work on our newest 'it' couple outing."

I blinked at him, wondering if I'd heard him correctly.

"You don't have to babysit me," I said.

"I'm not. I invited a friend over to hang out. Nes and Jenna will probably show up at some point."

"When did you talk to them?" I tried to keep my voice neutral, but this was another kind of pressure. Made out of caring, sure, but they'd talked about me without me.

"After Dane told me about the pictures. I wanted to be here for you yesterday, but I had that thing with Cassie and some things to do in the afternoon that took longer than I expected. Nessa's seriously pissed on your behalf, by the way."

"I know."

He stopped walking and turned me toward him. "And you think we're talking about you."

Much as I didn't want to, I forced myself to meet his eyes. "Aren't you? Feeling sorry for me, too, I bet."

"Not the way you think we are. You deserve privacy, Abbi. It's something all of us close to famous people crave. Probably because we lack it."

My chin jutted as my pride kicked in. "I can manage. It's not like I have a choice."

He leaned forward until his nose brushed mine. The unexpected gesture caught me so off guard, I wrapped my hand around his biceps to steady myself. He made a noise low in his throat and heat bloomed across my skin.

My eyes dropped to his lips, which quirked upward in a

self-satisfied smirk. He knew exactly what he did to me, and he liked it. Problem was, I liked it, too. And I was finding it harder to logic out why I shouldn't say yes to whatever he wanted.

"That's the point. You don't have to manage alone. The Times says we're a couple. Let me help while I can. And—"

He dropped his voice so he had to lean in even closer. Need shivered over my skin.

"You can always make me dinner to show your gratitude."

I shuffled back, my jacket dampening as the rain hit it. "Dinner?" I tried to state it but it came out more as a question.

"Tonight. At my place. But I should warn you, it'll be for at least six people. Dane and Nes are attached more often than not and wherever Nes goes, Jenna isn't far behind. Kai practically lives with us."

"Your life is already so full," I said, hoping I could use that as an excuse to back out of seeing him. I liked Clay, but my world was about to crash, and I didn't want to take him down with me.

"Tell me about it. Now, I expect that text with the rest of your schedule. I'll send you my address. You'll come to my apartment?"

"Clay, it's just that…I mean, people will assume when they see us together that, you know, you're sleeping with me."

He tucked me back into his side and started walking again. "Here's the deal. I've thought about this a lot, and the bottom line is I don't give a single fuck what other people think. I care about making sure you're not harassed, especially since I caused part of the problem. Oh, and dinner. I like to eat. Here's your car. I plan to hear from you within the hour. If I don't, I will come find you." His voice was stern.

"You have a life, Clay. It had to be better before you met me."

He reached up and tweaked my nose. "You're my friend. I take care of my friends, just like you'll take care of me if I need the help."

He winked, and it set off the same crazy fireworks in my chest as the last one had. "In you go. Tell your aunt hello. I enjoyed meeting her on Saturday."

Not knowing what else to do, I opened my car and climbed in. "You're bossy. Do you normally steamroll people like this, or do you just expect me to be a pushover?"

"Neither. I don't need to do more than suggest, because you want to hang out with me as much as I want to hang out with you. But you can thank me for my security services with food. I'll pick up some fish at the market."

I shook my head. "I'm not a great cook, but it'll be a pleasure to do something nice for you."

"Oh, it'll be mine, too. See you soon."

———

I was so engrossed in my thoughts, I had a hard time focusing on Aunt Bri at lunch.

"So you're talking to Asher's attorney?" she asked.

"I set it up yesterday when I went home." My thoughts drifted back to Clay and the way he watched me drive away. Standing in the gray mist, his face obscured by his hood, the blue of his jeans and the red of his jacket bright spots. I'd felt this tug to turn around. To cuddle in close and wrap my arms around him, not that he'd offered to do more. He kept saying we were friends, which was nice.

145

"Can I ask you something?"

Aunt Briar folded her hands on the table, her large sapphire engagement ring flashing when it caught the overhead lights.

"Of course."

"How did you know about Hayden? That you were in love?"

"Not where I thought you were going with this." She took a sip of her water. The waiter brought our soups and salads, along with a pile of onion rings. It was something Mom and I started years ago, and Aunt Bri insisted we continue, telling me no salad was complete without onion rings.

After smiling my thanks at the waiter, I faced my aunt. She and Hayden had been close, really close, before he left to finish his world tour. Unfortunately, Briar was left to deal with the paparazzi who'd wanted the scoop on a lovers' spat. She'd endured weeks of constant hounding before she and Hayden worked through their issues.

Now she, like my mom, had the look of a very happy woman. And for the zillionth time in my life, I longed for that feeling, whatever it was, behind the look.

If I was honest with myself, that was my real goal in life. More than becoming a vet, I wanted a man to love me as well as my mom and aunt were loved.

"It's just…well, Clay's been really nice."

Aunt Bri wiped her mouth with her napkin and leaned back. "So you've seen him again."

"Yeah." I dropped my gaze to the table, running my finger along the edge of the plate. "I want Asher's lawyers to talk to the administration. See about criminal charges."

"Why?"

"It's starting here." I hated saying the words. Pushing them past my closing throat was hard. So hard.

"No," Aunt Briar growled.

I pushed my uneaten food back. "Worse after the gala last weekend. My friends Nessa and Jenna had to walk me to class yesterday. Clay walked me to my car so I could meet you here."

"Are you serious?" Briar whisper-yelled. She leaned back in her chair, setting her fork next to her plate with exquisite care. "You're moving back home. You can take your courses online."

I shook my head. "That was my first thought, too. But I don't want to do that. I've already changed schools, given up on my original dream."

"Abbi, this is your *safety* we're talking about."

"It's also my happiness. I've made new friends. I like them, and they seem to like me, even with all my baggage. That's why I'm meeting Asher's lawyer. I want to fight back. Like I should have then."

My aunt's blue eyes were similar to mine, but right now they were harder than any sapphire I'd ever seen.

I grabbed her hand. "I'll wait until after your wedding. I don't want to mess that up for you."

"Abs, I'm not worried about the press. We can handle that part. Asher and Hayden both have PR teams for this kind of stuff, which we begged you to use last May. I want to know the real reason why you're willing to push back now when a few months ago you were too busy rolling over to consider another option."

Her eyes demanded the truth. Aunt Bri might not work in newspapers anymore but that didn't mean she'd lost her investigative instinct.

"It's not just those pictures and what they implied." My stomach tied itself up in knots.

Did I want to do this? If I didn't—there was the text Bethany sent me. I hadn't seen it until I'd pulled up in front of the restaurant, planning to text Clay the rest of my schedule.

I own the pictures and I own you. Don't go near Clay Rippey again.

I pulled out my phone, letting it scan my thumbprint, which made me shiver. So weird that I was trying to protect some part of my identity when social media had destroyed so much of it.

Without a word, I handed over the device, message open.

Aunt Bri read the text, eyes hardening. "Can I forward this to my phone?"

"Yes."

"So you think she posted the pictures?"

I nibbled my lip. How much did I want to tell her?

"No. She's a problem here, at Northern. Steve's the one who took pictures of me at Tech."

"Your mom said Sally was involved in that."

I swallowed down the worst of my fears, unable to share them. The shame and confusion were unbearable. Soon, I'd know just what to accuse Steve of.

"With the time that's passed…It's harder to bring a case even if Tech's opened an investigation."

"I think Sally stepped forward and shared the information she gave me with the administration there," I said.

"If that becomes public, the media attention will be intense. So, yeah, you might as well press charges."

I blew out a breath. "I don't want to run away again. I—"

Heat crept up my neck, blooming hot and bright in my cheeks. "I really like Clay. He seems to like me, too. Even with all the nasty conjecture about me."

Aunt Bri bobbed her head once.

"Is there more to this?" she asked, her voice low.

Tears pricked the back of my eyes. I didn't want to think about that. But I had two choices: either I faced my fears and learned to deal with them, or I didn't.

"Yes. There's more. But can we start here? I'll tell you the rest. I promise. I just need some time."

"I'll see what I can dig up." She sighed. "But it's not going to be easy, Abbi. Some of the kids won't be there anymore. These investigations are best done immediately."

"I didn't know the school would even consider one until I saw Sally a couple of weeks ago."

Briar sat back in her chair. "This may grow, Abbi. It's very likely it'll spider out into something much bigger than we expect it to be. Especially once we file court papers. You'll be inundated with questions. I'm not trying to scare you. I just want you to understand the reality of what this could become."

"I realized yesterday when this guy was talking about my girl parts in really crude terms that my silence was giving him permission to do so." I looked around the restaurant, gaze jumping from one group to another, unsettled, flighty. The opposite of what I wanted to be. "This isn't about Clay. I want to be whole again. I want to feel like my decisions, my feelings matter."

Aunt Briar took my hand. "Of course they do, sweetie. Of course."

Her eyes were full of concern and sadness. I'd gone through

the pictures when I went home yesterday, but I just wasn't ready to give those to Aunt Briar.

As soon as I sat down here with my aunt, I wanted to talk to Clay. See if he agreed with my strategy. I planned to ask Jenna and Nessa as well. I swallowed down the lump in my throat. Being part of a group, knowing someone cared about my feelings, was motivating.

"Will you start at the beginning? I'm going to need as many details as I can get to investigate this properly," Aunt Briar asked, her concern switching into professional interest.

"Ask away."

CHAPTER SEVENTEEN
Clay

I wasn't sure Abbi would actually stop by after her lunch with her aunt. She was determined to handle this situation on her own, which made me both proud of her and irritated. I'd offered my help *and* my public image, not something I gave over lightly. She was supposed to be enthusiastic about pairing her name with mine. Instead, she'd seemed nonplussed. Worried even. That was new. And quite the hit to my ego.

Leaving the restaurant. Still okay for me to swing by?

My response was instantaneous. *Yes.*

Much to tell you. Be there in half an hour.

Come straight here. I'm serious!

Was going to pick up some ingredients to make you dinner.

Warmth filled me as my smile grew. She was planning to stay and make me dinner. I typed back: *We can pick up whatever you need together. See you soon.*

K.

Twenty minutes later, I opened the door to Abbi's knock. Damn, she was a sight. Her eyes were still guarded, but the rest of her face seemed more relaxed.

"Hi," she said.

I grabbed her hand and pulled her into the apartment. Dane had texted, letting me know he and Nessa wouldn't be back until later because they'd decided to go on a sunset ride on the Ferris wheel. I had a couple of hours alone with Abbi, and while nerves fluttered in my belly, I looked forward to talking with her.

"How was lunch with your aunt?"

Abbi's eyes had been roving the room but they came back to me. "Good. That's what I want to talk to you about. She said to tell you hi. And to make sure you let her know about your gig schedule so she can tell Hayden."

"Nice of her. Want a drink?" I asked as I pulled her toward the couch.

"I'm good."

She sat on the edge of the cushion. Fine tremors built in her slender fingers. I sat next to her, our knees bumping.

"What's wrong?"

After a long moment, she raised her eyes to mine. "I'm going to press charges. Against Steve at least. Maybe Bethany, too."

"Takes some metaphorical balls, and I'm really proud of you for making the stand. I'll help with the stuff here." I sucked in my lip, thinking about my actions yesterday and this morning. "I should tell you, I've talked to the campus's victim advocate on your behalf. I asked Nessa and Jenna to file complaints as well. We added a recording of a conversation between Nes, Jenna, Bethany, and me to the file this morning while you were in your lab. Nes and Jenna wanted to tell you, but you had enough going on."

She brushed her hair back from her cheek, which was paler than when she came in.

"That's probably smart," she said. "It'll help build the case here. I'd like to hear the conversation."

"Sure."

Her eyes flashed up to mine again, held. The darkness there shook me, and I hated seeing her hurt.

"I'm going to take back my life. Part of that is because of you." She held up her hand when I opened my mouth. "And

Nessa and Jenna, and even the girl who talked to me after my calc class yesterday who slept with some guy last year, not knowing he recorded it on his laptop and later sent it to a bunch of his friends. *Of course* it went viral. She took a full bottle of pills because she was so overcome with the shame."

She sucked in a big breath. "There's one other thing you need to know." She pulled out a large manila folder. Her hand trembled so much the folder became a fan. Her mouth settled into a firm line.

"Bethany sent me a text. I don't know how she got my number, but it said she owned me and she owned more pictures. My aunt has the text, but I didn't give these to her yet. I will. Or maybe I'll give them to my mom so she can understand why I didn't want to say anything earlier."

She thrust them toward me. "I wanted you to see. So you understand what being attached to me in the press actually means."

I took the envelope, awareness prickling up my neck. Whatever was in there, I wouldn't like it. Abbi stood, her arms wrapped around her waist as she walked to the window.

"There may be others. I don't know what Bethany has. These are just the ones *I* know about."

I glanced up, wondering if I could really do this. Invade her privacy like this.

"You need to see," she said, not turning back.

When I pulled out the first of three pictures, I was glad she'd given me a moment. Rage and bile rose fast. I wasn't prepared for it. Not just because Abbi was in the photos but because no one should ever have to face this.

Abbi was naked, clearly passed out, on a bed. Surrounding her

153

was a group of men, all dressed.

The next picture was worse. Two of them men had their hands on her breasts. In the third, they'd spread her limbs open so she had no secrets from anyone or the camera.

My concerns reared up as I shoved the pictures back into the envelope. Much as I wanted to burn them and what they represented, they were her best defense to prove she hadn't been a willing participant. *I don't remember.*

No wonder she hadn't fought back. This wasn't a simple case of cyber bullying. Those pictures showed intent. *Criminal* fucking intent.

"Did they rape you?"

She didn't turn around. "I don't know."

"How can you not know?" I demanded.

She looked so small and lost. My heart seemed to tear apart as I watched her gather her emotions and pride. Not that she'd done anything to be ashamed of, but the men in the pictures sure did.

I'd have to figure out some way to deal with them. Right now, though, I was worried about Abbi. She needed a friend, and I'd promised to be that for her. Even if it killed me, she'd have someone to trust. To lean on. Eventually, I'd tell her that her past didn't change how I saw her.

Except it did. Because the people responsible for those pictures, for putting her in that situation, had taken a chunk of her she'd never offered.

"Not enough apparently. I woke up on a bed. Naked. I had vomit in my hair and it was all over the bed."

"And you don't remember any of that?"

"I remember Steve being there. He woke me, actually."

I tensed, struggling to keep my grip from being too firm. "And what did he want?"

"He wanted to get me out of the house. I was in his room. I could barely function. He helped me dress. Not because I wanted him to, but because I couldn't do it myself."

She bit her lip and then ducked her head. I ran my hand over her hair like I used to with Cassie when she was feeling the effects of her chemo.

"Did he say anything else?" I asked through gnashed teeth.

"He said he hadn't meant for it to go so far, that there were too many of them and he couldn't stop it. That it was good I'd gotten so sick, that it grossed the guys out. He said I had to leave. The first round of pictures appeared later that day."

"He shoved you out of the house?" I couldn't keep the censure from my voice. The guy was a complete ass.

"He offered to walk me home. He'd offered me a change of clothes, but all I could process was the fact I was naked and it was, like, four in the morning. I just wanted to get away. To think."

"Did he try to talk to you about it again?"

She tucked tighter into herself. "Once. He sent a text. Said there were more pictures and we should meet."

"But he didn't offer to help? Or tell you what had happened."

Abbi shook her head. "I blocked his number. I didn't want to talk to him." She glanced up, her eyes worried, searching. "I kept the text. In case I needed it. I probably should give it to my aunt."

I squeezed her a little. "Not a bad idea. You haven't had any memories surface?"

"Nothing. My head hurt for the next couple days, and I had a hard time eating. We did a date rape lecture as part of our orientation. My symptoms were like GHB. It's a clear liquid that anyone could've poured into my drink."

"And you never told anyone?"

She pulled out of my arms, her frown fierce.

"What was I going to say? I was drugged, fucked, and left to choke on my own vomit? But I don't remember any of it? That I can't point to the people who did it? That my ex kicked me out of the frat house in the middle of the night?"

"I get that those pictures paint a terrible picture, but why didn't you say anything?" I asked, my voice soft.

"Mom was finishing a book."

At my look of disbelief, tears filled her eyes.

"She was so happy. This is the first time she's been happy in years. My dad…he didn't make her life easy. She doesn't talk about it, but all I remember is her being sad. I don't want to send her back there, to that place."

"She wouldn't want you shouldering this alone."

"I know she's worried about me. I didn't want to add to that. Plus, the media was all over me with just those 'walk of shame' pictures. I mean *all over*. Sixty phone messages in an hour. Hundreds of emails. I couldn't walk outside without flashes from cameras. Can you imagine what it would've been like if I said I was date raped? My word against who knows how many people ready to stand with Steve?"

"You don't know that. You can't just let them get away with that, Abbi."

"I know. I'd been planning how to deal with this. I just needed a little more time. But your sister's speech made me think. What if I don't have the time? What if this is my last day? Then I want it on record what Steve did." She nodded toward the folder. "Those are his band mates. I want them to know they can't get away with that."

I scrubbed my hands over my face. "You got checked, right? What did the doctor say?"

"I couldn't go anywhere on campus. I was afraid Steve, then the media, would find out, and then there'd be stories about an unplanned pregnancy or an abortion or something equally as salacious. I went to San Francisco and got one of those Plan B kits. I tried to get in with an OB there, but they didn't have availability unless it was an emergency. I couldn't tell them it was—not with those pictures hitting every national media outlet. Someone would have sold me out. So I waited."

"To make sure you weren't pregnant." My stomach rolled. I'd never been through that with a girl, but Colt had. He'd been nearly out of his mind when his high school girlfriend's period was late. "Please tell me you've been checked."

She didn't meet my eyes. "I tried again when I got home at the end of the semester, but at first, the media was too involved in my every movement. I didn't want to go to a clinic in Sydney because I was worried about what the press there would say. By the time I got back, I had four weeks until my annual. It's next Monday."

CHAPTER EIGHTEEN
Abbi

I blew out a breath and waited, my body tensing more with each passing moment. If he didn't say something, I'd break.

"And you thought—what? That I'd stop being your friend because you actually need one. That hurts, Abbi."

"Sally wouldn't talk to me after my junior year in high school. We'd known each other since the third grade and all of a sudden, one day, she wouldn't return my calls.

"When Asher suggested we move to Seattle for my senior year, I was totally fine with that because of Sally's defection." I picked at my thumb's cuticle, unable to look at Clay.

"So you moved to Seattle and went where?"

"Cleveland High. That wasn't the area Mom and Asher wanted to move to but I liked the STEM courses. They got me in there. I got a lot of flak for that."

Clay sighed.

"Everything was fine until that stupid 'she's so pretty, why doesn't she want to be a cover model' article came out. Students came out in droves, pretending to be my friend. If I told them anything, it'd end up all over the school, social media. I'd hoped college would be different. And it was. Tech was worse. So much worse."

He touched my cheek with his thumb before cupping it with his palm. "If it's okay, I'd like to hold you and let you know you're not in this alone."

"In some ways, I've been alone for years," I said, blinking against the tears that threatened to spill out of my eyes.

He pulled me into his arms, snuggling me close against his chest. I wrapped my arms tight around his waist, hugging him tighter still.

"No, Abbi. It just feels that way. I've met your family. You were never alone."

I don't know how long we stood there together. Eventually, Clay shifted. He kissed the top of my head and led me back to his couch.

"You okay?" he asked.

"Yes," I said, surprised. "I'm actually good. I mean, I don't want those pictures to come out, but I feel better to have shared all of this mess with someone."

"I'm glad you feel safe with me."

I smiled up at him, a genuine one. "You sure you don't want me to leave?"

His eyes narrowed and his brows pulled down in a low, angry V. But he cupped my cheeks with a tenderness I'm sure I didn't deserve. "I'm not leaving you to face this alone."

"Clay," I whispered.

He pulled back, but I clamped my hands around his wrists.

"Please. Don't pull back. I need…I want…"

I leaned forward and pressed my lips to his. Good. His lips felt so good. He cupped the back of my head, his thumb rubbing up and down in a gentle caress.

I pulled back in slow degrees, my lips clinging to his as surely as I clung to his wrists. He'd said he wanted to be friends, but I'd just laid some pretty heavy secrets on him. Time to step back and woman up. Give him the space he deserved.

"Sorry. It's been a while since I've kissed anyone, and you

159

make me feel safe."

"That's it?"

I blinked up at him. "What's it?"

Clay's lip flipped up in a little smirk.

"I'll spell it out. I want you, Abbi. You gotta know that. I wouldn't have asked you to dance if I didn't. I knew the media would write about us. But here's the deal: I'm not going to push you because first and foremost, I am your friend. I thought I'd made that clear earlier."

I smiled and rolled my eyes, trying to cover my hurt. It's not like I expected him to proclaim his undying love, but I would like him to show more interest in pursuing a relationship. This felt lukewarm instead of the raging libido I tried to suppress whenever he was around.

"What did you buy for dinner?"

Clay's eyebrow shot up under his bangs. "You are not changing the subject."

"I make a pretty decent lemon-and-herb salmon with couscous. Healthy but tasty."

Clay leaned in and nipped at my lower lip, and my throat quivered on the resulting moan.

"I want you, Abbi. But right now it feels like if I go further, I'm no better than those bastards who took advantage of you."

I pulled out of his lap, settling next to him. I looked down at my hands. I'd ripped the skin and cuticles on my left hand, leaving it scabby and gross.

"You want to know what the worst part about this is? Not that I could have an STD, though that would totally suck. Especially since it would've gone untreated for so long."

I swallowed and forced my gaze up to Clay's, needing to tell him the last of my secret. The piece that cut so deep into my heart.

"I was a virgin that night. That's the main reason I want to go to the OB/GYN."

"You've never had sex?" Clay asked. He kept his voice neutral, but I could hear the thread of surprise.

I gripped my fingers tight. I'd been so stupid.

"Not that I can remember, no." I forced my face up toward his. With Clay, I wouldn't lie. "I dated a guy for a while my junior year of high school, but the break up was traumatic. Then, I worried the guys wanted to be with me because of my famous stepdad. I wasn't willing to chance that. I took a bunch of courses at the community college so that I started at Tech basically a semester ahead. Because it was always my dream," I shrugged, "both the school and the degree. I wasn't going to hookup, not when I already felt pressure from the media just by being related to Asher and getting into a top-tier school."

His skin was gray-tinged. He ran his fingers through the short hairs at his nape.

"Thank you for telling me."

"I thought Steve actually liked me, but he ended up being the worst of the lot. I just want you to know trusting…It's hard. Especially now."

We sat in silence for a while, each wrestling with my revelations. "My mom told me to fight for my happiness," I said softly. I turned to cup his cheek. "I think you've already become that for me. Just so you know, I didn't plan to meet you. Or like you. Or…or need more than that with you."

He looked away. "I don't do relationships, Abbi. I like you and I desire the fuck out of you, but I…"

I wouldn't regret telling him all my secrets because I knew he'd keep them. Because of his background, he understood how hard it was to find someone to confide in, and he was too honorable to betray me. Of that, at least, I was sure. But I'd thought he wanted me like I wanted him.

"Listen. Please."

I couldn't meet his gaze and my heart slammed in my chest.

He swallowed hard, his eyes darkening with some pain I couldn't understand. "I've never wanted a relationship like Nes and Dane have. All that shit—the commitment to each other, the time, knowing we've got each other's backs—that just seems like a big ruse. At some point, it'll crash and burn." With each word, his features hardened, his determination to remain single evident.

"But you said you wanted to act as my boyfriend." Confusion built in my chest. "Isn't that the same thing?"

He smiled, shaking his head. "Nah. Whatever we do, we know we're not in a real relationship. It's for the paps. And to help your image."

Disappointment welled up, choking me, but I managed to say, "And we know it's all fake."

"Right." He smiled.

I bowed my head, pressing it against his shoulder. I needed the time to absorb his words and Clay stroked my hair, letting me adjust.

I was no catch, I got that. Over the last months, I'd become moody, cautious. Probably a huge pain in the ass. Definitely high maintenance. My throat tightened and my nose stung.

Two choices: run away or take him up on his offer for this fake something.

I heard a key scrape against the front door's lock. I jumped up, smoothing my clothes, my hands fluttering over my hair.

Clay stood, all easy grace and extreme male hotness. He scooped up the manila folder with the pictures in it and shoved it into my bag. "Why don't you put this in my room? Door at the end of the hall."

I grabbed the strap and scurried down the hall. Clay's room was large but not ostentatiously so. His bed was covered in a thick dove-gray silk duvet. My brow rose. Silk. Really. I guess it paid to grow up rich. There were other blankets and about ten pillows on his bed—a king, I'd bet. It looked comfortable, a retreat from the rest of the world. A place to snuggle.

My shoulders rolled forward as I realized I was lusting after Clay's bed like many other women had before me. He didn't want me. Not the way I wanted him. But he was willing to help me.

I set my bag in the deep armchair near the window, taking a moment to look out at the view. I needed to calm down. So many emotions rolled through me, and I wasn't sure which to latch on to. I pressed my hand to the glass, taking in the panoramic sweep of Seattle's Pike Market district.

"Abbi?" Nessa called.

"Coming," I said. Stepping out into the hall where Nessa hovered near Clay's door, I gave her a hug. "I thought you were going on the Ferris wheel."

Nessa shrugged. "Malfunction. But it's cool. Clay says you're making dinner. We can all hang out."

I smiled and started down the hall but Nessa's hand on my

arm stopped me.

"What's going on with you and Clay? Why were you in his room? I've never seen a woman in there."

"Ever?" I asked, pleasure enveloping me.

Nessa shook his head. "Clay's private. He kinda has to be with his dad. You know?"

"I was just putting my bag in there."

Nessa raised her brow. "Welp, I guess that's stating his intentions."

"It's not really like that," I sighed. "He's just helping me out, Nes."

"But you put your bag in his room," Nessa said, clasping her hands together under her chin. "So he must want you to stay. That's so sweet."

The doubt and disappointment slithered back through my mind, a poisonous snake hell-bent on destruction.

"If you say so."

"I do. I've seen the way he looks at you," Nessa said. "He wants you. Badly. But he cares enough to take it slow."

I nibbled the corner of my lip, wondering what she'd think if she'd heard Clay talk about how against relationships he really was.

CHAPTER NINETEEN
Clay

Abbi was more than capable in the kitchen. Once we realized she knew what she was doing, the rest of us fell back and watched her work. I grabbed a beer and offered another to Dane and Nessa, who accepted. Abbi declined, which didn't surprise me. If she was right and she'd been drugged, I sympathized with her desire to stay clear-headed.

"Where's Kai?" I asked.

"Sulking," Dane responded. "Jenna's going on a date with some lacrosse player tonight so he's holed up at his place."

"Why doesn't he ask her out if he's interested?" Abbi asked.

Dane shrugged. "He knows she isn't. Like, at all."

"She's still hung up on her high school boyfriend," Nessa said. "They have unfinished business."

"Something about betrayal," Abbi said, frowning. She finished scooping the herbs into a bowl with garlic and butter. Her gaze was thoughtful as she checked the asparagus. "She mentioned it on our ride down to Portland."

"Yeah, it was bad. I guess she had an OD incident in high school," Nessa said. "She has a slew of issues, but the depression is the worst."

"Is it better now?" Abbi asked.

Nessa pursed her lips. "I got the sense when she OD'd she was really messed up. And hanging out with a band—that's a lot of temptation. So she doesn't come to many of the concerts. She won't talk about it."

"That's too bad." Abbi sighed. "Offering up those vulnerable pieces of yourself, that's scary. But when you find someone you can share it with—"

Again, her eyes found mine, and I struggled to force down my desire for her. From that first moment when she'd walked across campus, I'd lusted after her. Knowing her secrets, her strength, I respected the hell out of her, but that need was tempered with the knowledge other men had seen her naked. Touched her and shared those pictures not just with each other but with the world at large.

The timer buzzed and Abbi broke eye contact, busying herself with finishing up dinner. Nessa grabbed the placemats my mom had bought as a housewarming gift and laid them on the table. I filled glasses with water and laid out the silverware and plates. Dane smirked, but I liked the effort our girls made. These little touches were what made the difference between just a meal and a home.

Abbi brought the salmon, couscous, and roasted asparagus to the table.

"Meant to tell you," Dane said as he took his seat next to Nessa. "Bo called about the show on Saturday. He wants us to expand our set. I guess the other band dropped out."

I nodded, considering our playlist, as I helped myself to the salmon Abbi passed me. "We'll need to practice the rest of the week to make sure we have a large enough repertoire."

"Figured. I've already let Kai know."

"You're going to come this time," Nessa said, turning to Abbi. She was two beers deep and her lids were heavy.

Abbi's eyes flashed to mine. I picked up her cold hand. "I'd like that. Please."

"But if this keeps going, the story will be about us and not your music."

Dane kicked back in his chair, his arm slung across the back of Nessa's. "You know the saying about the press."

"I don't want to overshadow your gig." She shook her head. "That's not exactly what I meant."

"I know what you meant," I said, leaning forward. "Look, I told you I don't give a fuck what anyone else thinks. I want you there." The words were right. I really wanted Abbi to be there because her presence would make me happier. I swallowed down my concern about what *that* could mean.

She studied me for a long moment, her eyes darkening. Then, with a soft voice, she said, "I'd like that."

"You should take Abbi out this week. So it's not as big a deal that she's there on Saturday," Nessa said. "You know, to give everyone time to get used to your amazing couple hotness."

I rolled my eyes and finished off my beer. "I'm taking Abbi out on Friday after we practice. We're getting sushi."

I ignored her raised eyebrows. I set my bottle on the table.

"And she's staying here, with me, this week."

"Guess we're eating better than usual," Nessa said, trying hard not to laugh.

"Am I?" Abbi asked. She looked amused.

Dane snorted.

"Dude, the first thing about dating. You ask. Always."

I shot him a grin. "I would, but Abbi gets nervous. So I figured I'd just let her know the plan. That way she doesn't have to overthink it too much."

Nessa burst out laughing. Dane shook his head and joined in. I turned to look at Abbi, who wore an expression somewhere between exasperation and pleasure. I picked up the hand I was still holding and kissed her knuckles, enjoying my role as much as my audience.

"Will you go out with me Friday, Abbi? On our first official date?"

She smiled, a bright wide one. "I'd like that. Except for one part: I'd rather not eat sushi."

I lurched back in my chair. Keeping hold of her hand, I laid her open palm on my thigh.

"How could you have grown up in Seattle and hate sushi?"

"First, I don't hate sushi. It's just not my favorite. Second, I didn't grow up in Seattle. I lived in Idaho for most of my school years. We like beef, potatoes, and corn."

"Looks like you're going to have to pony up for a fancy steakhouse," Dane said. He pointed his fork at me. "Good thing you asked."

Nessa and Dane insisted on cleaning up, but Abbi and I kept them company. The conversation flowed with lots of teasing. I watched Abbi open up more with each passing hour. This was the woman she'd been before her life shifted because of Asher's fame—the woman she was meant to be—the one I was going to help reestablish.

Abbi leaned into my side as we talked, and I liked her nearness. It was only about ten when Dane brushed Nessa's hair from her face. Her eyes were closed, her breathing soft and rhythmic.

"Guess she found you boring," Dane joked. He stood, lifting Nessa into his arms. She curled into him and he clutched her closer.

"See you tomorrow at practice." He strode down the hall. We

listened to the soft click of his door.

The easy comfort evaporated under the thickening tension. Abbi scrambled up. So much for thinking I'd fooled her into believing my slick boyfriend act.

"I don't have a toothbrush. Maybe it'd be best if I just went back to my dorm."

I stood and set my hands on her shoulders. She stilled, her body coiled tightly.

"I'm pretty sure I can find you a toothbrush. My mom brings over packages from Costco once a month." I took her hand, pulling her down the hall toward my room. Her footsteps faltered, but I kept a firm grip on her hand.

Past my bed and into my bathroom, I practically dragged her the whole way. I opened a drawer and offered her one of the many toothbrushes. She picked one out, her eyes wide with concern.

"I don't have anything to sleep in," she said.

"That is the exact opposite of a turn-off," I said. I couldn't help chuckling. She was cute when she was nervous.

"It's just…I've never done this before."

Her honesty was disarming, and I cupped her cheek, trying to soothe the fear building in those big, expressive eyes. "Neither have I. It's going to be okay, Abbi. You'll see."

Her smile was tentative but it was genuine. "Okay."

"I'll grab you a T-shirt. You do your thing while I make sure the front door's locked."

Knowing Abbi was in my room getting ready for bed had me all kinds of hot and bothered. I'd never shared my bed with a woman before. Abbi there, sharing my sheets, feeling my body heat, was both strange and appealing.

I took my time locking the front door and the back slider leading to our terrace. I picked up the four glasses on the coffee table and settled them in the dishwasher.

I walked back into my room, and Abbi stumbled back from the far side of the bed, clutching my duvet to her T-shirt-clad chest.

"Sleep on this side," I said. "I like that one."

I waited to feel creeped out by having a side of a bed. That meant serious, right? Like, a real relationship. Didn't come. She crawled into the bed and fluffed her pillow behind her head.

"You look good there." I hadn't meant to say that out loud. Mainly because I hadn't meant to think it.

She finally looked at me, her eyes dancing with laughter. "Your bed is really comfortable. I may stay with you just for more mattress time." Her cheeks reddened and she covered her mouth. "Oh, that sounded bad."

"Nope. Hot. Sounded hot. I'm going to get ready for bed now. See you in a minute."

Once I was behind the locked bathroom door, I tipped my head back and swallowed.

Intense desire ripped through me. Abbi, in my bed, laughing up at me…Shit, I hadn't been ready for that.

I pushed off the door and touched my finger to the wet bristles of her toothbrush, surprised by the growing bubble in my chest.

I caught a glimpse of myself in the mirror and rolled my eyes. "Just helping out a friend."

I ran through my night routine on autopilot, my mind on Abbi's soft, warm curves snuggled under my covers.

I couldn't help the semi-erection I sported as I walked back to the bed in my boxers and tee. Abbi's eyes glistened in the dark.

"You're quite the sight, Clay Rippey."

I slid into the bed and snuggled my hips to hers. "You feel good, Abigail Dorsey. We should make this a habit."

She stiffened against me. "I don't want to impose."

My fingers clutched at her waist. "Yeah, it's a fucking imposition to have you, a beautiful woman, all soft and willing in my bed. Tragic. For me."

"I just meant—"

I couldn't see her, but she had to be nibbling the corner of her mouth. I bent, searching, finding the spot for myself. Yep. She was. I tugged it gently, and before I realized my actions, I'd dipped my head closer and licked her lip. Abbi moaned. The sound was soft, closer to a gasp. I loved it. This, here, was just us. Learning her in a way no one else had.

I pressed her onto her back, my lips never leaving hers as I reached up to cup her cheek. I let my tongue plunder her mouth, just as I'd wanted to for days. Fine, weeks. I pressed my hand against the back of her head, tipping her head to give me better, deeper access to her mouth.

"I love the way you kiss me," I murmured. "You give me all of your mouth."

I ran my lips across hers, a slow, slick slide of desire. She shuddered and moaned. Kissing Abbi was addictive. My body screamed for more—more of her taste, her passion. More.

I rolled off, breathing harder than after a mile-long sprint. I shoved the heels of my hands into my eye sockets and tried to turn off my raging need.

"Shit, Abbi. Shit. I didn't mean to take it that far."

"I didn't want you to stop," she said. Her voice was quiet, a little uncertain. A dagger to my heart.

"That's why I had to."

She pressed her hand to my chest, her fingers splayed wide. I maneuvered my arm until it was wrapped around her waist. She was narrow, my arm easily curling back to her stomach. She lifted her head and placed it on my shoulder. I kissed the top of her head, nuzzling my nose through her soft hair.

"I've never held a woman for the sake of holding one. I like that it's with you, Abbi."

"I do, too." She yawned, her jaw stretched across my pec. I shifted, trying to ease the ache in my balls.

We were quiet, Abbi snuggled in closer as her body eased into sleep. It was magical, holding her against me, knowing she trusted me so much with her body.

I swallowed down another curse, because I shouldn't be thinking this way. I was Abbi's fake boyfriend, fulfilling a role she needed me to because I'd promised to help her through this scary time. As Abbi relaxed into sleep, I tried to will away the throbbing need from my crotch and the lustful thoughts from my mind.

Didn't work.

CHAPTER TWENTY
Abbi

At Clay's request, I'd spent the last three nights at his place. Three nights of getting a full eight hours of sleep, sometimes more, in Clay's bed. As usual, I woke with my back pressed to his front, his arms wrapped around me, cuddling me back into his thick erection. His breath was soft against my cheek. I was wrapped up in his scent and body.

I loved feeling safe and desired, was quickly becoming addicted to this new reality. But it was fake. And I didn't want our relationship to be just for the media. I wanted a shot at…well, at an us. A real one.

"Good morning," he said, nuzzling into my hair.

Clay was usually so controlled with his emotions, his every action, making me appreciate these glimpses into the man who lived behind his public mask.

I rolled over in his arms, linking mine around his neck. "It certainly is. I sleep really well with you."

His green eyes darkened as he searched my face. "You don't sleep well?"

I shrugged, wishing I'd kept my mouth shut. "Nightmares."

"From that night?"

"Not like memories," I sighed. "More like possible scenarios. Worst case."

"And this has been going on the whole time?"

I nodded.

"Christ, Abbi."

I leaned in and pressed my lips to the corner of his. He stayed stiff and unresponsive, his mind clearly on that night. I kissed him on the other side of his mouth, this time letting the tip of my tongue flick against his firmed lips. Somewhere in the past few days, I'd begun to believe he cared for me as I cared for him.

"I'm sorry, I shouldn't have brought it up. I was trying to tell you how good waking up with you is."

His arms slid up my back to cup my shoulders, his thumbs rubbing the back of my neck.

"I like it, too."

"I could tell." I giggled, pressing my hips tighter against his hard shaft.

"Stop that."

I slithered against him until we touched from chest to feet. He gritted his teeth, trying to hold back a moan. I smiled as he failed.

"Shut up and kiss me, Clay."

"Abbi," he said with a sigh.

"It's practice. For our fake date. So we look totally into each other." I rolled my eyes, tried to keep my voice sardonic.

He laughed as I'd hoped he would, flopping back on the bed, arms thrown wide. I took him in: over six feet of muscled male, his green eyes bright with mirth. His shoulders were broad and his shirt had ridden up so I could see his navel and the deep V on either side of his boxers still tented with desire for me. His legs were long, well-muscled, covered in soft brown hair.

I clambered up his body, letting my hips land on his thighs. He groaned as I cuddled him between my thighs. We stared at each other, desire spiraling up with each beat of our pulses.

"I want you, Clay."

He reared up, cupping the back of my head and kissing me

before I finished my plea. His mouth was ravenous as he rolled us to our sides. His large palm slid over my cotton-clad breast and I arched into him, needing more. He tugged my nipple, pulling it to a stiff peak.

"Can I see you?"

I pulled my shirt up, Clay's big hands shoving the material so it bunched over my ribs. He moaned when the cool air hit my breasts. He tugged the shirt over my head, tossing it toward the foot of the bed.

"I've wanted to do this forever," he said, lowering his head until the wet heat of his tongue laved my breast. I moaned, low and long when he took it in his mouth. I threaded my fingers through his hair, pulling him tighter to my body. My other hand slid over his shoulder and down the ridge of muscle on his back.

He moved to my other breast, his tongue licking before his mouth suckled me to greater pleasure. I scored my nails up his back, and he grunted, his hands sliding over my body.

I writhed, wanting more. So much more.

"Abbi, I really think we should wait." His voice was hoarse.

"I can't, Clay. I need you. Please. Please."

I slid my hand down to cup him through his boxer briefs. His erection grew larger and pulsed in my hand. I explored him with gentle, inquisitive fingers before sliding my hand under his waistband. He threw his head back, his teeth gnashed.

I licked the cords in his neck before I moved down to nibble on that spot at his shoulder I'd discovered he loved. He started to roll away just as I palmed him, a small exclamation forming as I learned his length and girth. He shuddered in surrender, his hands sliding from my waist down over my hips.

He leaned in and kissed his way along my jaw, my eyes, down my nose, taking my mouth in a long, slow drugging kiss that was too sweet. I murmured into his mouth, trying to tell him what I needed.

But Clay knew I needed slow drugging kisses followed by long, tongue-tangling ones. He knew I needed him to kiss his way down my chest and belly, taking his time to learn the contours of my ribs and the indentation at my hips. He knew I needed to climb slowly, with such sweet sensual promise.

And I did. Because Clay asked me to. My need built as he took his time, caressing my thighs and the curves of my rear before moving back up to my breasts. His eyes were intense and dark when he finally rose over me, braced between my splayed thighs.

I'd never wanted anything—anyone—as much as I wanted Clay. He'd played me more skillfully than his banjo, and I vibrated with desire. He leaned down and kissed me again. Another one of those long, slow kisses as he tugged my panties down my legs. I wrapped my thighs around his hips, urging him closer.

"You sure, Abbi? I'll stop." Despair laced his voice. These words cost him.

"Don't stop. I need you inside me."

He inched a finger into my ready, willing body. I moaned, loving how he filled me.

"You're so tight," he moaned against my mouth.

I shifted my hips in a restless motion. He stilled, looking at me. My breasts ached and my sex clenched hard around his finger. My nails bit into his shoulders, and he grunted. He trailed kisses down my neck, hovering over my pebbled nipple.

I arched my back and he cupped my breast, eyes on mine as

he slowly licked across my sensitive peak. His fingers toyed with me, just inside my entrance, rubbing, circling my swollen flesh.

"Not yet. We're taking this slow. It's your first time, Abbi."

First time. Not first time I'd remember. I tugged at his hair until he brought his lips up to mine. I kissed him the way he liked—rubbing my lips against his in slow, light brushes. He licked my lips until I opened for him, sucking his tongue into my mouth.

I ran my fingertips over his eyebrows, the morning scruff of his beard, down his neck to his shoulders. He broke the kiss and ran his fingers up my rib cage, his thumb brushing the underside of my breast.

"Clay," I cried, my head falling back as I struggled against his teasing. His lips closed over my nipple and I clutched his head to my chest, my feet rubbing up and down his calves. "Oh, God. Oh."

He chuckled, as he sucked on my breast.

"Glad to know you think so highly of me."

He moved to my other breast, nipping and licking. I bucked under him, my breath so ragged.

He was going to tease me up to a climax. I didn't want that. I needed him now. I slid my hands down his sweat slicked-back, feeling his muscles quiver under my touch. Good, he wasn't as unaffected as he seemed. I cupped his buttocks, pulling him tighter to my core. He retaliated by rolling my nipple to the roof of his mouth. My body tensed, on the edge of something amazing.

"That's right, Abbi. Come for me." He swirled his finger over my clit, and I exploded. I rode out the thick pulses with my mouth pressed to his collarbone, mewling his name over and over.

He kissed my temple before rolling to his side. "That was so hot."

I stretched, rubbing my cheek against his chest. "Mmm hmm."

He ran his hands down my back, cupping my hips. His thumbs rubbed over my hipbones to the hollows that led to the apex of my thighs. I lifted one of my legs so my knee rested on his hip. I rubbed against his hard length.

I leaned forward and kissed his chest. I hooked my fingers in the waistband of his underwear. "You have condoms, right?"

"Yes."

"Where?"

He nodded to his dresser across the room. "Top drawer."

I kissed him again, teasing him with my tongue and my fingers, keeping both light. He shifted, probably to pull me back into his arms, but I rolled from the bed.

CHAPTER TWNETY-ONE
Clay

Disappointment filled me, along with a surge of desire. Damn, Abbi had a sexy back, all soft, smooth skin. Her hair caressed her, just like I'd like to do, ending a couple of inches above her narrow waist. My dick twitched again, tighter, so achy after three days of cuddling. Sleeping with Abbi was beautiful torture. I shouldn't enjoy it so much.

"Stay right there," she commanded.

I stacked my hands under my head. "No problem. Loving the view."

She threw me a smile over her shoulder and I groaned. No way I was recovering quickly from this hot-and-heavy make-out session.

"You can love it even more in a minute. In fact, I'm going to insist you do."

I cupped my aching balls and gritted my teeth. Abbi was innocent in a lot of ways, no matter what some assholes had done to her body. I hadn't planned to be the one to ease her into intimacy, but I wasn't turning her down either. Abbi knew the score, knew where we stood. So if she wanted to offer me her body, I was damn happy to accept that gift.

She pulled a couple of the foil packets from the opened package, and she seemed to pull into herself. I knew she was thinking about where the rest of the condoms were. I bit back a curse as she set the empty box on the dresser top with care.

"You must be good," she said. She smiled, but this time it didn't reach her eyes.

"I borrowed some from Dane." I shrugged. "A man can hope." I sat up, ready to swing my legs over the bed and gather her back into my arms. Not to have sex, though I wanted to, but to hold her.

"Stay there." She licked her lips as her eyes traveled my body. I lay back, watching her cheeks heat and her nipples firm.

Good to know I did it for her as much as she did for me. She walked back toward me, her gaze getting hotter.

She started at the foot of the bed, condoms clutched in her hand and she crawled over my feet and legs. She stopped at my straining cock to look at me from under her lashes. "Seems like we have a situation."

"Abbi."

She kissed me right there on the tip through the thin cotton of my boxer briefs. Her warm breath and the heat of her mouth felt so good. I barely resisted the urge to thrust into her mouth. She kissed me again, a little surer of her power.

I'd never been with a woman as inexperienced as Abbi. There was something mind-blowingly hot about watching her come into her sexuality. But, at the same time, I didn't want her to feel pressure to be what she thought I wanted.

I wasn't sure it was what I wanted. Playing her boyfriend was totally different from *being* her boyfriend.

"We're going to wait," I gritted.

"Why? Don't you want me?" She sat back, confusion fading the sexy flush from her cheeks.

"Do you see my dick?"

She considered me before kissing her way up my chest, stopping to flick her tongue over my abs, then again on my nipples.

When her teeth clamped around my ear lobe, I groaned and my hips thrust up, seeking her warmth.

"Seems like you do want me."

"Dammit, Abbi, you know I do."

"Show me, Clay. Please."

Shit. Her eyes were wide with need but also vulnerability. She thought I was turning her down because of what those douchebags did to her. My cock was more than happy to let her know that wasn't the case, but still, I worried Abbi would regret having sex with me if we did this.

"I trust you, Clay."

And there it was. She trusted me with her secrets and her body. And I was more than a willing accomplice.

I grabbed one of the condoms still clutched in her hand. I put it to her mouth. She frowned at it, then me.

"Rip it open. With your teeth."

She smiled, then did as I asked. Sexy as hell.

I pulled off my boxers and rolled on the condom. I lifted her hips. She had her hands on my shoulders for balance. I positioned her where I wanted her and then moved my hands up to cup her hips. "When you're ready."

I groaned as she sank down a little, testing our fit. She was so tight. The tip of her tongue poked between her teeth as she lifted her hips and spread her thighs wider. Her pupils were so big, they swallowed the blue of her eyes. Her breasts rose and fell in rapid succession. She sank down harder this time. We both stilled. I stared up at her, my eyes just as wide as hers.

"Fuck." I leaned up so my cheek rested on her breast. Her heart raced in a quick rhythm.

"That hurt." She said, her voice dazed.

I looked up at her. "Still?"

She shook her head. "No." She licked her lips, her eyes even wider than they were before. "Does that mean I was still a virgin?"

"Yes," I groaned, thinking about the gift she just gave me. I pulled her down to my chest and held her. I'd just taken her virginity. "That's what it meant."

She rested her forehead against mine. "Oh. Clay." Her back shook. "God. I'm so glad it's you."

"Me, too, Abbi." I had to kiss her. Claim her. Now. She was *mine*. I was the only man who'd been here, inside her.

I kissed her, lingering at the place right in the middle of her lips she liked me to lick. I gathered her close in my arms, and then I twisted. She held on, her elbows on my shoulders, her fingers fisted in my hair as I rotated so she was on her back.

"I'm going to move now," I said, looking deep into those blue eyes. Her lips, all swollen from my kisses, parted as I slid out of her. I pushed back in, deep. She arched against me, and I leaned down and bit her just above her shoulder. She cried out and clenched tight around me. Slow. I had to take this slow.

CHAPTER TWENTY-TWO
Abbi

Knowing my body was still mine…the relief was enormous. But the feel of Clay rocking in and out of me was beyond intense. Good, no great. He altered his hips so the friction shifted forward. I clawed at his back, trying to contain the feelings pouring through my body.

He cupped my breast as he kissed me, his tongue forcing my jaw open wide so he could mimic his hips' action. I arched up into the next thrust, straining to get closer, to hold him tighter. He found a smooth rhythm, and I wound up, up, up.

He pulled back, his chest heaving as he slid his arms under me, hands cupping my shoulders. He slammed into me. Hard. He growled, low, primal. The sound was so hot my thighs spasmed. He slammed into me again and my body heated, rising higher than before.

"Clay," I cried.

His mouth dropped to my shoulder and he sucked hard. One more thrust, and I was over the edge, falling, twisting, panting with my release. Clay groaned.

He collapsed onto my chest, his breathing as ragged as mine. I trailed my fingers up and down his back, loving how his narrow, tight waist flowed up into those broad shoulders. He lifted onto his elbows, and I murmured at the loss of his weight on me. He shook his head. Hard.

"Hey," I said.

He leaned down, brushed his lips over mine. The caress was soft, sweet. I smiled into it, and he pulled back, questions forming in his eyes.

"That kiss was sweeter than our, um, sex."

Clay laughed. He rolled to his side, and I winced as he slid from my body. He pulled me tight against his side.

"This is more than just sex, Abbi." He brushed my hair out of my face, his thumb tracing the curve of my cheek.

My cheeks heated but I grinned at him. "I think it's you. You're a pretty stellar teacher."

He stilled. His gaze followed his fingers as he traced them down my face to my lips. "I don't get off on screwing virgins. And whatever you've heard, I'm not that big into hookups either."

I ducked my head, embarrassment flaming up my neck. "I didn't mean it like that."

He cupped my cheek so I had to meet his eyes. "I want you. *You.* And I'm really fucking glad I was your first. But not for the reason you're thinking." His eyes darkened and his lips twisted down in a sardonic grimace. "Okay, maybe for that reason, too."

"I like that, too," I whispered.

He ran his thumb down my cheek, over my bottom lip. "I'm relieved they didn't rape you, Abbi."

Tension I didn't know I was still carrying slid from my shoulders. "Guess barfing on myself turned out to be a good thing."

Clay sat up, pulling me up by my shoulders so I straddled him. "Don't joke about that, ever. They wanted to hurt you. The fact that they failed…that's awesome for you, but they'll probably try with some other girl. Someone like my little sister."

His fingers dug into my shoulders, but I got where his anger was coming from.

My nose stung as his words swirled through my mind.

He'd just implied I meant as much to him as his sister. The little girl he went home to see almost every weekend. I wanted to tell him I loved him, but I was scared.

He blew out a deep breath as he petted my hair. "How about we shower?"

My body warmed. "Together?"

His grin was downright lascivious. Oh, I liked this side of Clay. "If you're up for it."

I glanced down. "Looks like you are."

He picked me up, leaving me no choice but to wrap my legs around his waist and hold on.

"You have no idea."

———————

I was late to class. Clay dropped me off with another scorching kiss. He'd promised to pick me up after, muttering something about commitments. As I stepped away, he cupped my bum, fondling the curve. I couldn't stop smiling and sighing.

"See you at three," I said.

"You better believe it. We've got our hot date. And I think we should try body art."

I frowned a little, trying to grasp his meaning.

"I'm going to like licking honey from your neck almost as much as your inner thigh," he murmured against my ear.

I gasped, my body tightening. I wished I hadn't felt the need to come to school today, but this lab was important—a quarter of my grade—and I didn't think my excuse of making love for the first time would hold up with my instructor even if it was Clay's brother. My stomach rolled in a painful push. *Especially* because it was Clay's brother.

Colt noted my entry, his eyes skimming over my relaxed expression and tousled hair. He turned away, but I caught the faintest smirk. I scurried to my seat and settled in as quietly as possible.

I worked through my lab, finally understanding the molecular component we'd been studying for the last few weeks. As everyone packed up, Colt caught my eye. He motioned me toward his desk. I nodded, dawdling over cleaning my station and shoving my binder back into my messenger bag.

My legs wobbled as I walked up to Colt's desk.

"How's the hazing around campus?" he asked.

Relief flooded my head, and I had to blink against the sudden lightheadedness.

"No one really bothers me because I'm usually in a group or with Clay."

"Glad to hear that," Colt said, his mouth easing tension. "So you and my brother?"

"Is that a problem?" I asked.

"No. It's great. Clay." Colt dipped his head at the same time Clay moved in behind me, close enough for me to catch his woodsy scent.

Clay slid my bag from my shoulder, lifting it to his before he threw his arm around my waist.

"I sent you a text," Clay said, "to let you know Abbi and I are going out tonight. In case you get any media requests for information."

"Good to know," Colt said. His brows pinched tight over his nose. "I'll have to talk to the dean, make sure it's all good that I'm teaching this class if you're dating my brother."

I looked down, twisting the hem of my shirt. Fake-dating Clay was complicating lives quickly.

"I don't want to cause you any trouble," I murmured.

Clay's fingers tightened in a possessive clasp at my waist. "You're not. Colt's just doing his CYA work."

I forced my gaze back to Colt's, trying to swallow the unwelcome dryness in my throat. "Are you sure it's not a problem?"

Colt's brown eyes were kind, though his expression was thoughtful. "Honestly, I don't know. But I'll haul ass upstairs and talk to Dean Mosconi now. The fact that everything is open and transparent will help. Anyway, I was thinking more about you, Abbi. I don't want anyone to think I gave you a grade you didn't deserve."

I tucked my hair behind my ear. "Seems kind of far to stretch. Me, sleeping with your brother, means you give me better grades."

"I see your point." Colt stood, picking up his battered leather satchel. He was young and hip, the antithesis of the normal science prof. He made it to the door before turning back and looking at us. "Don't worry too much about the social media hoopla. Just a bunch of trolls looking to rip someone else down so they don't feel so shitty about eating bags of chips in their parents' basements."

I smiled and waved. "Your brother's pretty cool."

"He has his moments. So this is a science lab."

"It is. Do you have a sudden need to learn chemistry?"

Clay's lips twitched. He turned me so our bodies aligned. His hand splayed across my lower back, pulling me tight against his chest and hips. I raised my eyebrow when his thickening bulge pressed against my belly.

He leaned down and pressed a kiss to the corner of my eye. I sucked in a breath at the jolt of need that sizzled through my body.

"I already have lots of chemistry with you."

I rolled my lips into my mouth but I wasn't able to stifle the giggles that erupted. "That's a terrible line," I managed to gasp.

"It was amazing. Like me."

I rolled my eyes as he took my hand, pulling me from the classroom. Kai hailed us as soon as we exited the building.

"I'm hungry, and I need a ride. My car's in the shop."

"Abbi needs to run by her dorm to pick up some clothes and such," Clay said.

"Then we'll feed my poor neglected stomach," Kai said.

Clay grabbed my hand and pulled me down the sidewalk toward my dorm, ignoring the looks of avid interest and even some of the catcalls thrown our way.

Kai wasn't as cool. "Fuck off," he yelled after hearing a particularly racy comment about what I could be doing with my hands.

Clay's hand tightened around mine, but he kept walking forward, even as his jaw tensed.

"You dealt with this at Tech?" Kai asked. "By yourself?"

"It was worse."

"How was it worse?"

"They'd touch me."

"Wow, Abbi, you're really living up to your reputation," Jenna joked as we walked by her open door.

I rolled my eyes, but Clay was ready to snap. "That wasn't funny." His voice was tight with anger.

"Abbi knows I'm teasing. Right?"

I opened my door and gasped.

The room was trashed. The worst wasn't the shredded bedding or even the broken picture frames on the floor.

"Holy shit," Jenna said. "That's so uncalled for."

Words were written in red spray paint on what was left of my mutilated bed and all the walls. They'd even written on my desk and chair. I was glad I'd brought my laptop with me when I stopped by a couple days ago to pick up some more clothes and class notes. Otherwise, I was sure the words would be written there, too.

But even those weren't the worst. Those were words. No, what kept me transfixed were the pictures. The pictures I'd shown Clay.

I didn't want to do this. Not here. Not yet. Clay and I were supposed to have a date tonight. A normal night. He was supposed to tell me this morning meant something to him, that we were together for real.

Much as I didn't want to involve the police because this would get back to my mom and Asher, hurting them more, I pulled out my phone.

"I'll call," Kai said, his voice gentle. Jenna touched my shoulder. "Abbi? Why don't you come into my room?"

I didn't move. Instead, I stared at the pictures taped to the walls, placed strategically so I could still read the words below. Ugly words, shameful words.

This was what people thought of me.

Clay swung me around, dragging me down toward Jenna's open door. I was shaking so hard, walking was difficult.

This was Tech all over again. Except this time, I had friends and they'd seen the pictures and the words.

I bolted to the bathroom.

Long after I'd emptied the contents of my stomach, I sat there, shivering. Those men had their hands on my body. It's why I was sure one of them had raped me. But they hadn't. They'd just used me.

I'd really thought I could leave it all behind. I pressed the heels of my hands to my eyes, wishing I could block out the rest of my life just as easily.

"Abbi?" Jenna's voice was hesitant. "I'm worried and so is Clay. Will you come out now?"

I didn't want to. I wanted to hide, to pull back inside myself again.

But that hadn't worked, not if copies of those photos were on my dorm room walls. So my only other choice was to move forward.

"Just a minute."

I stood, my legs still shaky but my fortitude firmly in place. I rinsed my mouth. After washing my face, I met my gaze in the mirror. I had choices, but only one path.

I stepped out of the stall and met Jenna's worried gaze. "I brought you a clean toothbrush."

I hugged her, quick and hard. "Thank you."

She hugged me back. "You'll get through this, Abbi. Just so you know, Nessa and I—we're sticking by you. Clay is pretty firm he's in this with you, too. Even Kai's out for blood. And he doesn't care about anything."

"He cares about you. In fact, he likes you," I said.

She waved her hand, dismissing that. "He likes that I don't like him."

I took the toothbrush and cleaned my teeth.

"I need to call my mom. I don't want her to hear this from some reporter or gossip site."

Jenna walked me back to her room. Clay sat on her bed, his hands linked between his spread knees. He stood when I entered, coming close enough to touch me. He didn't. Was he disgusted with me?

"Those were the same pictures, right?" he asked. "The ones your friend gave you?"

I nodded, my throat tightening with the need to cry.

"I need to call my mom. She's going to be so upset."

"For you. She's going to hurt because someone did this to you, Abbi."

I winced, pulling back. But Clay cupped the back of my head in that way I loved. The way that made me feel so safe, cherished.

I leaned in, needing his smell and the solid wall of his chest against my cheek. He played with my hair, his body tense. I knew he was thinking what I was—more people would see those pictures. This time it would be the police, but once I filed the report...I shuddered again.

"Will you stay with me? I don't want to do this alone."

He leaned forward and kissed my forehead. I let my eyes slide closed, loving the feel of his lips on my skin. He pulled back slowly, his hand sliding down over my hair. "You're not alone. You never were."

Much as I wanted to burrow into his large body, to absorb his strength, I wasn't ready to show that much vulnerability. Not yet. Even with Clay. Some lessons were just too deeply ingrained. I dialed my mom's number, standing there as close to Clay as I could without actually touching him.

"Hey, Abs. What's going on?" Mom sounded cheerful.

I couldn't say it. I just couldn't tell her. Clay slid his hand up my arm, over my shoulder to the base of my neck.

"Abbi? Are you there?"

I met his gaze. The difference here was stark: I lived my life, or I let others dictate it for me. Clay waited for me to make the choice, his eyes swirling green with emotion.

"Hi," I said. "I have some news."

"You're okay?" Her voice rose. Panic bubbled behind her words.

"I'm fine." And I meant it. I smiled, and Clay brushed his thumb along my jaw. "I'm actually really good." I sighed. "But my room isn't. Someone broke into it today. Well, maybe last night. I'm not sure."

"What? Why? Were you there? Are you hurt? Did you call the police?" The wheeze built in Mom's voice, a sure sign she was about to have a panic attack.

"I'm fine, Mom. I promise. I'm with Clay and Jenna and Kai."

"You're with Clay." Mom released a gusty breath. "Tell him thank you for me."

"I will. But I need to tell you this wasn't a break in to steal stuff." I swallowed hard, my eyes firmly fixed on Clay's. His thumb continued its gentle caress. "They wrote words on my wall."

"Oh, Abbi," Mom breathed. "Honey."

"The worst part, though, are the pictures from that night. At Tech."

"I'm coming over there," Mom said. "Right now."

"Please don't. Not because I don't want to see you but because that'll just make it worse for me."

192

"Abbi." Mom sounded lost, a little broken. "You're sure I can't come there?" She cleared her throat. "Asher said to come home. We'll talk about this some more."

"I will. Tomorrow. First thing. But tonight, I'm going to stay with my friends."

That set Mom off. More than anything else, she'd been as frustrated and hurt as I was by the difficulty I'd had since she and Asher got married. She sniffled harder. "I'm so glad you have friends again."

"It's going to be okay, Mom." I smiled at Clay, who smiled back slowly, a bit unsure. "I'm going to be okay." His smile widened and his eyes lit up.

"Cops are here," Kai called from the door.

"Did you hear that? The police are here. I'll text you when we leave campus. I'm staying at Clay's tonight. So are Jenna and Nessa," I rushed to add.

"I love you, Abbi. Be safe."

"I'll text you later."

"Do. I'm going to worry about you."

"Love you, Mom. Same goes for Asher and Mason."

CHAPTER TWENTY-THREE
Clay

We didn't leave the dormitory until close to midnight. Abbi looked exhausted. For the first time in hours, I could breathe deeply. Much as I wanted to grab her hand, I refrained, unsure where she and I were after this latest shockwave.

I wanted to go back to the simple, happy place where I could ease my lips and tongue over her body and know it was mine alone. Which made me the world's biggest asshole. Abbi hadn't posed for fucking Playboy, trying to garner fame with her body. She'd been drugged and violated.

But I'd quickly realized I didn't want to deal with that reality.

She'd told me. She'd showed me. I'd been okay with the theory. I wasn't so okay with the knowledge that every time I looked at her, someone else was looking at her, too. Fine. I was fucking pissed. And jealous, which made me angrier because I'd never been jealous before.

I'd stood in the hall of her dormitory as she packed a bag of clothes, which I now held. She'd insisted on carrying her messenger bag herself.

"We're going to Clay's now," she said to her mom as we walked down the steps of the dorm and out into the cool, dark night. Shit, I couldn't imagine how anxious Dahlia and Asher had to be right now. "I'll call you tomorrow. Afternoon? Okay. Yeah, that shouldn't be a problem. Let me ask him."

"My mom wants me to come over tomorrow. You want to come, too?"

I tried to gauge her reaction but couldn't in the dark. "Do you want me to go?" I asked.

The next light along the path spilled onto her face, showing her uncertainty. I stopped walking and cupped her cheek with my free hand. Her skin was soft, smooth. Her eyes drifted closed like she couldn't believe I'd want to touch her.

"Do you want me there?" I asked again.

"Yes." Her lip trembled. "I want you there. But that's selfish. Maybe it would be best if I went home now and you could go back to being normal."

The weight in my gut pressed even harder. Hadn't I just been thinking that? Abbi's face was pale. She was tall but so small at the same time. And she was carrying such a burden.

"Look at me," I said.

Her lashes lifted, and I looked into those eyes—eyes I'd never, ever forget. Vulnerable eyes filled with fear and hope.

"I'm here for you, Abbi."

She turned her face to press her lips to my palm. The kiss was gentle, a thank-you. But it turned me on, much to my disgust. I removed my hand before I totally embarrassed myself.

She put the phone back to her ear. "Clay's coming with me."

My hand fisted on the handle of her bag as I listened to her making plans for us. Because we were together. I had to look away so I could get my expression back under control. I swallowed down my need to bolt. I'd promised. I wasn't going to be like my dad and run.

I wasn't my dad.

Sure, I'd planned to help her with the media, but now someone—probably Bethany—had upped the game. Forced me deeper into this than I wanted to be, but I'd continue to play the role.

195

Except this morning it hadn't been me playing a part. It had been magic. We'd been so comfortable together.

"Love you, too. We'll let you know when."

She hung up the phone, tucked it into her pocket.

"Let's get you home," I said, my voice gruff.

She flashed me a smile. How, in the midst of all this terrible shit, could she be happy? She laid her hand on my chest and I stopped walking again.

"Thank you, Clay. You being here, I'm so thankful for you."

She slid up onto her toes and kissed me. A soft peck that went straight to my crotch. I dropped the handle of her suitcase and gathered her in my arms and kissed her, claiming her mouth with mine. I wasn't willing to share her, not now. And she needed to understand that.

I pulled back, shocked I'd been so aggressive. Abbi touched her lips, then her cool fingers touched mine.

Driving to my apartment took about fifteen minutes. Kai and Jenna had left the dorms hours ago, but I'd waited for Abbi to finish with the police and the university administrator. My eyes burned and my throat felt drier than the wheat fields of Eastern Washington in the summer.

"You hungry?" I asked as we headed up the elevator.

"I don't know."

I walked to my door, but before I could pull out my key, it opened. Nessa was there, pulling Abbi into a hug.

"You're here. We were worried."

"I had to talk to the police. Twice. Then the Northern staff and your good friend Jan, the victim advocate."

"We ordered pizza," Jenna said, peering around Nessa. "Come

in and grab a slice. It's cold, but it's food."

I grabbed a couple bottles of water from the fridge and handed one to Abbi. She nibbled at a piece of veggie-laden pizza, looking lost in thought. Jenna leaned forward like she wanted to ask a question.

"Where's Dane?" I asked, sighing as my butt hit the chair. I was tired.

"He and Kai ran an errand," Nessa said, her eyes darting back to Abbi.

"Please tell me they didn't go talk to Bethany," I groaned, setting down my slice of pizza.

The door opened. "Talk, no," Kai said. He snagged a slice heavily laden with meat, same as I had. "She wasn't there."

Nessa stood and wrapped her arms around Dane, who looked as raw as I was. He pulled Nessa down into his lap with a sigh.

"I swear she wasn't this crazy when we met," he said. "I'm so sorry about this shit, Abbi."

Abbi set her pizza down. "No one's blaming you. We don't know for sure she's even responsible. It could very well be Steve or one of his gross friends. But thank you for looking out for me."

"Oh!" Nessa scrambled up on her knees. "Bethany said her cousin goes to Tech? Remember, Clay?"

I nodded as I chewed. "She did. Maybe there's a connection there."

Dane tugged at his lower lip. "I'll make some calls."

"Me, too," Kai said, face solemn. "We got your back, Abbi."

She nodded, her gaze taking in all the faces in the room. She stopped last at me. "I haven't had so many people care about me in a long time. It's nice."

I grasped her hand and pulled her down the hall toward my room. I stopped long enough to grab her bags, thankful I had a bathroom attached to my bedroom. I didn't want to deal with more emotion or people tonight.

I closed the door behind me, locking it. I wrapped my arms around her, tucking her in close, the way she seemed to like best.

"How are you, really?"

"I'm good," she said. She sounded surprised and relieved. "I don't have to hide anymore because I'm scared those pictures will come out."

Her arms wound tight around my back, like she was comforting me. But I was supposed to be comforting her. Hell, this was confusing.

"Go brush your teeth, whatever you need to do to get ready for the night."

I waited until she was in the bathroom before I slammed my fist into the mattress. Not once, but many times. I tunneled my fingers through my hair, trying to calm down.

I hated those pictures. I hated the douchebag who'd taken them and the ones who'd participated. I hated that the police were—right now—touching them, examining them. I'd think about that while we were together, and it was *not* a turn on.

"Fuck," I groaned. I hit the bed again.

Abbi ran her hand down my back. "It's okay."

I turned, surprised to find her in her bra and panties. Her hair was pulled up into a messy bun. I studied her: face washed clean, getting ready for sleep. This version of Abbi was immediately my favorite because it was *mine*. No one else was going to see her like this. I'd make sure of it.

I grabbed her waist and pulled her against me, bending my head to slam my lips against hers. She grunted but wound her arms around my neck, opening to me immediately. I eased the kiss, running my lips side to side over hers in a whisper-soft caress.

"I don't want you to be upset about those pictures."

I leaned my forehead against hers. "See. That's the problem. *I'm* supposed to be comforting *you*."

She cupped my cheeks tilting my chin down so she could look in my eyes. She hesitated for a long moment. "I've had months to figure out how I wanted to deal with the shame of it—and that's what this is about. Making me feel terrible for being a woman."

"I—" My eyes darted away. "I don't like sharing you with anyone. I don't like men knowing how you look naked."

"I don't like it either. But I can't change the fact someone took the pictures. All I can do is stand tall and not let them take another piece of me along with those photos." She took a deep breath. "Maybe...would you take the day to hang out with me tomorrow?"

I nodded. We'd hole up here and focus on each other. "Do you know how to make waffles?"

She smiled. "Yes. Mason loves them. You, too?"

"They're my favorite. With whipped cream."

Her eyes widened as she saw where my eyes had dropped. I had to get away from her before I pushed this further. She was vulnerable, and I wasn't going to be another asshole who took advantage of an emotional woman.

"Grab a shirt if you want one. I'll be right back."

I trudged into the bathroom, lamenting my need to act like a gentleman. I got ready for bed—I had no idea what took women so long and was pretty sure I didn't ever want to know. Then I took another couple minutes to give myself a pep talk.

Much as I wanted to brand her sexually so that she couldn't remember anything or anyone's touch but mine, that was a purely Neanderthal reaction. One I needed to get the hell over. Because we weren't really even dating.

We were complicated. More so now that my desire to protect Abbi was mixed up with my desire for her.

Taking a deep, calming breath, I walked back into my bedroom. I stopped when I noticed Abbi sitting on the edge of the mussed bed, picking at her thumbnail. She looked small and sad.

"What's wrong?"

CHAPTER TWENTY-FOUR
Abbi

I slid off Clay's bed and picked up one of his shirts he'd thrown over the back of his chair. It smelled like him, and I had to resist the urge to bring the soft cotton to my nose. Clay grabbed my hand.

"What are you doing?"

"The look on your face…I was thinking maybe it would be best if I left."

"Why?"

"I told you I was a mess. And now I'm hurting you. I hate that, Clay. You've been through enough with Cassidy."

"You're not leaving. I want you here."

"No, you don't."

His nose quivered as his eyes narrowed. "Don't you goddamn tell me what I want!"

"You could barely look at me. You're waging a war in your head, and it's exhausting for me to watch it."

"I want you, Abbi. I want you to stay here in my bed."

"But—"

"Do you want to that, too?" he bellowed. The voices in the other room fell silent.

I should be afraid; he was shaking with anger. But it was directed at the people who'd hurt me. I put my hand on his chest, feeling the rapid beat of his heart. "Yes. I want that, too."

His arms slid around me, pulling my bra-clad chest tight to his naked one. He dropped his cheek to the top of my head. "You make me crazy."

"I don't mean to."

He held me for a long moment. "Will you stay with me?"

I pressed my cheek harder against his chest, inhaling that clean, woodsy scent. I shouldn't. Now that I'd seen what these pictures were doing to him, I should cut him loose. I closed my eyes, tears burning my nose and eyelids. The media, the pictures, my life, everything was only going to get worse.

"Please." His voice was soft.

I sucked in a deep breath and forced the need to cry down. "Yes."

———◆———

I woke slowly, feeling languorous as I stretched. I'd slept—really slept, which shocked me. My mouth tipped up. We'd both been exhausted by the time I finished showing Clay how happy I was to have him in my life.

"Morning, sleepy head," Clay said, smoothing my hair off my neck and kissing me there. I shivered.

"It is a good morning."

He chuckled again. "It's almost over."

I tensed, trying to sit up, but he kept his arm around my waist. "What? How is that possible? What time is it?"

"Just after ten. You slept like the dead."

"I never sleep late," I said, shocked. "Must have been all the orgasms." Clay's tongue licked its way up my neck to my earlobe. He sucked on it gently. I moaned.

"I'll take that. I wanted to call your mom but it was impossible to break into your phone. She called a couple of hours ago. I told her you were still sleeping. She said to call her and reminded you about stopping by later."

"I'll call her later." I twisted the sheet between my fingers.

He cleared his throat. "What do you want to do today?"

"This." My words were breathy, barely there.

He chuckled. "Good. Me, too." He rolled me over and kissed me, his mouth hungry against mine.

I gripped his biceps and kissed him back, my tongue dueling with his.

He finally broke the kiss. "We gotta slow down, Abbi."

"Why?"

"Besides the fact I want you so badly I can't see straight?"

"I can fix that."

He rolled over and threw his arm across his eyes. "I should've waited the last time. Much as I liked sexing you up."

I eased out of bed. He didn't move. I slithered out of my panties and bra and then crawled back into the bed, right on top of him. He opened his eyes wide when he slid his hand down my bare back.

"So here's the deal. I wanted you two months ago. I want you more now." I met his gaze, his pupils dilated. "I care about you, Clay. Like, a lot."

He flipped me over, pinning my wrists to his bed. His tongue found my jaw and I arched my neck up into him. He made a thick, humming sound and worked his way down my throat toward my chest.

"You are gorgeous," Clay moaned. Desire had pebbled the pink tips of my breasts to hard points. He pulled one into his mouth, lapping it with his tongue. I liked the sensation but it was clearly more of a turn on for him. Sensing my hesitation, Clay nuzzled his head between my breasts, and my hips shifted up to cuddle him.

"Turn over," he said. I complied and he licked and kissed his way down my spine. I shivered as goose bumps popped up all over my skin. He kneaded his hand on my left bottom cheek, his teeth scraping along my right one. I moaned, shoving back toward him.

He laughed. His hand snaked back up to my breast, tweaking the nipple. This time I lurched back against him again. He worked those soft, warm lips over the back of my thighs, down to the sensitive skin behind my knees.

My breathing had shortened to puffs of need. When he slid back up my body, his bare chest in contact with my back, I couldn't help the moan. He felt too good. He pulled me up to my knees, my back against his chest as his fingers slid from my breasts, circling my navel before finding the indentions inside my hip bones.

I looped my arm behind his neck, pushing my chest out. Clay's chest rumbled with the sound as his left hand came up to claim my breast again. He weighed and massaged it in his hand.

His other hand slid between my thighs. I trembled as he rubbed his thumb over my clit, seeking my desire. I was wet, plumped, ready. He inhaled sharply as he slid a finger into my welcoming body.

"You feel good."

I pressed my hips back into his thighs, feeling his thick erection against my back. I rubbed again, needing more, wanting more. Especially when his finger pumped in and out of my body.

My legs slid open farther and Clay slid another finger into me, his thumb flicking back to my swollen bundle of nerves. I jerked against him, needy.

He kissed my cheek and I turned to find his lips. I opened for him and his tongue slid past my lips to tangle with mine. The dual sensation of his tongue in my mouth and his fingers in my body rippled heated pleasure through my muscles.

He broke the kiss and reached around me to his bedside table. He pulled out a condom, and I watched, fascinated as he rolled it on. He slid his hand up and down himself, his eyes sliding closed as his nostrils flared.

His obvious desire for me made me feel powerful. I cupped him and his eyes shot open, finding mine.

"Do that again," he groaned. I did, and he pushed his hips against my hand. I slid my hand over him like he'd done and he growled.

"I need to be inside you. Right now."

"Yes," I murmured against his lips.

He pulled my hips back against him. I blushed as I realized he wanted me on my hands and knees. I leaned forward, catching the headboard so I could ease my body down to the bed.

"Like that," he grunted, one of his thighs pushed between mine, spreading my legs. "Hold on tight."

As he said the words, he slid inside my body. My stomach muscles and even my throat tightened as he eased into me. It was as though I didn't want him to leave—ever.

"Abbi." His hand landed on top of mine where it gripped the wood of his headboard.

He slid out and I pushed back, wanting him filling me up

again. His hips thrust forward and I moaned, deep and long.

"I like hearing what I do to you," he whispered in my ear.

"More."

He bit my earlobe as he pulled back. His lips moved in a lazy trail down my neck as he pumped back into me. My fingers slid against the headboard, my breast hitting the cool wood.

I yelped at the shock of the coolness against my sensitized skin. Clay slid his hand around my waist. His arm was thick, corded with muscle and covered in short dark hairs that tickled my belly.

He picked up the pace a little with each thrust. His breath shattered in my ear. I spread my legs wider, needing more. His chest rumbled against me as he dropped over my back, forcing me to land on my hands on the mattress. The next thrust had us both moaning. He was so deep. I loved it, and I told him so.

That broke his restraint and Clay's teeth found my shoulder as he gripped my hips, slamming into my willing body. I pushed back into each of his thrusts, searching for that pleasure coiling deep in my belly. When it finally released, I screamed his name. Loud. My throat hurt as I started to sink down, my muscles so relaxed I couldn't hold them up anymore.

Clay lifted my hips, positioning me so he could continue pounding into my body. I took him, marveling at his stamina. He grew even bigger before he stiffened. His balls pulsed against my thigh as he grunted his release. Finally, he sighed, falling next to me on the bed.

I rolled into him, and he wrapped his arms around me. I giggled at his racing heart.

"What's so funny?"

"You're so quiet when you come, and I'm not."

He smiled, kissing the tip of my nose.

"I like you screaming my name. Total turn-on."

"I like how you feel sliding in and out of my body," I said, running my thumb along the short whiskers on his jaw.

"Abbi. Stop it. You're making me hard again."

I kissed that spot in the middle of his chin.

"Good."

He narrowed his eyes before rolling me over onto my back. "You asked for it."

I stretched up to him. "No. I asked for you. Inside me."

Clay's nostrils flared as he stared down at me. "Oh, you'll get me. Again."

"And again and again?"

He didn't answer, he was too busy kissing me.

CHAPTER TWENTY-FIVE
Clay

"So your family…" I said.

Abbi turned toward me, wearing an embroidered cotton tee and low-slung panties. I had to resist the urge to pull them off with my teeth. I wanted to take her back to bed and hear her scream my name in that breathy voice she used in the throes of passion.

Yep. Hard.

"What about them?"

I blinked back the daydream and pulled on my jeans, hoping the layers of clothing would help reduce my reawakened desire. No such luck.

"Are you going to show them the pictures?"

Abbi sat on the edge of the bed so I settled next to her. She fiddled with the hem of her shirt until I stilled her hands. She leaned her damp hair against my shoulder, and I could feel the fine tremors moving through her narrow frame.

"I need to." She tipped her head back to meet my gaze. She faced her fears and the hard situations with equal determination. That was one of the reasons I loved Abbi. I stilled, my thumb resting on her chin as I considered her face.

I didn't love her. I just…cared about her. As a friend. That I was having the best sex of my life with.

"My mom's going to want me to stay there."

"No." The word tumbled out before I thought it through— before I understood the consequences of what I'd just said.

Abbi raised an eyebrow, waiting.

"You should stay here. With me." What. The. Fuck? Did I really want that?

My gaze lingered on her long legs. I wanted her in my bed, no doubt there. But…in my life?

"There's so much we don't know about each other," she said as if reading my mind. "I mean, what if you leave dirty socks on the floor or like to get up at five a.m. to jog?"

I ducked my head.

"So that's a yes to both of those?" She laughed again, standing to grab some jeans from her bag.

"I don't always do either. What are some of your bad habits?" I asked, shocked by my interest. Standing, I went to my dresser and pulled out socks. Glancing around my room, I breathed out a sigh of relief. I didn't have any piles of clothes on the floor. They usually made it to the hamper in my closet.

"I hate five a.m. Six thirty is much more civilized. Oh, and I don't drink coffee very often…"

"What the hell's wrong with you? Aren't you American?"

She grimaced. "Like that's a new one. I need to doctor it up until it barely resembles a dark brown liquid. Think milkshake color. It's so bitter."

"Not the good stuff."

She flipped her hair back and padded into my bathroom. I marveled at the sexy swing of her hips. She popped her head back out, brushing out the tangles in her long hair.

"Not changing my mind."

"We can add stubborn."

She stuck out her tongue, and I chuckled as I went to collect my shoes. I moved her bag into my closet and hung up the pants and tops, surprised by how right her much smaller clothes looked next to mine. I tucked her lingerie onto a shelf and placed her shoes on the floor after scooting mine over with my foot. Stowing her bag, I met her in the bedroom.

She had on some lip gloss but nothing else. "I'm probably going to cry," she said with a shrug. "Seemed stupid to put on mascara."

"I like you all fresh-faced. A lot. Your skin's soft." I rubbed my thumb across her cheek. "But right now I'm starving. So let's get something to eat."

I led her out of my room. Quiet as the place was, I assumed everyone was gone.

A note stuck on the door confirmed that. *Reminder: Gig at Tractor Tavern tonight. Practice at 5 sharp!*

Kai. Good thing he'd reminded me. This gig was a huge coup for us—one of the hottest places to play alt-country in Seattle. The best part was the owner had called us because he'd seen a concert at another place a couple months back.

I'd still like Abbi to come to my concert, see us play. We might not be as good as Asher's band, but we were talented.

"Bagel?" I asked, holding up one of those everything ones. "Not as much fun as the waffles, but we have a schedule to uphold."

Abbi blushed, but the look she threw me was pure heat. Yeah, teasing her meant teasing myself. I busied myself with popping the bread in the toaster. I knew she'd seen the note. The large black letters were hard to miss. She didn't say anything, though, and I didn't bring it up.

"Do you have peanut butter? I prefer it to cream cheese."

I pulled out the jar and she grabbed a bottle of water before slathering her bagel. She brought my plate over while I heated the water for my pour-over. At Abbi's raised eyebrows, I shrugged, unapologetic. "Yeah, I'm a coffee snob."

We ate in relative silence, me waiting for my cup of coffee before eating my bagel. Abbi's face grew more and more pensive. She took my plate as soon as I finished eating, loading it into the dishwasher.

She rubbed her hands over her hips. "Do you think we can go now? I'm getting nervous."

I walked around the bar and pulled her into my arms. "This is your family, Abbi. They'll love you, no matter what."

She clung to me, just like Cassidy used to when she went out too deep in the swimming pool. Finally, Abbi shuddered and loosened her grip. I tried not to wince but I knew I'd have bruises.

———◆———

Asher's house wasn't what I expected—it wasn't as showy as the place I'd grown up in. While it was large with an open concept, it was in a neighborhood with other family homes. The house was sided in a rusty red, a modern take on the traditional Northwestern architecture. As soon as Abbi's mom opened the door, I could see the back lawn, a bright jewel-green that led to a long, weathered dock into Lake Washington.

"I'm glad you're here," Lia said into Abbi's hair, holding her tight.

Abbi returned the squeeze while I stood to the side, uncomfortable because of the emotion pouring off the two women. Abbi pulled back, brushing her hair back and took my hand.

"You remember Clay."

Lia smiled, and I was struck by the similarities. While Abbi's eyes were nearly violet to Lia's gray, the two women were the same height and had the same color hair. Lia wore hers shorter and layered, while Abbi's hair was longer, and she sported bangs.

Lia pulled me in for a hug, reminding me once again of my mother. I patted her back. Lia pulled back and led us into the house.

"Asher will be down in a second. He had a call about some new project. He decided to barbecue," Lia said, her voice conspiratorial. "I think to show off in front of Hayden. Those two are ridiculous. We may end up calling for pizza."

"Where's Mason?" Abbi asked.

"He's at Simon and Ella's, playing with Jeremiah. We thought you might want to talk to us first."

Lia nibbled her lip just like Abbi did when she was nervous.

"You want a drink or something?"

"Water's great."

"Hey," Asher said from the stairs. He strode forward and wrapped Abbi in a big hug. I was happy to see her clutch his shoulders, obviously glad to see him. He kissed her cheek before holding out a hand to me.

"Good to see you again, Clay."

"Thanks, you, too."

"Clay's band has a gig tonight," Abbi said. "At Tractor Tavern. He's going to dedicate a song to me." She smirked at me, and I couldn't help but grin as I shook my head.

"I am *now*," I said, chuckling. "I wasn't sure if you still wanted to come."

Abbi rolled her eyes. "That's what girlfriends do—support

212

their guys."

I lifted her hand to kiss her knuckle, hoping it covered my grimace. Girlfriend. Moving in together. I'd lost total control of my life.

"We'll see if we can get a sitter. I'm sure Hayden and Simon would like to hear you play, too. Want me to call Liz, Dahlia? You can see if Simon and Ella want to bring Jeremiah here for a sleepover."

"Sure," Lia said. "I'll text El in a sec after I get the kids a drink."

I had to bite the inside of my cheek to keep from laughing. It had been a long time since anyone called me a kid, even my parents. And Lia was younger than they were by nearly a decade.

We trailed her into the kitchen. She handed each of us a glass.

"The suspense in killing me, Abs," she said. "The paper was fairly tight-lipped about the story, and Clay didn't add much."

Lia looked pale and Asher hooked his arm over her shoulder, leading her to one of the broken-in leather couches. They sat and looked over at Abbi.

Abbi took my free hand and led us to the other couch. "I need to go to the car for a minute and grab something."

She turned and headed out the door, leaving me alone with her family. Awkward didn't begin to cover the moment.

"You don't have to come tonight," I said, setting my glass on one of the coasters.

"Actually, we do. For Abbi," Asher said. "But also because I've wanted to hear you guys."

"How is she, Clay?" Lia asked, leaning forward. Her gray eyes were filled with worry. I wished I could reassure her, but I didn't think either of them would like platitudes.

"She's doing better than I would in her situation. And, just so you know, I want her to move into my apartment. I have much better security than the dorms. I live there with Dane Anderson—he's our guitarist. His girlfriend Nessa and Abbi are good friends."

Lia nibbled her lip again. Maybe I shouldn't have led with asking Abbi to move in with me. These were her parents, no matter how cool they were.

"I think that's a good idea," Lia said, eyes moving to the door. "She trusts you. Something she hasn't done in far too long. I get that she doesn't want to live here, though I'd love to have her home again." Lia's eyes closed, her lashes sweeping her cheek as she shuddered.

"Do you think she blames me?" Asher asked. His deep voice was filled with concern, even a little hurt.

"I don't. I never did," Abbi said as she walked back into the room. "I love you, Asher. You know that."

Asher looked relieved, like really, deeply. I was glad to see so much caring between them. I knew Abbi was going to need it. She held the manila envelope to her chest and I could see her hands shaking.

"I love you, Asher, but please, don't look at these." She cleared her throat, her words still thick. "Not while I'm here at least. I'm sure you'll need to at some point, but—"

She held the envelope she'd shown me on Tuesday. The pictures were copies of the ones we'd seen on her walls yesterday. She thrust the envelope toward her mom then came to sit down next to me. I picked up her hand, squeezing just a little, before settling my palm atop hers on her thigh.

"I need to tell you what I remember from that night."

CHAPTER TWENTY-SIX
Abbi

Telling my parents was easier than I expected. They listened, Mom gripping Asher's hand as tight as I gripped Clay's.

Steve no longer had the power to hurt me. Not just because I hadn't been raped, but because the pictures were out there now; maybe not completely public yet. If they did come out, I could point the finger back to him, thanks to Sally. The communication exchanges between the two of them were also in the folder. Aunt Briar had copies of all the information, and she'd texted me yesterday to say she'd talked to Sally.

Steve and his friends would have to face the consequences for what they'd done.

My mom's face was pale but she didn't seem close to having a panic attack.

"You're so good for her," I told Asher.

He nodded, a little absently. "When did you realize more than one person was involved?"

"I didn't."

"Clarify," Mom said.

She was holding it together, but not by much. I frowned but she made a motion with her hand. I continued whether she was ready or not.

"I told you Sally contacted me? She told me she'd suggested Steve take pictures of me and sell them to some media outlet."

Dahlia looked down at her hands, clearly upset.

"And that was the night you can't remember?" Asher said.

I nodded. "I think someone put GHB in my drink—and before you ask, I had water. There's no way I should've passed out, and there's no, no way I couldn't remember that night unless they did something to me. I had strep, remember? A really bad case. I ended up needing two rounds of antibiotics."

Lia set the envelope down on the coffee table before knotting her fingers in her lap. "Why didn't you tell us then? Once you realized there were more photos?"

I bowed my head. Clay ran his hand over my hair, waiting for me to gather enough courage. "I was ashamed. I didn't know how far it had gone. If they had, you know, raped me. And all I could think about was the press. More cameras, more stories."

"Oh, Abbi." Mom stood, rounding the coffee table before pulling me into her arms. She hugged me tight like she used to when we found out Dad was sick. "I love you," she said, her voice low and gruff with emotion.

"It was stupid, but I was scared. I was naked when I woke up, so I knew there had to be more pictures once the first came out. The ones in the envelope—Mom, they're bad," I whispered.

"They hurt you." Asher's hands locked between his knees and his face pulled taut with anguish. "I'm so, so sorry my fame led to that."

I dashed the tears from my cheeks. "But it didn't. Maybe in the beginning. Because I let them." Anger shot up from my stomach. Anger at my weakness.

"I let them," I whispered again.

Mom pulled me around to look her in the face. "What Steve did was horrible. Unconscionable. Briar, Hayden, Simon, Ella... we all want to help. We need to make sure he doesn't do it again."

"That's what Clay said. I'm sorry I wasn't stronger. I should've told you." Tears blurred my eyes. "I just wanted you to be happy. You were finally happy. Asher's the best thing that's happened to us in years. I didn't want to mess your relationship—"

Asher stood, a little shaky, but he wrapped his arms around both of us, and I knew he was hurting, too. I'd done that.

"I just wanted you to be proud of me. It got so messed up. I just wanted to make you proud."

CHAPTER TWENTY-SEVEN
Clay

Lia stepped back and Asher tipped Abbi's face up, kissing her forehead.

Abbi pressed her cheek to his chest, eyes squeezed tight. "Thank you for being my dad."

"Always, Abigail."

A tear streaked from the corner of Asher's eye that he didn't bother to wipe away. He hugged her tighter, and I moved toward the kitchen. This moment was private, and I didn't need to witness more of it.

Lia fell into step next to me, leaning in. "You're the reason Abbi was willing to mention this?" She held up the envelope.

I shook my head, uncomfortable with her suggestion. "She was ready."

"This is a lot of emotion. You look like you could use a breather. Maybe a beer? I know Asher will approve. He's going to want one once he gets his equilibrium back."

"Thanks." I trailed behind her, noting how homey the kitchen was.

Her lips curled up in a small, sad smile. "Thank *you* for giving Abbi back a piece of herself." Lia shivered, rubbing her hands up and down her arms. "How anyone could…Horrifying."

"Abbi!" Mason shrieked, running into the house. Lia turned away, shoving the pictures into the built-in kitchen desk drawer.

"So sorry, love. He broke away, the little demon." A petite woman with round, rosy cheeks and sparkling brown eyes glided into the room. She pecked Lia on the cheek before turning toward me. "And who might you be? Big, strong, and simply divine. I'm guessing you've netted our darling Abbi."

"Erm." I rubbed the back of my neck, shocked by how discomfited I was with the woman's comments. Abbi came up next to me.

"Stop, Aunt Ella. You're embarrassing Clay, and I really want to keep him."

"I would, too, darling." She waved her hand. "But that would make me a disgusting lech."

"You're something. I wish it was perverse," Simon Dorsey said, smacking a kiss on her cheek.

"So, Clay, this is the rest of my crazy family."

I smiled, overwhelmed but charmed.

Hayden clapped me on the back. "They take getting used to."

"Be glad I love you," Briar said, pinching his butt as she walked by to hug Abbi. "Good to see you, Abs. Clay." She nodded in my direction. "I hear you're performing for the crazy clan tonight."

"And for the first time, ever, I'm nervous," I admitted.

"Because of all the raw musical awesomeness in one place?" Hayden asked, opening the fridge and pulling out a container. "We are amazing. Crikey, Lia. What happened to my lemonade?"

"I haven't had a chance to make more," Lia said, kissing his cheek.

"Fair dinkum, woman. You know I live for that stuff. Now I'm going to have to drink one of Asher's lightweight Yank beers."

Abbi squeezed my fingers. "Let's walk down to the lake." She tugged me toward the doors.

"Shouldn't we say something?"

"So polite," Abbi teased. "They understand you're over-whelmed. You look ready to duck and cover. Plus, my mom wants to tell Aunt Bri, Uncle Simon, and the rest of the crew what I told her, and I don't want to be there for the rehash."

We walked across the soft grass toward a low gate. I opened it for Abbi. We walked to the end of the dock, and I sighed, the peace of the lake sliding into my chest.

"This place is great."

"I like it. Different from our place out in Rathdrum."

"Where's that?" I pulled her down to sit next to me on the dock.

"Idaho. We lived there from the time I was nine until Mom and Asher started dating when I was seventeen."

"Do you miss it?"

She started to say something but hesitated. "No," she said, surprise lacing her voice. "I don't."

I brushed her hair from her lips. She smiled, pressing a kiss to my thumb. The late afternoon sunshine caught her hair, making it glow red. I was struck by the perfectness of the moment.

"Thanks for bringing me here today."

"I'm pretty sure that's my line. I'm so glad you were tenacious in your pursuit of being my friend."

I chuckled. "I'm not known for my staying power. My longest relationship before you was about—oh—fifty minutes."

Fear slid into her eyes. "I guess I'm lucky then. To be graced with your presence still. For almost a week."

The breeze picked up, pushing her hair back into her face. I brushed it back, catching it in my fist. "I told your mom I want-ed us to move in together."

She wet her lip with the tip of her tongue. "How'd that go over?"

"She seemed open to the idea."

"My mom's been waiting for me to fall…" She peeked at me from the corner of her eyes, probably gauging my reaction to her words.

I knew what she'd been about to say, and as much as I cared about Abbi, I wasn't willing to go there. Not yet. Love, for me, meant what I'd once thought my parents had—finding and connecting with each other despite the media and fans and the craziness of raising three kids and coping with Cassidy's cancer. When I'd realized their relationship was built on lies, something fundamental inside me snapped.

I managed to check the shudder that started at the base of my spine. I wasn't willing to buy Abbi a ring and start popping out kids. Or even think about it.

"I'm twenty-two. Moving in together is one thing, but marriage could wait a couple of decades, easy."

She ducked back, away from me. "Yeah. Totally. So…I want to hang out with Mason before we have to go to your gig tonight."

"Abbi," I caught her shoulder. "That came out wrong. I care about you. More than I have for any other woman. Ever. But—" I blew out a breath. I hadn't talked about it with anyone. Had never planned to. "I used to believe in love. Like in that old movie, *The Princess Bride*. My mom loved that one and made us watch it every Christmas break."

"I'm sure there's some connection between your folks and us, but I'm not following what this has to do with some movie."

"Wesley chases after Buttercup, fighting giants and evil princes for her. Because they had true love. I always saw my parents' relationship like that. My dad turning down easy lays or a bathroom blowjob because he loved my mom."

Abbi wrinkled her nose. "Not sure I like that comparison, but okay."

"Except he didn't actually turn women down. He was just discreet. I caught him once. At the studio." I exhaled hard. "Then, the day we found out Cassie's chemo was failing, her body was failing, my parents had some fight. I don't know what it was about. Colt texted me about it. Dad left Mom there at the hospital, all upset. The doctors didn't expect Cassie to make it through the week. Worst case, she wouldn't make it through the night. I got there in time to see my dad drive off. I followed him, thinking he might need me."

I swallowed down the bile that always accompanied thoughts from that day. "He drove into town, not to our house. He greeted some woman in a hotel lobby. Took her hand and led her to the elevators." My voice broke. Shit. The betrayal was fresh, a kick to the gut I couldn't handle.

"I'm sorry, Clay," she whispered, snuggling her cheek over my heart.

"He showed up at the hospital a few hours later, relaxed and showered. He'd changed his clothes. He smiled and kissed my mom's temple. Fucking kissed her and Cassidy like nothing had happened."

I didn't realize I was squeezing Abbi's waist until she wriggled backward.

"So you think your dad ran off to screw some woman while your mom and sister were at the hospital?"

I looked up at the ponderous gray clouds hanging over the house. Or were they over me? I hated how sordid it sounded when she said it out loud. "Yes."

"Have you asked him about it?"

I shook my head hard. "Hell no."

Abbi rolled her lips into her mouth as she pulled slowly out of my arms. "How can you be sure that's what happened?"

"Seriously? Abbi, he came back *showered*. He had to have fucked her." I twisted away from her, needing space. Needing to hit something. "God! He cheated on my mom when my sister was struggling to survive. That's not what love's supposed to be."

Abbi stepped in front of me, halting my jerky march. She placed a hand on my heaving chest, smoothing her palm over me. Soothing the ache.

"Did you believe those pictures about me, Clay? When you first saw them? Did you think I was the school slut who decided to bang half the male population in one night?"

I cupped her cheek, looked into her eyes. "Kinda." I hated admitting it. "I mean, you looked drugged but I figured you'd had too much to drink but knew what was going on." Shame washed over me. Wasn't that just another way men took advantage of helpless women?

"Most people did. Didn't matter that I'd never done something like that before. That I look sick and lost in those pictures. You saw that. You talked to me, got past the sordidness of it all until you saw *me*."

My shoulders tensed. Abbi going through that, alone, pissed me off. I pulled her back to my chest, wrapping my arms around her. Needing her there to comfort me as much as her.

"That's different."

"Is it? How can you know if you don't ask? I chose not to give details because I didn't know what to say. I didn't know how to ask for help. That was wrong, and I regret not telling my family sooner. They would've helped me."

"You didn't do anything wrong," I mumbled.

"Maybe your dad will confirm he had an affair. But what if there's an explanation he's never given you because he has no idea you saw him go to that hotel?"

"Abbi—"

She cut me off. "What if you've believed he cheated because it's your nightmare? Waking up in that frat house, assuming those guys…that was rock bottom for me, Clay. Except it wasn't. I found out later people *believing* I'd do that to hurt my family because there were rumors that I hated my mom's new husband, that was the worst. Because I'd never, ever do anything to hurt the people I love. Not on purpose."

I didn't want to meet her gaze. I didn't want her to see what her words were doing to me. My choices were to retreat or to attack.

I stepped back, toward the lake.

"It sucks that you make sense. It's just…I don't want to know. Not really."

Abbi threaded her index fingers through my belt loops, pulling my hips closer to hers. I stilled as her floral shampoo drifted up, wrapping around my heated mind. Calming me. I'd resent the hell out of her for it if she'd done it intentionally.

"I get that. Some truths suck."

"More like blast away at your foundations."

We were quiet, both of us turned to look out at the water. My body, warmed by hers, started to relax. I wrapped her in my arms and she settled against me.

"I've always known I was wired to love someone like the people in that movie you mentioned." Her voice was soft but sure. "With the pictures and the media hell my life's going to be…It's asking a lot of you, Clay. I don't want to force you into something you're not ready for."

I let my fingertips drift up over her mouth, her cheekbone, past her eyes. Up over the top of her crown to cup the back of her head. Once again, Abbi humbled me. She'd been bullied, lied to, drugged…the list kept going. But she stood here and told me she was strong enough to step back if I didn't want to commit.

My hand tightened into a fist in her hair.

"I—"

She whispered something then, pressed a lingering kiss to my T-shirt. I stiffened, afraid of the words, the delivery of them. She slithered from my arms to move back up the pier. Away from me. She wouldn't ask me again. I knew it. She'd just…leave.

My heart slammed hard into my ribs. She waited at the gate, her slim back straight, her hair falling almost to her waist. Beautiful, yes, but more. Abbi was so much more than simply another pretty face.

I released a breath.

We were young. Plenty of time to see where this led, and anyway, she was moving in with me. We could keep it to something more than friends. We'd figure it out.

Because Abbi not in my life…The closest analogy to the way it made me feel was when I'd thought Cassidy wasn't going to make it.

I strode toward her, desperate for our connection. I rubbed my thumb over her lower lip, and her breath bathed my finger in its warmth. I wanted nothing more than to sink into it, into her. To find that place where she didn't question and I didn't worry.

I needed that place.

"Come play with me, Abs!" Mason hollered. "I made that new level. I think you can build horses and stuff."

"Absolutely," she called. She stepped out from my embrace, leaving me cold and lonelier than I could ever remember.

CHAPTER TWENTY-EIGHT
Abbi

I'd thought making love with Clay would somehow magically solve my problems. I knew it was stupid, but I'd always believed in my mom's romance novels. The act of actually making love—not just sex—was the elixir the characters needed to persevere.

I was naïve.

The fear in Clay's eyes when I'd come close to mentioning the big "L" word shocked me. I'd seen his parents together and would have thought he wanted the same type of closeness. Once he explained his reasons, his anger toward his father wasn't surprising. Clay was loyal.

The relief I'd gotten through the day warred with the embarrassment of Clay's reaction. Spending the afternoon with my family when they obviously wanted to ask me more questions made my head ache.

"I'll come over with my folks," I suggested when Clay stated he needed to get to his rehearsal.

His brow furled but he nodded. He pulled me into the deepening shadow on the front porch, his big hand cupping the back of my head. I sighed and relaxed into his large, warm body, my headache fading a little.

"You're really coming?" he asked.

"Wouldn't miss it. I'll need to get a shirt and have you sign it." I slid my hands over the tops of my breasts. "Here, so people know you've claimed me."

"You're not mad at me?" he asked.

Interesting. Clay was uncertain.

"Why would I be mad?"

"Because I didn't handle our conversation well, down at the lake." His fingers gripped my skull tighter, his other hand digging into the sensitive skin at my waist.

"Ask me to stay with you tonight."

"What? No, I want to talk about how I screwed up earlier. I hurt your feelings, and that wasn't what I meant to—"

"Yes, Clay, I'd like to stay with you tonight. I'm thrilled to know I'm going home with you. That, of all the women there, you chose me. That we'll sleep together and I'll get to wake up with you in the morning."

"You don't have to do that just to prove—"

"But I'm not coming right now because there're four more hours until you go on stage, and I'm scared to be alone in the bar, especially right now. Plus, I need to talk to my parents about how to proceed with the case. I want my family around me when I'm at that bar, so I don't feel so exposed."

He leaned his forehead against mine. I was surprised to feel the small shudders working their way through his shoulders. "When we met at the library…I get it now," he said. "I don't want to be the reason you're hurt, Abbi. I don't know how to keep the reporters from taking your picture tonight, digging into your past. I don't know how to keep them from writing about you, whatever half-truth bull shit they want."

"Someone really smart told me not to give a fuck what other people think."

Clay shook his head, his eyes still filled with sadness. We hadn't had enough time together to be us, and there was so much working to pull us apart. Relief swept through me when he tightened his hold.

I rose up on my tiptoes and kissed him. A slow, lingering kiss that carried the promise of more and flirted with the depth of my need for him. He grunted as he gathered me closer, tilting his head to take the kiss deeper. Here, he couldn't lie to me any more than I'd try to lie to him.

Maybe we should only communicate in kisses from now on. I opened my mouth wider so my tongue rubbed deeper against his.

"Gross!" Jeremiah complained.

"You, too?" Mason said with a long-suffering sigh. "I thought you were cool."

I broke away from Clay, laughter tumbling across my swollen lips.

He leaned back in and kissed me again as though he wasn't ready to let me go. "I'll see you in a few hours. And Abbi?" he murmured against my skin.

"What?" I asked, shivering with pleasure when his teeth closed over my earlobe.

"I'm serious about wanting you to move in with me. I don't want a night here and there."

Wow. He melted my heart with those words. I didn't think moving in was a good idea—not yet. Not with the pictures hanging over my head—a guillotine waiting to slash through my self-worth.

He turned and waved at the boys who'd moved to one of the large trees in the front yard. I sighed and watched him jingle his keys in his hand. At his SUV door, he turned back.

"What song should I dedicate to you?"

I smiled, some of my old mischief poking up. I'd missed this side of me—the playful side I hadn't let out because I was afraid of what people would say.

"Something that convinces me to agree to your proposal."

He winked. So I had to blow him a kiss. He chuckled as he slid into his car.

"He's good for you," Mom said, coming up behind me, sliding her hand over my shoulder. "I like him, you know. You have to be cold. I brought you a sweater."

"Thanks. For believing in me when I couldn't believe in myself."

"Ah, honey. That's what moms do."

I wrapped my arm around her waist. "Just the good ones."

"Briar said the pictures will help. I don't understand her tracing voodoo, but she's good. I gave them to her. I don't want them here, at our house, with Mason. They're really horrible."

"Yeah, they are. I was scared, not just that you'd see them, but that you'd believe them." Tears pooled in my eyes.

"I'll never fully understood how isolated you had to feel. That's the problem with emotions. They're big and they're personal. But I like seeing you more like my daughter again. I've missed you, sweetie."

"I've missed you, too. I slipped so far, you know? I'm still freaked out about the pictures leaking." I swallowed, trying to work past the emotions balling in my throat.

"Asher's called his lawyers again and explained the new details. We should be able to work out a deal about the pictures staying private. I think that's the biggest cost, potentially. The fact you're unconscious is going to be in your favor."

Mom hugged me tighter. I wrapped my arm around her waist and held on.

"Thank you for trusting us. Just so you know, everyone stepped up."

The tears didn't come. I didn't need the release, I guess. Or maybe Clay had helped heal the vicious tear I'd let Steve rip in my soul.

"Thanks for coming tonight. Clay's excited."

"I'd support that boy in just about anything he wants to do." She turned and brushed my hair off my forehead. "He gave me back you."

CHAPTER TWENTY-NINE
Clay

"You're late," Kai grunted.

"I'm also the reason Asher Smith, Simon Dorsey, and Hayden Crewe are coming to our performance tonight."

"Seriously?" Dane asked, eyes bright.

"Yep. Asher's bringing Abbi later."

"Sweet," Kai enthused. "We need to practice."

"Wait. I'm calling Nessa," Dane said, bouncing up and down. "She'll let the paper know. Should swell the crowds."

"I want to add a song to the set list," I said.

"Now? That's a terrible idea," Kai said.

"Quit whining. I'll play the piano, and you already know the harmony."

"We don't have a piano," Kai said. "Christ, Clay. What are you thinking? This isn't a huge venue and we don't have extra pianos laying around."

"Relax," I said. "Take a breath. Seriously, dude, you need to loosen up."

"Kai's right. There isn't even room on the stage for an upright, let alone a good baby grand. And we don't have one," Dane said, shoving his phone back in his pocket.

"Which is why I'm borrowing one of my dad's old but still really good keyboards. Sure, I'd prefer the grands, but this is going to be fine. Colt's going to bring it over in the next hour. He said he's told his friends about the show and to expect a big turnout. Before you ask, my parents can't come. They took Cassidy to Disneyland. She's wanted to go for years."

Dane's face softened. Like pretty much everyone, he had a soft spot for my little sister.

"Focus!" Kai yelled. "We don't have that long to tighten up our songs."

"So I want to play the new one we started practicing this week."

Kai groaned. "It's not ready."

"It will be. We know the parts. The lyrics are tight and you've got the chord progression locked in."

Dane's lips curled with skepticism. "Are we sure it's ready?"

"Is this why you want the piano?" Kai asked.

"Yes. Abbi deserves it."

———◆———

I didn't get a chance to see her before we went on stage. I broke two sets of strings—one on my guitar and the other on my banjo. Kai muttered about this being our worst practice ever, thanks in part to my fumbling fingers. They'd chalked it up to nervousness, but they were wrong. I didn't want to admit to my epic stupidity this afternoon with how I reacted to Abbi.

My chest tightened as the clock ticked closer to our start time.

Why hadn't I played it cool? I should've just rolled with her comment, hugged her close and kissed her. I should've…I squinted as the stage lights came up, trying to find her in the crowd. It was way bigger than usual with bodies packed in tight between the stage and bar, thanks in large part to Abbi's family's influence.

Damn, I was nervous. So unusual. I hadn't ever been nervous on a stage.

There she was. Right below me. Everything settled down. I

winked at her and she blew me a kiss.

The music was tight, and we hit all the cues. The eight songs Kai and I had written went over well. Alt-folk was gaining popularity, and while most of our songs fell into that category, we straddled the alt-country line, thanks to growing up children of the Internet generation. We played "Open Road" by Roo Panes because Kai's voice fit it so well. Dane sang a kickass version of The Shadowboxers's "She Forgives," which he dedicated to Nessa, who, standing next to Abbi, beamed back at him.

While R&B would never be my strongest style, we got the harmonies right. We'd discovered that when we really felt the lyrics, style didn't matter so much.

My turn. Nerves fluttered through my gut. Maybe this wasn't a good idea.

I didn't play piano at gigs often—not that I couldn't; I'd taken to most instruments with an ease that never ceased to amaze my parents and piss off my brother.

I never sang alone because I'd grown up on some amazing harmonies. They added depth to the listening experience. But Abbi had asked for a song, and it was a small price to pay for having her here tonight.

"So I have some special guests here tonight. My girlfriend picked out a pretty cool stepdad. Thanks for coming, Asher," I said with a nod in his direction. His arm was curled around Lia's waist as she sat next to him. He raised his free hand in salute.

I let my fingers drift across the first notes of the song I'd written about Abbi. "I don't play many ballads. Simon's much better at that than I am."

"You just need practice," Simon yelled.

234

I laughed. "Just so. I'm a little nervous because Hayden Crewe's here, and I'm definitely not up to his level of competency of the piano." I waited for the laughter to die down. "Abbi, you told me to sing something to make you say yes."

I focused on the keys, my voice a little unsteady as I worked my way through the first verse.

With every heartbeat, I breathe you in,
Soft, not too sweet. Your eyes see my sin.
You've lived through your own kind of hell
Been burnt by friends, not really,
If they're willing to sell you. Oooh, oooh

I hit the chorus and felt the words deep in my gut, just as I had when I wrote them. My fingers relaxed on the keys, the words pouring out.

With each breath, the fever in my blood grows—
My heart flips when you look at me like that
'Cause I need you now, just where we're at.
Oooh, oooh.

Abbi's eyes softened to that deep violet I loved so much. I winked. I was pretty sure she blushed, which was awesome.

Many sounds of silence sealed in the jar
Shoved 'neath the bed or back too far—
Filled with the truths but bits of who
They tried to rip and shred from you.
Oooh, oooh
But with each breath, the fever in my blood grows—
My heart flips when you look at me like that
'Cause I need you now, just where we're at.
Oooh, oooh.

235

Kai and Dane joined in, their voices harmonizing with our instruments and each other for the last verse and chorus.

I found you, not what I expected.
Your back of steel has been well-tested
The many sounds of silence pressing from every side—
Still, you keep going; Fighting against every lie
Oooh, oooh.
With each breath, the fever in my blood grows—
My heart flips when you look at me like that
'Cause I need you now, just where we're at.
Oooh, oooh.

Someone clapped. Simon. Hayden wolf-whistled. Lia, Briar, and Ella hollered as they wiped their eyes. And Abbi. She was right in front, where I could see her, smiling up at me.

CHAPTER THIRTY
Abbi

Nessa leaned in. "He's really into you."

"No more than I'm into him." I watched as Clay thanked the crowd, ribbing Dane who was struggling to get his amp unplugged from his guitar. He was so smooth. Such a consummate performer.

And if it panned out well, he'd have a very nice record deal by the end of the school year. Dread and excitement mingled in my chest, causing it to tighten. Music was Clay's dream. One I'd have to learn how to support, just like my mom and aunts did. Neither of them wanted the limelight, but they championed their men while still balancing their own needs. I had no idea how, but I'd have to learn.

Clay turned those sexy eyes back on me, the corners crinkling with humor. His eyes dropped to my mouth.

I blew him a kiss. Nessa sighed.

For Clay, for us, I'd work through my fear. I didn't have a choice, really. He'd done so much for me. And giving up Clay wasn't an option.

I just hoped I was strong enough to deal with whatever the media decided to serve up about me this time. The wait was terrible. At least when the story hit, I'd respond.

Mom touched my shoulder. "We're heading out," she said.

"Okay. Let me tell everyone bye. Nessa, do you and Jenna want to meet my family?"

They both nodded, wide-eyed. At the table, I introduced my friends, who stumbled over their words. I rolled my eyes, unsurprised by their flustered responses. It took them a while to remember Asher and Hayden, and even my uncle Simon, who was still building his ever-growing following, were just people.

"I heard one of you is dating the guitarist," Hayden said. "Quite a musician."

"Thanks," Nessa said, her voice higher than usual. "He's a very nice person."

"Always good in a guy," Aunt Ella said with a wink. "I'm dragging Simon off, love." She stood and kissed my cheek. "Your mum is keeping Jeremiah because she's a doll. I'm going to sleep until noon. Tell your bloke bye for us. He knocked off my knickers."

"You'll be up by seven," Simon said with a chuckle, giving me a hug. "And no more talking about knickers."

"Seven will feel amazingly late," Ella responded. "Give me my moment."

"So glad I don't have a kid to deal with," Hayden said, standing and stretching.

"Just Princess, who wakes us up at five thirty every morning," Aunt Bri complained.

"She settles down fine. You just need to know how to pet the girl," he said with a wink, causing Jenna to sway and whimper.

"Bye, Abs. This was fun," Aunt Briar said, hugging me. "I'll call you as soon as I know anything," she whispered into my ear. "It'll be soon. Your mom and Asher are pushing forward."

I nodded. "I'll call you all tomorrow."

"Come over. Bring Clay and your friends," Mom said. "We'll do a cookout."

Jenna grabbed my hand hard enough to make me wince.

"Excellent! Another barbie. Count Bri and me in," Hayden said. He turned to me, slinging his arm over my shoulder in a friendly hug. "These guys, they'll do well."

"Absolutely," Asher said. He kissed my forehead, and I wrapped my arms around his middle. "We love you, Abbi," he murmured into my hair. He stepped back. "You okay getting home?"

I nodded. "Love you, too. I'm good. Clay's taking me. Thanks for coming. I know Clay appreciated your support."

Asher smiled and slid his hand around my mom's waist.

"Talk soon, honey," Mom said, hugging me again.

"Love you."

"Whew. That is one helluva a family you got there, Abbi." Jenna sighed, collapsing into the chair. "I mean, crap on a stick. They're even nice."

I giggled, my nose wrinkling at her image. "They're pretty overwhelming. I wasn't sure Clay would be able to withstand their combined force when he met them all this afternoon. At least in social situations, they spread out. Well, usually."

"I can see why. That's a lot of personalities. And holy hotness," Nessa said, fanning herself. "It's like you're related to all the beautiful people."

I grabbed one of the seats nearby. "How long does it take the guys to break down?"

"Not too long."

I wanted Clay to take me home now. I wanted to lay him back on his bed and kiss every inch of him. Him singing for me, that had clicked the final piece. I'd known for a while I was falling in love with him, thanks to his misplaced and sometimes grudging help. Now it was irrecoverable. Irreversible.

I loved him. Hard. Like one of the heroines in my mom's books.

He didn't feel the same. But no matter what happened, I'd be so thankful to him for helping me stand up to the emotional bullying.

Hands slid across my shoulders, a thumb pressed into my neck. I started until I smelled Clay's bodywash. I already knew his woodsy scent, and it both calmed down my racing heart and revved my body temperature up.

His chuckle vibrated against the back of my head as he bent down, pressing his lips behind my ear. I shivered, my response to him visceral. I couldn't stop it any more than a pilot could halt a plane midair. A pulse started to beat between my legs and I gasped when his lips slid up to my ear.

"I liked seeing you here. I liked the way you looked at me like you do when I'm about to sink deep inside you. Made it hard to concentrate on our songs. Then you parted your lips, like you did just now, and I kept thinking how they part when I kiss your navel. How you moan just like that when I bite your earlobe."

He bit the sensitive tip. Reckless, wild need scorched through me and I stood and spun, my arms around his neck and my lips on his.

"Crap, that's hot," Jenna muttered behind me. "I really need to get me a guy."

"I give Abbi a nine for that move," Nessa said, laughing.

Clay cupped the back of my head in that way of his, cradling me closer. His tongue ran the seam of my lips, parting them so he could glide in with leisurely strokes. I clutched him tighter and followed him through our personal dance.

Sighing, I pulled back slowly, a bit at a time so that just our mouths separated. "I like you dedicating songs to me," I whispered against his chin.

240

"I'd never guess," he chuckled, kissing the tip of my nose. "I wrote it for you. You ready to go?"

I glanced back at Nessa and Jenna, both of whom were listening. Nessa shooed me off.

"Go. Have fun. Jen and I are going to hang here for a while."

"I can stay here, keep you company."

"With that level of unsatisfied sexual tension? Nope." Jenna shook her head, eyes dancing. "This is part of our wind-down. Three a.m., baby."

She winked. Clay leaned down and collected my bag, grasping its handles in a fist.

"Bye, ladies. See you soon."

"What about your equipment?" I asked.

"Stored in the back of my and Dane's SUVs. Let's go. I need to kiss you more. More of you and more times."

"You got a plan there, captain?"

His lids slid lower over those smoldering green eyes. "Oh, yeah."

"Good. I like a man who knows where he's going."

CHAPTER THIRTY-ONE
Clay

Tonight, I hadn't been sure about our music, something I was always sure of, until I saw Abbi. Which either made me unstable or lovesick. Concerned as I was about falling in love, I wasn't sure I had it in me to stop it from happening. Sure, she'd said she was falling for me, but she hadn't even agreed to move in with me. Which was why keeping the media off her back or saving her from Bethany was so much easier than admitting I wanted her in my life.

"You okay? You got all quiet and pensive."

I threw her a grin, surprised by how much the simple touch of her hand to mine calmed my insecurities.

"I enjoyed your performance tonight," she said, turning her head toward me. "Thank you for the song. I got so hot when you looked at me, singing to me."

And just like that, the desire was back, scorching. Good thing I'd just pulled into the building. I'd planned to take those sweet, soft lips, but her neck called to me. I kissed her racing pulse. Moved up to her jaw. Cruised along that strong line until my lips were over hers. She moaned as she dropped her head back into my hand, trusting me to support her.

She opened for me, and my hunger built. She'd been through so much, had her trust in people smashed over and over, yet she was here, with me, letting me love her.

I eased back, stared into her dreamy eyes. That was the third time I'd thought of love and Abbi together. She blinked at me, and my face tightened. "We're here."

A frown built between her thin, russet brows. I opened my door and walked around to hers. By the time I'd come around the car, her confusion had flushed to hurt. She ignored my hand as she stepped from the car. She stood next to me, silent and small, shrinking back into herself once again.

"I can just call a cab and go back to my dorm."

"No." The word was harsh. "Dammit, Abbi, stop doing that. I want you here."

And I did, desperately, even though it meant opening myself up to more of these feelings I needed to stop having.

She followed me into the elevator and into the condo.

"I don't know what's going on with you, Clay. One minute you're obviously very into me, but the next, you slam up this wall. I can't keep up."

She was so brave. Those words were steady but she'd forced them out of the fear I'd seen building since I'd pulled away on the pier earlier. Problem was, I didn't know how to protect her heart, my heart, and keep moving forward with us.

I couldn't let Abbi go. I couldn't let her fall in love with me. Everything was so jumbled. So I kissed her, trying to tell her I was here with her. But I wasn't.

I was too afraid of what could happen, what I'd seen happen with my parents.

And she knew it.

———◆———

"How was the interview?" I asked.

Abbi worried the skin around her thumb. I pulled her hand

away, holding it. She squeezed back lightly. "I think it was okay. I don't know how to gauge these things."

"Briar went, right?" I hadn't been able to—I had a class and then rehearsal for another gig—the frequency of our shows had been way up since Abbi's family came to the Tractor Tavern last month. Abbi hadn't asked me to get out of rehearsal either, and I hadn't offered. Maybe I should have. But we spent so much time together already, adding to it seemed like crossing some line.

The attention focused on Abbi and me, whether from the media or fellow students, grew to near insanity over the past month. Not only did people stop us to ask for our picture and autograph, some stopped us to tell us who we'd be better with, especially me. I hated the way they treated Abbi, but there wasn't much to do about it except keep her close, which had the added benefit of me getting to love her sweet body all over campus and at all hours of the day.

"Yeah. Briar and my mom were there. They said it went well."

I raised her hand to my mouth and kissed the back of it. "Then it did."

The interview caused a stir as we'd expected. But I wasn't prepared for just how intense the scrutiny would be. For the next few days, neither Abbi nor I left the building without a recording device or camera shoved in our faces.

During those days, the enormity of Abbi's case hit me. I was in the middle of one of the biggest lawsuits of our generation. Not really the publicity I wanted, but I'd promised Abbi I wouldn't walk away. If I did now, I'd be the world's biggest douche.

We spent most of our time in my apartment, leaving only

when necessary. I hated the inability to come and go as I pleased. Fame became its own prison.

We'd managed to bypass the wall of reporters at my apartment and walked across campus toward the science building. I planned to drop Abbi off at her class and then head over to the music building for some piano time. The song I'd written her had blown up on YouTube and Dane, Kai, and I planned to lay down the track next weekend at my dad's in-house studio.

"Hey, Clay."

Margie. She was pretty. Tall, slim and sleek. "Hi," I replied, already stiffening. While I hadn't seen Bethany in weeks, the other females I'd spent time with before meeting Abbi made a point to seek me out, much to my displeasure. Abbi had been cool about their interest, but this was one of the reasons why I feared relationships. Abbi was bound to get mad or jealous. That's what girlfriends did. And I wasn't prepared to deal with those emotions, even if I did like hanging out with Abbi.

"You ever get tired of her, you know where to find me," Margie said with a wink and an arm squeeze.

"I'm standing right here!" Abbi called. "Is that girl for real?"

I looked away, grumbling.

Abbi stopped walking. Since my arm was around her, I stopped, too.

"You slept with her, didn't you?"

I kept my gaze down and nodded, hating the heat creeping up over my ears. As I'd expected, Abbi had keyed in on Margie's knowing smile. But I didn't have anything to be embarrassed about. Neither Margie nor I had been seeing someone at the time, and I didn't even know Abbi then.

I caught the hurt flash across Abbi's face before she schooled her features back into blandness. "I thought so," she said. She'd become a pro at hiding behind her media mask. I hated that most of all.

"She didn't mean anything."

Abbi sighed. "That doesn't make me feel better, actually."

"But I'm supposed to be cool with half the world—maybe all the world—seeing you naked?" As soon as the words were out of my mouth, I knew they were the wrong ones.

It was eating at me, growing stronger every day, and I didn't know how to stop it.

"What do you want me to say? You know I don't want pictures of me out there. Any of them."

That was the shittiest part. How could I be angry with her for something she hadn't done willingly?

As far as we knew, the new round of pictures hadn't been sold to the media yet. But the initial ones were circulating again—the ones where Abbi was being tugged into a room or the ones where she was topless, kissing some guy. More like him kissing her. Those I hated. They'd touched her, fondled her, violated her.

But the worst part was how jealous I was that they'd seen her.

Why did this whole relationship thing have to be so confusing? I glanced after Margie, wishing I could go back to the casual fling. Abbi's eyes rested on me, and her hand fell from mine.

"Come on. I'll get you to class."

She stopped to pull her phone out of her pocket. "Asher," she said to me. "Hello?"

We started walking again, but she stopped, swaying a little.

"He did what? A plea bargain. Wow." I took her bag and pulled her out of the oncoming pedestrian traffic, letting her finish her conversation. "Yeah, I understand. It *is* good news." She listened. "Okay. Love you."

She hung up but continued to hold her phone, her face pensive. "I think I'll skip class," she mumbled. I turned, walking us back toward the parking lot.

"About the case?" I pressed my key fob to open the doors to my SUV.

"Yeah. Steve's team offered a plea bargain. No jail time for him."

"How's that good?" I asked, anger bubbling in my gut.

"It isn't. Not really. But his dad's a big lawyer in LA. Runs some powerful law firm."

I opened the backseat and tossed in our bags. "So?"

"Once his father saw the evidence, he didn't give Steve a choice. Part of the deal is that Steve has to give the names of the men in the photos so they can be named in the suit and I can ask for restitution." Abbi waved her hand. "I don't care about that. I want what they did on their records. We'll get that out of the deal because Steve's going to be expelled from Tech and the school is cooperating with the investigation, promising to punish the other students involved."

"Without jail time," I said, frowning.

Abbi leaned against the side of the vehicle, a frown tugging at her brows. "Right. But in exchange, Steve's father will pay all the legal fees incurred thus far."

"Not a huge incentive when you've got the money part covered."

"Which is what Asher's lawyers told them. The biggest win is the injunction Steve's father has already put on any and all photos, stating the pictures could not be sold to the media." Abbi's whole body loosened with relief as she said the words.

"That's fabulous news," I said. My shoulders loosened as well. I knew some people had looked at the pictures, but my hope was that the general population wouldn't see them.

I kissed her hard. Then I pulled back, looked into her eyes, and kissed her again, softer, sweeping my lips across hers. "Let's go out."

She smiled up at me. "'Kay. I know just the place." She plucked the keys from my hand and sauntered toward the driver's seat. "Coming, Casanova?"

I grinned, thinking how hot Abbi-in-charge was. "Oh, I plan to."

She giggled as she started the car. After a few minutes, she pulled into a parking space near my favorite sushi place.

"You don't like sushi," I said.

She beamed at me. "We never got to go."

"We can do something else."

"Right now, I'm so happy, I could eat anything. You've helped me through so much, Clay. Let me buy you a spring roll."

I laughed as we walked into the place, ignoring the photographer who'd taken our picture. Even Abbi relaxed during the meal. Admittedly, she didn't eat the raw fish but she did have a big bowl of soup that she proclaimed delicious.

The ease of our lunch wasn't new but the longer I spent with Abbi, the more I could see us, in ten years, compromising like this. Like my parents did. I set my sushi down, my stomach in knots.

I didn't want to be my parents. I didn't want to betray Abbi like my dad betrayed my mom. More, I didn't want to spend the rest of my life trying to please someone who'd eventually break my heart.

"Let's get out of here," I said.

Abbi frowned but she followed me, her trust pissing me off. Which is why I made the next hour about getting off. Sex I understood. Sex I liked. Sex with Abbi was mind-blowing.

As always, Abbi gave me her body, but more. She gave me her emotion, but I shied away from just how deep her feelings went.

"You went somewhere, Clay." She was curled into my side. I was on my back, arm curled around her waist.

"I'm right here, holding you," I said, but the sinking feeling I'd been living with for weeks threatened to crash over me. So much for believing I'd hidden my concerns from her. That was the problem with dating a sensitive woman—she seemed to hone in on my every emotion. Considering how all over the place I'd been these last few weeks, I wished she didn't.

"No, you just shut me out."

"It's more than sex, Abbi. You know that."

She slid from my bed, pulling her shirt over her head. Picking up her panties, she slid them up those legs that had so recently been holding me tight.

"Is it? You don't want it to be."

"Don't put words in my mouth," I grumbled.

"I don't want you to resent me, Clay. But you do already. Like on Friday when you wanted to hang out with Kai. I wasn't mad about that, but you expected me to be."

"I didn't think you'd be mad," I said, standing to pull on my boxers and jeans. "Why are we getting dressed?"

"I saw the way you looked at that girl today. The one you hooked up with before. You looked at me like that. Now. In bed."

"I didn't."

"Please don't lie to me, Clay," Abbi said, her eyes taking on that sheen that meant tears were imminent. I stepped closer, my arms around her. "I can't live with that."

Her lashes dropped, covering her eyes as she took a deep breath. I wanted to comfort her, to tell her I just wasn't ready, to give me time. But I wasn't sure I wanted this. Not yet, and it was so much faster than I'd expected, my feelings so much bigger.

Her lashes lifted and I stared into her beautiful eyes. Each time she looked at me, it stole my breath. She saw me, even my flaws, and she kept looking.

After a moment of searching, she raised her hand to my cheek. Her palm was small, fragile, but like the rest of Abbi, it held a strength most people wouldn't imagine.

"I love you." The words were strong, her eyes unwavering.

I reared back, sweat blooming over my skin. No. She couldn't. It was too soon. We'd just really started going out.

Her lip curled up just a tiny bit like I'd confirmed something for her. She stepped back and picked up her bra, jeans, shoes, and bag. Before I processed what she was doing, Abbi was in my bathroom, door shut.

"What are you doing?" I asked. My chest hurt.

"I'm leaving," Abbi said as she opened the door.

"But you're supposed to—"

"My dorm's been cleaned for a week. I'm going back there. Maybe to my parents' this weekend."

"You can't." The panic was building. My hands shook.

"I am. You don't want me here, Clay. You've been battling your feelings for me from the beginning."

"I care about you, Abbi. I want to protect you, keep you safe."

For the first time, anger flared bright and hot across her skin. Her mouth tightened and her eyes turned cold and hard. "That's not enough for me. I'm not a charity case, Clay. I won't let you reduce me to that."

"I don't think you're a charity—"

"Don't you? Aren't you trying to fix things for me like you wished you could for Cassidy? Except I'm not a child. I'm an adult. I want a man who wants *me*." She thumped her chest. "My moods, my body, my laughter, but most importantly my heart. Who doesn't look at another woman's ass with longing while he's standing on a street corner with me."

"So you'll just walk away from me? From everything I've done for you?" Anger was building now, pushing past the fear, simmering off the last of the panic. I welcomed it; the sick feeling finally faded from my gut.

"Yes." The fight left Abbi's shoulders and she collapsed into herself. "Can you honestly tell me you'd want me here with you every day? Can you tell me you look forward to my voice? To whatever stupid thought flits through my head? That you want to do something, like buy me a new pair of running shoes, just because you'll get to see me smile?"

I blinked at her, unsure how to respond. I did want those things—sometimes. But I was only twenty-two, and we'd been thrust into a really intense situation. Our every move was scrutinized. If one of us wasn't smiling in a photo, we were about to break up or I was cheating. I'd seen a header on one of the gossip sites while I was playing on my phone earlier asking when we'd get engaged.

"See, I want to do that with you, Clay. For you." Abbi's lips quirked up again. "I always knew I'd fall in love, and it would be better than one of my mom's books because the man I loved would be exceptional. You are definitely that," she said. She slipped in close and kissed the base of my throat. "You're funny, caring, sensitive and you have one of the most defined moral compasses I've ever come across.

"You're the best of friends. You protected me from Bethany and the media, just like you promised. But now, you don't have to do that anymore because the case just closed."

Relief swept through me. She was right. I didn't. She mashed her lips together and tipped her head back, looking at the ceiling. Then she stepped back and slipped on her sunglasses, creating another barrier between us.

"The woman you finally choose to let in will be very lucky."

She stepped through the front door, pulling it shut gently behind her.

"What just happened?" I whispered.

"You broke Abbi's heart."

I whirled around. Nessa and Dane stood in his bedroom's doorway. Tears streamed down Nessa's face, and Dane wouldn't meet my eyes. If something big and horrible wasn't about to break inside of me, I would've been upset they were listening.

"Me? She walked out on me."

"It's not like you really gave her a choice, Clay."

The thing inside me was breaking. Pain shot through my chest. I hurt. The way I'd hurt when Cassidy looked up at me, her small head gleaming bald and her green eyes scared. She'd said, "I'm not sure how much more fight I've got in me, Clay. You're going to have to take care of Mom. You know Dad can't deal with big stuff. He'll throw himself into work and destroy the family if he's allowed to."

My palms slammed against my knees as I tried to work my way out of the memory. She'd been right. Sort of. Dad did throw himself into another woman's arms.

I'd told him that I'd been in that part of town to run errands. I told him I'd happened to see him coming out of the hotel later. He hadn't explained, and I hadn't asked him why he'd cheat on my mother while she was sitting in a hospital chair next to her dying child.

Because I didn't want them to fall apart. Instead, that secret had been eroding my trust in love—in Abbi—for months before I even knew her.

My legs gave out and my butt landed on the edge of my coffee table.

Nessa rubbed her palm over her cheek. She kissed Dane and pulled out her keys. "I'm going to see if I can talk to her."

Nessa walked out of my apartment, too. She didn't bother to say goodbye.

The silence built, accusatory. But what the fuck? I'd asked Abbi to move in with me. That was commitment. I'd told her I cared about her.

"Do you want to tell me I'm an asshole, too?" I finally demanded when the waiting overwhelmed me.

"Nessa and I know you didn't intend to hurt her," Dane said. "I just never thought you'd let fear ruin your life." Dane went back into his room, shutting his door behind him.

CHAPTER THIRTY-TWO
Abbi

I made it to my car and all the way back to my dorm before the enormity of what I'd done slammed over me. I'd broken up with Clay. The man who'd held my hand at my OB/GYN appointment. The man who'd asked me to dance even though I'd been slut-shamed by the world. The man who sang me songs about being his hero.

I'd thrown all that away because I was frustrated he wouldn't admit he loved me. For a smart girl, I made really stupid decisions.

Opening my dorm room, I wrinkled my nose at the new-paint smell. I went to the window and threw it open. Then I sat on the bed I hadn't slept on in weeks. I wanted to take the last two hours of my life back. Do them differently. Hurt less.

"Abbi?"

I looked up to see Nessa and Jenna standing in the doorway. I guess I'd been too distracted by my thoughts to shut the door completely.

"You want to talk about it?" Jenna asked, crawling up the bed to lay her head in my lap.

I looked down at her big brown eyes so full of sympathy. She understood better than anyone.

Loving someone who didn't love you back was a level of hell no one should experience. Tears filled my eyes. Jenna wrapped her arms around my middle and cried with me. Nessa sighed from the doorway.

"Guys suck."

"Not Dane," I sighed.

"Him, too. He screwed Bethany."

"What? Again?" I asked, shocked.

Nessa curled her lip as she shook her head. "Once was enough. I just hate that he ever touched that girl. Good thing she's disappeared."

I held out my arm and she slid onto that side of me. We lay back, a pile of limbs and tears.

"We should do something," Jenna said, sitting up.

"Like what?" I asked. My thoughts remained sluggish. I kept reliving my conversation with Clay over and over in my mind.

"We could get raging drunk," Jenna said, biting her lip. "Forget our worries for a few hours."

"I don't drink," I reminded them.

"I'm not saying we have to drink to pass out," Jenna pointed out, somewhat reasonably. "Just enough to feel good."

"That isn't a good idea," Nessa said. "She's sad. Liquor won't help with that."

Jenna huffed, her cheeks pale beneath the drying tear tracks. "Dunno. Seems to work fairly well for me." She smiled but it didn't reach her eyes.

She had secrets—ones that probably started when I began staying the night at Clay's. She'd been the fifth wheel; being left behind by friends wasn't easy. But I was here now, and I intended to stay here. With Jenna.

"Let's order ramen and binge-watch some reality TV shows. Those people's lives are always way more messed up than ours."

"Ramen?" Nessa asked. "Mmm. I'll call the place around the corner. They have a really cute delivery guy."

Nessa pulled out her phone, just as I hoped she would. She

couldn't resist the siren call of good ramen.

I lifted my hips a little so that Jenna fell onto the bed next to me. "What's up with you?" I asked.

"Pretty sure that's my line," she muttered.

"I think I'm still in shock. I mean, I dumped Clay Rippey. I'm certifiably insane."

"True. I've read the stories."

I whacked her with my pillow before turning so that my face was near hers. "What's going on, Jenna?"

She plucked at my bedspread. "Nothing bad. Or at least not too bad. I've been lonely. So I started hooking up with Charles."

"What?"

She looked away and shrugged. "He's fun."

"He's a mess. Dane said he's one of the coke pushers."

"He likes to have a good time. Nothing wrong with that."

I didn't know what to say. "Jenna, this doesn't sound like you."

"I've been sad," she said.

So we did what any self-respecting young woman does when she's hurting: We ate too much and stayed up way too late watching the worst of reality TV.

———◆———

The next day—well, late afternoon by the time I finally woke up enough to get out of bed—I picked up the rest of our trash. I was postponing calling my mom because I knew I'd lose it when I did. I settled for a text, letting her know I'd be hanging out with Jenna tonight after I did some homework.

Except I found it hard to concentrate. I pushed the window

open farther, trying to get rid of the faint traces of paint scent. As I shoved against the sill, I saw a girl down in the quad squeal and throw herself into her boyfriend's arms.

Jealousy rose, striking faster than a rattlesnake. And way more deadly.

My fingers fumbled with the window ledge as I tried to hold myself up. I failed, collapsing onto my floor. I pulled my knees up to my chest and huddled there, wishing I hadn't walked away. Hoping he'd call.

He didn't.

Finally, probably hours later, I stood, stiff, my muscles screaming, and picked up my earbuds. I shoved them in, blasting the Supernaturals' songs. Asher's voice calmed me, and I finally opened my biochem notes.

CHAPTER THIRTY-THREE
Clay

I'd blamed my age, the craziness of her case and the pictures, anything but the fact I was scared to end up like my dad. Scared to love Abbi and fuck it all up because of the fear.

Abbi deserved that truth. She'd given me hers even though it was ugly and hurt her deeply to share.

I shut down the thought. I hadn't seen Abbi in three days, and I was like a junkie going through withdrawal. I couldn't sleep. I forced myself to eat, work out and practice, but it wasn't the same. I needed to wash my sheets, but I'd held off, hating losing that last bit of her from my apartment. Maybe my life.

When I'd run into Margie yesterday, I backed away fast.

"What's up with you?" Kai asked. "It's like you had a Bethany sighting."

I frowned. "No. Still no sign of her. Do you think she had another breakdown?"

Kai shrugged. "Why'd you run away from Margie? She is definitely still into you."

I ran my hand over the back of my head. "She isn't Abbi."

Kai looked me square in the eye. "None of them will be."

I was trying to man up, make things right. Calling my dad had been hard. Talking to him would be worse.

I opened the door when Dad knocked. I'd thought about meeting at a coffee shop but a public place meant people could overhear this conversation; I didn't want my mom hurt and embarrassed by what I had to ask.

"Want some coffee?"

"What's wrong, Clay? You look like hell."

"Abbi and I broke up." I sighed, pouring him a cup of coffee I'd set up earlier. I fixed another for myself. My caffeine addiction was out of hand, but it was pretty much all that kept me functioning.

"What? Why? Even with all the media attention, you seemed good. Solid."

"She said she respected herself too much to be with a guy who wouldn't love her back."

Dad's brow wrinkled as he processed that sentence. His eyes darkened, a signal he was upset with Abbi. He tapped his fingers on the rim of his coffee cup.

"She's right. About me not admitting to loving her."

Dad's eyes flew to mine, shock radiating off him. We'd never talked about this kind of thing before. Mom had handled emotions when we were little. Later, I just stopped talking.

"So what's the problem? Just tell Abbi how you feel."

"I was…no, I *am* afraid."

There. I'd said it. I sat my mug on the table, uninterested in the thick, rich taste. My fingers tunneled through my hair. But I forced my eyes to meet his. Abbi was much stronger than I'd given her credit for. Meeting his eyes was near impossible.

"That day at the Four Seasons. You went up the elevator with a woman. Colt told me about your fight with mom so I followed you, thinking you might want someone to talk to."

Dad just managed to set the coffee mug on the table before it spilled. "That was a bad time," he managed, his voice raspy.

"I saw you at your studio. That woman was a redhead."

I stood because the energy pouring out of me needed the release. I paced, waiting. He didn't say anything.

"So let me tell you what I know. You've had multiple affairs and one was the same day we were waiting for Cassidy's last-chance meds to save her life."

"True."

I swung around to see his face. It was lined, each crease deepening as I watched.

"When Mom needed you, you were in bed, fucking another woman." I swallowed the lump building in my throat. It was that thick, ugly thing that had been destroying my insides since Abbi walked out. "If you could do that to your family when we needed you, when Mom needed you, that's not love. And that's what I know. What you taught me. That you run when it gets hard. Or that it's never going to be love like in Mom's movie."

Oh, shit. The words reverberated through my body. The thing gaped wider, threatening to suck me in.

"Look at me, Clay."

I didn't want to. But I'd made the accusations. I stopped pacing and raised my head.

His face was even more haggard. "You're right. I fucked up. Literally. There's no why—not the first time or even the second."

I flinched.

"Sex was easy, fun. But when Cassie was so sick…I couldn't fix any of it!" He yelled, his throat straining. "I'd promised your mother, God, Buddha, anything and anyone I'd be faithful. And I was until I couldn't save my baby girl and my wife was fading before my eyes. Goddammit, Clay, I was angry."

"I've been angry since then, too." I fell back against the couch cushions. "Angry with you. That you gave up on us."

His head fell into his hands, causing his hair to stick up. Gray threaded with the dirty blond, no longer an even mix.

"You think you're scarred from my affairs, is that what you're saying? You can't love a beautiful young woman because you think—what?—you'll end up like me? Fucking some woman you've just met? Or, worse, meeting a woman you don't even care about at a swank hotel while you have one ear listening for the phone to ring. Waiting for the call that'll tell you your daughter's dead?"

"Yes!" The thing opened even wider and I was in it. "Wait. No. I don't want to be like you. That's the whole point. *I don't want to be like you.*"

"Then don't." Dad sighed.

Colt and I used to play a game when we were little. We'd loop a rubber band to a door handle and then pull it back as far as we could to hear it snap. This moment was the snap.

I didn't have to be my dad. Could it really be that easy?

"I've made mistakes, Clay. I've done many, many things I'm not proud of. Those affairs are at the top of the list. And just so you know, I've told your mother."

If I hadn't already been sitting, I would've collapsed.

"Are you…Is everything okay?" I asked, hesitant.

A small smile flitted across Dad's face. "So now you're going to tiptoe around this shit?" He took a deep breath. "I broke her trust." He met my gaze, his hazel one serious. "I can't fix it either. I expected her to leave, but we were still reeling from Cassie's recovery. We've seen a therapist. Lots of times. He said it's not uncommon for extra-marital affairs during times of deep stress."

Dad held up his hand. "I'm not explaining away what I did. Hell, I'm not even trying to sugarcoat it because I screwed around a few times before Cassie *was* sick. But those words helped your mom. She said bad decision-making happens. We're working through it. We'll keep working through it. I hope."

"Have there been other women? I mean, since…"

He leaned forward and grabbed my hands in his. The calluses on his palms grated over my skin, but his hands were warm and reassuring. No bigger than mine now, but still my dad's hands.

"No."

I sank deeper into the cushions, my second biggest fear unrealized. I wished my father hadn't broken his vow, but…my muscles clenched. My mom knew and they were dealing with it.

"I respect the hell out of your mom, Clay. She's stronger than I was. Than I am. I'm not sure I could get past her with another man."

He squeezed my fingers, let them fall back to my lap as he stood.

"I feel a million times worse that my mistakes have weighed so heavily on you. Marriage isn't always the easy choice, but I don't regret marrying your mother. I can't—not just because she gave me three of the best kids, ever. But because she makes me laugh. Sitting next to her, sometimes that's better than the best concert I've ever performed. It's quieter, softer, more intimate."

His words echoed Abbi's. Neither were romanticized. They were the reality that was building a life together. Because there wasn't any certainty, no matter if it was a life, like Cassidy's, or a marriage, like my parents'.

"I'm supposed to say something about fighting for what you believe in," I said. I picked up my coffee and drained it.

"That's utter bullshit. Some things you can't fight. Look at

Cassidy. We threw money and the world's best doctors at her Hodgkin's. What ended up kicking its ass was your mom's love. She simply wouldn't let Cassie give up."

He swallowed, a thick wet sound. "And I have to live with knowing she was there, loving our baby, while I was self-destructing. That's hard to swallow. There are days I can't swallow it. I can apologize, and I do. But it doesn't change how you feel, how your mom feels. It's months of therapy to get us to this point—and me vowing to never, ever cheat again. I have to forgive myself now that your mom's making peace with my infidelity. I really don't know what I did to deserve her, but I sure as hell won't let her go."

I gripped his shoulder, hard. Then, thinking about Cassidy, I pulled him to me and hugged him. I hadn't hugged my dad in way too long.

"I know I ambushed you."

"No more than I did you."

I stepped back, dropping my arms. "I'm afraid."

"Of what?"

"Not being enough for Abbi. Loving her when she doesn't want to love me back anymore. Screwing it all up somehow."

Dad cupped my cheeks in his. His eyes were red-rimmed like I expected mine to be. "There are no guarantees. Ever. For anything in life. So my question to you is, is it better to have some time or to live with the regret of not knowing?"

"What if I cheat with a groupie? Sex is so available."

"I can't answer that for you, Clay."

I rubbed my aching chest.

His phone beeped an alarm. "I have to go. I promised to pick Cassidy up from school."

"Thanks, Dad."

He paused at the door, his shoulders lower. Turning back, he met my gaze. "Actually, thank you. I hated keeping that secret. It weighed on me more than I realized. Not that I'm ready to tell Cassie yet, but I'll talk to Colt. He's finally getting over his break up from Kara."

I nodded.

"And Clay?"

"Yeah."

"I want you to talk to someone when you're wrestling with these big problems. If not me, someone else. The worst feeling is feeling alone." He grimaced. "That sounds like a bad after-school special."

He let himself out of my apartment, and I settled back on the couch, thinking about what he'd said.

CHAPTER THIRTY-FOUR
Abbi

"You ready?" Jenna yelled over the stereo. "Charles said this place is happening."

I don't know why I'd let Jenna talk me into this. I hated clubs. The only reason I'd ever stepped foot into a bar was to hear Clay play.

I was tired of sitting in my dorm room, moping. Waiting for Clay to call. He hadn't. Nessa said he hadn't left his apartment in days, not even to go to class. I hated that I'd hurt him, but I hated his stubbornness more.

At least the press hadn't picked up on our breakup yet because everyone wanted to talk about the plea bargain I'd signed yesterday—never mind the gag order on the details.

Jenna popped a chocolate into her mouth and chewed, humming to the song.

"Who sent you those?" I asked.

Jenna shrugged. "They're yours, actually. I found them outside your door. I figured Clay must've sent them. They're really yummy." Her smile was vapid.

Damn Charles for getting her involved in whatever it was she was doing. I picked up the box, looking for a card.

"Here," Jenna shoved one of them into my mouth. "So good, right?"

I frowned, chewing the chocolate.

"Are you ready to party?" Nessa yelled, gyrating her hips in some crazy parody of a model catwalk. She looked amazing in a short skirt, one-shoulder tunic blouse, and high-heeled, black lace-up boots.

I looked down at my simple keyhole blouse and skinny jeans. Nowhere near as sexy as Nessa's outfit or Jenna's tiny black strapless dress, but I was covered and comfortable. I wasn't ready to flash as much skin as my friends. Baby steps, as Aunt Bri would say. The first step was to go out. I'd worry about looking attractive for a guy later. When my heart was no longer slashed to bits.

Jenna whooped and I swallowed the chocolate. It was saltier than I expected. I picked up my water and chugged.

"Let's get this over with," I said.

"What kind of attitude is that?" Jenna asked. "Have one of Abbi's chocolates, Nessa. They're so good."

Nessa nibbled at one, her face contorting into a grimace.

"God, that's awful." She chucked the rest of it in the trash. "I hate when they mix sweet and salty."

She snagged one of Jenna's makeup wipes, cleaning her fingers. "Great. Now chocolate's ruined forever."

"Where are we going?" I asked.

"I forgot," Jenna said. Her eyes definitely appeared glassy. I'd talk to Asher about it. He'd know someone discreet to take Jenna to talk to. First was getting her away from Charles.

"Let me text Dane where we're going. You okay if he drives us back later?"

I wasn't but I just shrugged not wanting to push my anger at Clay over on Dane. The whole situation was already awkward for Nessa and Dane, trying to bridge both of us. I was smart enough to know I'd be the one to fall away—Dane and Clay had the band to keep them together.

By the time Nessa parked at the club, I didn't feel good and

Jenna couldn't walk a straight line.

"This is a bad idea," I said to Nessa.

"I need to throw up," Jenna whimpered.

"Help me get her inside. I'll take her to the bathroom."

I paid our entry fee and started forward. My head was off. Each turn of my head was like a slow-motion psychedelic rainbow.

Nessa was on her phone, her arm supporting Jenna's waist.

"Can you come get us?" she said. "Jenna's on something. I don't know. But I think she gave some to Abbi. She looks weird, too."

She hung up.

"Get some waters, Abbi. I'm taking Jenna to the bathroom."

I headed to the bar, trying to keep everything in focus. I bought the waters, blinking against the bright lights. I shoved the bottles into my bag and drifted toward a nearby table. I dropped my over-flowing bag on the table, looking for Nessa. We needed to leave.

I swayed as the world tilted again.

"Hey, watch it there, princess."

Some guy's voice. I didn't want him. There was only one man I wanted. And I'd left him.

"Clay. I need Clay."

"I'm Harrison, and I'd be happy to help you out, babe."

I clutched his shirt. "I don't feel good." I licked my lips. "I need my phone. I need to call Clay."

"How about you need me instead? I'm sure I can make you forget."

No help. I stepped away from the table, intent to get to Nessa, wherever she was. Bathroom. I needed to make it to the bath-room. Someone bumped my shoulder and I spun in a slow circle. The world kept going, careening over.

I tried to clutch the table but missed. My chin slammed into the wood as I went down. I bit my tongue hard and my head snapped back. The last thing I saw as I hit the ground was the guy's shocked face.

"Clay," I said again, but my mouth hurt and I wasn't sure I was clear. The black was eating at me, pulling me under.

CHAPTER THIRTY-FIVE
Clay

I scanned the bar but didn't see Abbi, Nessa or Jenna.

"You sure we're in the right place?" I asked Dane. "Hell, it's a meat factory."

He and Kai scanned the area, too, concern puckering both their foreheads.

"Let's just find the girls and get out of here." Kai shoved into the crowd first as we scanned the booths near the dance floor. It was so crowded, finding the girls there would be impossible. Kai grumbled, obviously thinking the same thing.

A group of guys stared down at the floor near a table. One stepped back. There, on the ground, was a jean-clad leg with a pair of buff high-heeled boots. Boots Abbi had worn just days ago.

My chest ripped open. "Abbi!"

"What?" Kai yelped.

I didn't bother to answer, just kept forcing my way through the crowd. I bellowed her name, but she didn't stir. A guy was leaning over her.

Kai and Dane were at my side, forming a wedge so we could finally cut through the crowd. I dropped to my knees. Blood poured from her chin and her mouth.

"What did you do to her?" I yelled. I pulled her up against my chest. Her head lolled back and she choked. She choked on her own blood. What was I supposed to do?

I lifted her forward and opened her mouth. Blood poured from her lips.

"We didn't touch her, man." One of the guys was talking to

Kai, who looked ready to kill.

"Call an ambulance," I said.

"Already did, dude," the guy said.

Dane's phone rang.

He pulled it out. "Where are you?" he barked into the phone.

Nessa's voice slid out of the speaker, loud and nearly hysteri-cal. "In the bathroom. Jenna's convulsing. What do I do?"

Kai spun around and pushed off through the crowd.

I rocked Abbi, not sure what else to do. I put my fingers to her neck but I didn't feel her pulse. "No," I pressed harder. "I can't find her pulse."

One of the guys crouched next to me and put his hand on her chest. Instinctively, I knocked it away. "Don't touch her," I yelled. "Abbi, you have to wake up."

"I'm checking for her heartbeat," the guy said.

"Calm down, Clay. We're going to help her." Dane was on my other side. People were clustered around us, whispering. Some were crying.

The guy's face was pale. "She's not breathing."

"I can't give her mouth-to-mouth. Not with all the blood in her mouth." My breath hitched. I was suspended over an abyss. Everyone scrambled back. Someone tried to pull Abbi from my arms.

"I'm an EMT. You have to let go so I can help her. Let go, sir." His words finally filtered through my fogged thoughts.

"She's not breathing. And there's so much blood."

The guy had on gloves and opened Abbi's mouth. "Bit her tongue when she fell. How much did she have to drink?"

"I don't know. I just got here. There's water in her purse." I pointed at the water spilling from her bag.

The EMT looked at me like I was crazy, but he was working on her, getting a gadget to help her breathe, so I didn't hit him.

"It's true, man."

I turned to see the man who'd been crouched at Abbi's head when I got to her.

"She had a bottle of water. I noticed because I wanted to buy her a drink." The shorter man shrugged.

"She's mine," I growled.

"She's stable," the second EMT said.

"There's another one in the bathroom," another EMT said. "Convulsions."

"You go," the EMT crouched over Abbi said. "I've got to get her to the ambulance."

"Can I ride with her?"

"Yep. Upfront. Let's go."

I stood up with cautious movements. Once I was sure my legs would hold, I turned to Dane, whose face was way too pale. "Tell Nessa where we are."

Dane waved me off. "Go. I'm going to stick around with Nessa and see how Jenna's doing. Call us and we'll meet you." His face and voice were grim.

I ran to catch up with the gurney.

———•———

I'd been sitting in the ER waiting room for nearly an hour by the time Lia ran in. She was out of breath, her eyes dark with worry.

"Clay, you're covered in blood." Her breathing escalated. "Abbi?" she wheezed.

"I don't know anything. It's her blood."

Lia started to sink to the floor, even whiter than Abbi had been earlier. I caught her and settled her in a chair.

"You okay?" I asked, nervous as she struggled to breathe.

"Panic attack." She dropped her head to her knees and I patted her back, feeling awkward and clumsy and like the worst fuck-up ever. I hadn't called Abbi in a week. If I'd just told her how I felt, she'd be asleep in her bed or mine.

Asher barreled into the room. He pulled Lia up into his arms and she clutched his shirt, her back shaking as she wheezed.

Asher spoke softly into her ear, petting her hair. I watched them for a long moment before I dropped my gaze back to my linked hands.

Eventually, Lia said, "I'm okay now. We need to find out what happened. What they're doing."

Asher settled her in the chair next to me, his face pale and concerned. "What happened?"

I wanted to hit something; shout, curse the world. Anything but what I had to say to Abbi's parents now.

"I don't know. Nessa called Dane, said he needed to come pick them up. That Jenna seemed high or something. We were looking for the girls when these guys moved back and Abbi was on the floor, bleeding. She fell," I said quickly as Lia's eyes grew wider. "Hit her chin, busted it and bit her tongue."

"I'm going to talk to someone," Lia said.

"I'll come with you," Asher said, concern evident.

They walked toward the nurse's station, Asher's arm cinched

tight around Lia's waist. She leaned into him, obviously needing his support.

Lia asked some questions, all of answers seemed to agitate her more. I dropped my head in my hands.

"Hey, man, any news?"

Kai. He slammed into the chair near mine. His long legs sprawled out. "No. Not on Abbi. What about Jenna?"

"Took them a long time to stabilize her. She threw up a lot. I guess that's a good thing? I don't know. They're thinking alcohol poisoning."

His brows were pulled low, his mouth pinched. He didn't like to think of Jenna drinking so much she made herself sick.

"Abbi's parents are here. Maybe we can get some information about her. Jenna's folks are in Austin, right? How are we going to find out anything on her?" I gestured toward the nurse's station, where Lia was facing a tall, fiftyish man with thinning, graying hair.

"Nessa called them. I was kind of hoping you'd know something about Abbi that would apply to Jenna. Nessa and Dane will be here soon, by the way. Nessa had to change—Jenna puked all over her."

I stood.

"Just hold up there," Kai said, gripping my shirt. "Something you need to know."

I looked down and saw how haggard he appeared. My legs shook and I slid back into my chair.

"We talked to the police after you left. They'll come here, too, man. The reporters were out in full force, interviewing anyone who'd open their dumbass mouths."

My stomach dropped. Abbi was going to hate that. She'd

just gotten to a happy place—whatever happened tonight wasn't going to keep her there.

Lia was still talking to the doctor, Asher holding her protectively in his arms.

"Nessa said Jenna was eating this chocolate. Chocolate she said was from you for Abbi."

"I didn't send her any chocolate."

"We know. So the other thing Nessa and Dane went to get were the chocolates. Nessa said they tasted weird."

"Weird how?"

Kai shrugged. "Nessa said she thought Jenna had a few of them. She was in some kind of seizure by the time I got there. The EMT was worried."

"And they won't tell you anything?"

He shook his head. Lia and Asher came back over, both their faces pale, eyes dark with worry.

"They're treating it like an overdose," Lia said. Her face crumpled, and she started to cry.

"Abbi?" Kai asked.

"Overdose?" I said, sitting up straighter. "No way."

"No fucking way," Kai repeated.

"That's what we told him," Asher said, pulling Lia onto his lap. "But the doctor said she had a ton of GHB in her system."

"Can you tell them to check Jenna for the same thing?" Kai asked, standing quickly. He looked uncertain.

"They know. She's in bad shape."

Asher's gaze darkened further, fury in each taut line of his body. "Someone slipped it into something they ingested, obviously. The doctor said she wasn't drinking, so that's something."

"The chocolates," I mumbled, shock still sizzling through me.

"Did they pump her stomach?" Kai asked. "Get all that poison out of her? If they did it for her, maybe they did it for Jenna."

Asher shook his head. "Didn't have to. Abbi vomited, too."

"Like that night at Tech." My grip on the cheap plastic chair had the chair shaking.

Lia whipped her head toward me. "That's what I told the doctor," she said, her voice scratchy. "But what are the chances of something like that happening twice?"

"Slim. Especially since it had to be the chocolates."

"What the fuck are you talking about?" Asher asked, his anger growing with each word.

Kai leaned forward. "Nessa said Jenna found chocolates outside Abbi's dorm room today. She was eating them while getting ready. She had some kind of a seizure as soon as they got to the club."

"There's something else you should know. Jenna's been hanging around Charles. He's known to peddle."

"Hard shit?" Asher asked.

Kai and I looked at each other. "I don't know. Maybe. The fraternity is always full of girls. A couple of them have left school after being at the frat house for a party."

"I'm going to talk to the doctor. Let him know about Jenna." Lia bolted off Asher's lap.

I sat, the quiet pounding inside my head.

Asher was as protective of Abbi as she was of him, her mother and Mason. No wonder she'd worried about their reaction. Asher wasn't just angry, he was about to explode.

I licked my lips. "There's one more thing," I said. He swung his gaze toward mine, eyes narrowed, nostrils white. "Abbi had a run-in with Bethany a few weeks ago. She's um, well, clingy. To the band."

Asher nodded once. I wasn't sure if he was telling me he'd heard me or he wanted me to go on.

Kai cleared his throat. "Bethany's been real jealous of Abbi. Because she wanted Clay. We think she was behind trashing Abbi's room and this. She's, well, she's delusional."

"Are you saying she gave Abbi the chocolates?" Asher asked.

I spread my hands on my knees. "I don't know. But I wouldn't be surprised."

"What good would it do for a girl to drug Abbi like that?"

I considered all these options. "I've been thinking while I was waiting for you to show up. I made a complaint about Bethany a few weeks ago. We banned her from our concerts. I haven't seen much of her in recent weeks. Not since Abbi's room got messed up and the pictures…" I cleared my throat. "I kinda forgot about it because then Abbi did that interview saying she was going to be working with the local universities on their date rape policies and we were inundated with journalists."

The muscle in Asher's jaw jumped. "So what's this got to do with your groupie?"

I flinched. "She's not *my* anything. I don't like the girl."

Kai gripped my shoulder. "Maybe nothing. But she's the only one I can think of who'd have a reason to hurt Abbi. And Bethany's tight with Charles. The pusher we told you about."

CHAPTER THIRTY-SIX
Abbi

Mom looked tired. Her eyes were red-rimmed. I frowned at her. I hadn't seen her so haggard since Dad was sick.

"What happened?" I winced. My tongue and chin hurt. Bad.

"You fell," Mom said. Her voice was harsh like she'd been crying. Guilt seeped up my chest. "At the club. Do you remember any of it?"

Looking around the room, I considered her question. There were a bunch of big bouquets. So many, the ugly beige walls behind them were barely visible.

"They're from Briar and Hayden. They'll be home soon to see you. Those are from Clay's parents. That one is from the girls in your dorm."

What? Really?

"You must've made an impression," Lia said, a smile flitting around the edge of her mouth. But her face is too gaunt.

"Clay?"

"He just left. He's going to be upset he missed you." Mom wrinkled her nose. "But he needed to shower and change. He was covered in your blood."

My mouth fell open, and I winced at the pain radiating from my jaw.

"Try not to do that. You have a lot of stitches in your chin. Only six in your tongue."

I must look like Frankenstein. I moaned.

"It's not so bad, really." Mom sniffled. "They did a lot on the inside to minimize scarring. We thought you weren't going to wake up."

"Why?" I asked. The word came out more garbled than I'd intended.

Mom picked up my hand, squeezing my fingers between hers. "You had a bad reaction to the drug. GHB."

I started. She squeezed harder. "The doctor said the second time you get the drug is usually when you see the side effects like yours. Plus, the volume in your system caused you to stop breathing."

My eyes flew to hers. Holy…no wonder she was so worn out. "I didn't—"

"We know, Abbi. Someone put it in the chocolates you and your friend Jenna ate." Mom's eyes narrowed to thin slits of gray.

I hesitated for a moment, dreading the answer. "Jenna?"

Mom looked down, her face filled with sadness. "She's in a coma. She had a lot more of the drug in her system than you did."

I closed my eyes, trying to tease out what she wasn't telling me. I'd read about GHB once I realized it was probably the drug Steve slipped me at that party.

"Will she make it?"

Mom inhaled sharply through her nose. Her eyes were red and fresh tears filled her eyes. "She might not wake up."

"Like ever?" I asked, horror building, pressing, painful in my chest.

I stared up at the ceiling, trying to process what Mom told me. Jenna—sarcastic, loving, hurting Jenna.

"Any idea who did this?" If I suspected Bethany, then I knew Clay, Kai, Nessa, and Dane would've already explained the situation there. Perhaps Steve, but he was supposed to be at his parents' house in LA for the next six months—part of the plea we'd reached.

"They'll find them, Abbi. This case is getting national attention."

"Them?"

Mom brushed my hair back from my forehead. "You feeling okay? Need anything? I pressed the button and let the nurses know you were waking up."

"Who's them?" My fat tongue was really annoying.

A nurse bustled in, lifting my arm to get my pulse. She checked my eyes, my tongue, the bandage on my chin.

"Up for some water? You were really dehydrated after all the vomiting. Good thing you did, though. You had a lot of the drug in your system."

I accepted the straw and sucked.

"Drinking a little will also help with the taste in your mouth."

I winced but managed to keep the liquid flowing down my throat. Heaven.

"She's doing well, Mrs. Smith. The doctor will be by soon."

Mom nodded. I stayed focused on her.

"Who's them?" My mouth was working a little better so I asked the second question. "Who drugged me?"

"Bethany and her cousin Steve."

CHAPTER THIRTY-SEVEN
Clay

I was back at the hospital in under two hours, an amazing feat considering I had to drive back to my apartment to shower and change and then head over to the police station in another part of Seattle.

Abbi's eyes met mine as soon as I stepped into her room. I walked toward her, thankfulness warring with concern. The doctor said she might have long-term effects from the amount of GHB in her system, as might Jenna.

Abbi had quit breathing. That could mean brain damage. That was the concern I'd refused to consider. Abbi was so smart. So dedicated.

"Hey," she mumbled, turning her face way. Her eyes didn't focus on mine for long. My heart expanded to an uncomfortable size in my chest. I hadn't considered her not remembering me.

I settled into the chair, reached forward for her hand but stopped just short. Maybe she didn't want me. Bethany attacked her because of me. Did she know about the media firestorm yet?

She gripped my fingers in her cold hand. My gaze finally rose from our connected fingers to her big blue eyes. "There's my girl."

I leaned forward and kissed her. Just a quick brush of my lips before I pulled back. Her lips were soft, a little chapped.

"I'm sorry, Clay." She formed the words slowly, her brow furrowed in concentration. "I heard Jenna hasn't woken up yet."

Her tongue. Right. The doctor said it was going to take a few days for the swelling to go down. Relief flooded my limbs, leaving me weak. Abbi alive, intact, that was a miracle. The rest we'd have to deal with. Soon.

"Her parents have talked to the doctors. They called Nessa to tell her they're on a flight. Should be here in a couple hours."

"You'll tell me when you know something?"

I cupped her cheek. "Yes. I'll tell you anything you want to know. I'll never lie to you, Abbi. I know you hate lies."

I stared at her while she looked up at the ceiling tiles.

"Mom said it was Bethany who put the drugs in the chocolates."

How long would she struggle to make her syllables? She sounded so un-Abbi-like. I gripped her hand tighter. I'd need to tell her Charles had squealed loud and fast once he realized what Bethany did with the GHB. Good thing he was locked in a jail cell.

"They found her."

Abbi raised her eyebrows, interest shooting through her blue gaze.

"Steve, too?"

I rested my head against the edge of her bed. I didn't want her to see me fall apart. Her hand moved to my hair, fingers sifting through the strands.

"Clay?

I waited through another beat. "Yeah. Steve, too." I raised my head to meet her gaze. "It was Bethany's idea to drug you again. She talked Charles into it. Slept with him. The whole deal. Charles said she kept talking about getting back with me." I shuddered.

Abbi closed her eyes, swallowed hard. "Not surprised."

"The police are shutting down Charles' operation. It was big. Worth millions." I was a shocked by the scope of Charles's business. I'd completely underestimated the guy.

"Bethany and Steve?"

"They're going to do jail time. Serious jail time if we get any kind of say."

Abbi nodded.

"I'm sorry, Abbi. I wanted to call you this week but I didn't know what to say."

Her fingers moved to cover my lips, and she shook her head just a little. I pressed a kiss to her fingers, needing to show her how much I loved her. Words I hadn't said. Hadn't realized how much I needed to say.

"I miss you so damn much. I want us to be together. Like you talked about."

Her eyes grew bigger and bigger, her mouth dropped open and she grimaced. She put a hand to her chin. I scooted closer.

"I should have told you before, but I was afraid. Not to commit to you. Not really." I hoped that cryptic statement would be enough for her to get the words I struggled with. I blew out a breath, forcing the words past my tightening throat. "I love that you love me."

"The fame?" she asked.

I hesitated before nodding. If my dad wasn't famous then that woman wouldn't have been as interested in him.

"It was a lot of pressure, yeah. I don't want to be defined by what people want to see. I was unwilling to commit—you were right about that—because I worried I wouldn't be what you needed."

"But?"

"Being without you is so much worse. There are other things I want to say." I glanced around, hearing the squeak of someone's shoe right outside the door.

Her lips flipped up just a little in that smile I'd begun to think of as Smartass Abbi.

"Will you tell me? When I leave here?" she asked.

"I plan on telling you a lot, so yeah."

"When I'm healed. Tell me then."

"Why?"

Her eyes lit up in that way I loved, the one that told me she's plotting sexy times in my future.

"Looking forward to it."

———◆———

Nessa, Dane, Kai, and I spent hours at the police station and even met with prosecutors to discuss what they knew about Bethany's obsession and the lawsuit we'd filed against Steve.

Word traveled like wildfire through Northern about Charles' drug bust, Bethany's arrest, and Jenna's continued hospitalization. Dane, Kai and I were bombarded with calls, texts, and social media messages, made worse when Nessa and Abbi turned off our phones. The deluge of questions and comments was too much.

Jenna woke about the time her parents showed up. Kai told me about it because I was still in Abbi's room. Mr. and Mrs. Olsen decided to take Jenna home for the rest of the year to recover, and Jenna didn't argue. She was still too ill from the effects of the drugs in her system.

Abbi had declined all interviews this morning, the first she could speak normally, too tired to try to field more questions thanks to her new position as the face of an international GHB court case.

The media was eating up each account and churning out new sensationalized details faster than I could click through the sites—which included the pictures of Abbi from last spring, but those led to a massive increase in awareness to the date-rape drugs with colleges, and universities in the Northwest were pledging money and education to focus on preventing incidents like what happened to Jenna and Abbi. Jan Silver was the first one to donate.

"Too little, too late," Nessa said, her lips twisting into a seriously pissed expression.

While I agreed, I chose to remain silent.

Asher, Lia, and Abbi were organizing a foundation that worked with the university's counseling departments to help the victims of Rohypnol and GHB. She had another few weeks to make a decision as to whether she wanted her name and time associated with the project, but she planned to do it, stating she could channel her notoriety, turn it into good.

Now, nearly a week after Nessa's call that night, I took the stairs at Abbi's parents' place two at a time. I walked into her room, noticing her flannel pants and rumpled pink tee. Her feet were encased in fuzzy socks and her hair was half falling out of her ponytail. Tape covered the stitches in her chin. I wrapped my arms around her, needing the closeness.

"You look gorgeous."

She shook her head, giggling self-consciously.

"C'mon. I want to take you somewhere."

"I'm in my pajamas," she pointed out.

"Which works great for where we're going." She shook her head violently, and I worried about her opening the wound.

"Fine. Grab a change of clothes. But we're leaving in two min-utes." Her ponytail slid further to the side. "Maybe three so you can use a hair brush."

She pulled the hair tie out and grabbed a skirt and a pretty blouse from her closet. "Boots would be good for later. Sexy ones," I added with a wink.

At least they'd be good if she agreed to my plan. I'd fight through the paparazzi frenzy to take her to dinner.

Hustling Abbi out the door, I snagged her keys as I stared at her long gorgeous legs.

"Where are we going?"

"You'll see."

"Clay," she sighed.

Part of me wanted to give in. "Give me this one. Please."

"Fine."

"Close your eyes."

She huffed but she did it. She crossed her arms over her chest, pulling the white jacket tighter around her torso.

We pulled into the parking space a few minutes later. "Keep them closed."

I walked around and helped her from the car, grabbing her purse before leading her into the elevator. We both ignored the faint snick of the camera lenses.

"Closed," I growled into her ear when her lashes fluttered.

The elevator dinged and we walked out into the hall. My heart fluttered as I opened the door. I pulled her in and closed the door behind us. Flipping on the light switch, I said, "Okay. Open your eyes."

She did. Her eyes swept the room.

"Do you like it?"

"This isn't your place. Wait. What's my stuff doing here? Is this—are we moving in together? Again."

I pulled her back into my arms, needing to feel her warmth and smell her light herbal fragrance. "Yes. It's all done. I gave the other apartment to Dane and Kai. Nessa and Dane will have more privacy because Kai's gone a lot more than I am—he goes back home now that his brother's back from Afghanistan. And you and I will live here, together. It's on the same floor as my old place, so we can see everyone often."

I lifted her knuckles and pressed a soft kiss to each of them. She didn't respond to my overture, too busy taking in our mingled items splashed across the room. I glanced around, satisfaction warring with nerves. "If it makes a difference, my mom and yours decorated the place. They're excited."

"You didn't like me staying with you before. Not really."

Panic built in my chest. "That's not true," I said. The words tumbled out, nearly tripping over each other. "I liked you in my space too much. It drove me crazy how much I wanted to spend time with you. That's why I pulled away. I was only happy when you were, and that freaked me out."

"So then why the sudden change?" she asked. "I don't want to move in together because you're worried I'm going to die. Or because you feel like you're making me happy."

I sank to both my knees. Her eyes widened. I chuckled as I pressed a kiss to her belly through her shirt.

"I'm not proposing."

She smiled, shaking her head. The pulse in her neck was going about a million miles an hour, but those big, searching eyes remained drilled into mine. My strong woman.

"Not that I won't, but I think we both need time to figure this love thing out."

I tightened my arms around her, hugging her tighter to me. "I love you, Abbi. I've been drawn to you since I first saw you by the fountain. I need to wake up next to you every morning and see your sleepy smile. I need to walk in at the end of the day and kiss you. I need to laugh with you while we eat breakfast and dinner. I need to comfort you when you're sad. Because I need you."

She cleared her throat, her eyes firm on mine. "Are you going to give me the tour?"

"Depends."

"On what?" she asked.

"On if you plan to stay here with me."

She snuggled into my embrace. "I need you, too, Clay. I'd like to stay."

I stood and scooped her into my arms.

"So you still love me, Abbi?"

"I always will," she whispered, pressing a kiss to my chest.

"We're starting with a tour of the bed."

Sure, this relationship wouldn't be perfect. We weren't perfect. But we loved and respected each other.

And I'd learned from my dad and from Abbi that, for right now, those feelings, that commitment, was enough.

EPILOGUE

"Congratulations," I whispered against Clay's lips. He kissed me, hard, ignoring the flashes from myriad cameras. We'd had months to get used to the constant scrutiny, and like my mom and my aunt said, you just had to keep living life.

"Seems like both forever and no time at all," Clay said with a sigh. He glanced around the auditorium. "Last time I'll be here."

"As a student, sure. But I've still got a couple more years of higher education. You'll come visit me between gigs, right?" I batted my lashes at him, enjoying the game.

Clay brushed my hair back from my cheek, his eyes softening as they met mine. "I'll always come home to you, Abbi. Always."

I smiled past the lump in my throat and pressed another soft kiss against his lips.

We'd changed—all of us—in the last six months. Jenna hadn't returned to Northern, but she'd left an indelible mark on our group—one I hoped she'd see when she visited us this month.

The national attention to my case brought attention to Lummi Nation as well, especially Clay, who'd taken the escalation in interest in stride. After looking at their options, he, Kai, and Dane decided to stick with a local, indie label that let them make the music they wanted. Asher and Hayden were helping them produce their album, and it was killer.

They were going to tour around this summer, doing a few festivals and some medium-size venues. Nessa and I would spend the summer with the band, none of us willing to be apart for long.

"I like the cap and gown look. Think I can peel it off later?" I asked.

Clay smirked. "I'm up for that."

"You will be," I giggled.

He leaned in and bit my lip, but then stepped back when the rest of our friends and family descended on us.

We hugged and accepted congratulations from the group, Clay never letting me leave his side for long. At first, I'd thought Clay was hesitant to let me out of his sight because of what happened at the club. But as time went on, I realized he found my presence comforting, which thrilled me.

"I'm starving," Mason cried clutching his stomach.

Everyone laughed.

"Some things never change," I muttered.

"We'll meet you at the restaurant," Clay said.

Clay's parents smiled as Cassidy skipped ahead, talking to Colt. Mom and Asher herded Mason away, followed by Aunt Briar and Hayden, who were holding hands and looking as in love as two people could.

I sighed, realizing I probably had the same dreamy expression on my face most of the time.

Nessa slid her arm around my waist and I hugged her back. Clay and Dane wandered off into the crowd, looking for Kai.

"So I didn't get a good look at your ring earlier. Let me see," Nessa said, grabbing my hand. On my left ring finger sat a narrow silver band that almost met together. In the middle was a large violet-blue diopside held in place by the silver. I thrilled as I looked at it. I'd never had a ring before, and this one was special, from the stone to the tension band.

Nessa whistled. "Clay done good."

"Yeah, he did. He says the stone fosters creativity, love, and commitment."

I smiled as Clay's arms slid around my waist, his simple silver band flashing on his right ring finger.

"I would have married her on the spot if she'd let me," he grumbled, causing everyone to laugh.

"For a guy who was so commitment-phobic, I like seeing you so invested," Dane said, slapping Clay's shoulder. "Not often you see a guy insist on his own engagement ring."

"I just needed the right woman," he said, squeezing my fingers as he brought my hand to his lips.

We ambled through the crowd toward Dane's SUV, talking about the graduation speeches, the upcoming tour. I glanced up just in time to see a telescoping lens directed at us. I reached up, turning Clay's face to mine and kissed him.

"What was that for?" he asked.

"The cameras," I said.

Clay glanced around, saw the one I'd noticed moments before. He dipped me back and planted a really hot kiss on my lips. He slid his tongue back into his mouth and I whimpered.

"Think he got the message?" Clay asked.

"I did," I panted. "Loud and clear."

Clay winked as he took my hand. "I love that you're a smart woman."

THANK YOU!

Dear Readers,

Thank you for choosing and reading this book. If you enjoyed it, I'd be grateful if you'd write a short review and post it on Amazon or your favorite book site. By taking a few seconds to leave a review, you not only help out your favorite authors, you help new readers find them as well—a total win-win!

This journey wouldn't be anywhere near as much fun without you.

ACKNOWLEDGMENTS

As always, thank you, Chris. Your unwavering support and love shine through in all you do. I'm me because you're you.

To my family, thank you for your patience with my dream—and letting me hang out in my head way too often.

LERA ladies and gentlemen, thank you for being so supportive, for making me love writing again and for sharing your knowledge so freely. You are the best-est.

To my AuthorLab writing pals: You keep me on task and keep me motivated. I love your commitment and passion. I love reading your posts and stories. And I love how diverse our group is.

To Bev, thank you for seeing the big picture—and making sure I see it, too.

To Nicole, thank you for the advice on Seattle—hoodies, not umbrellas!—and the fantastic copy edits that make the story shine. I'll get to Jenna's story soon. That's a promise.

To Jan, I loved working with you. Thanks for the thoughtful comments.

To Clarissa, once again the cover is gorgeous. I love working with you.

And to my readers and reviewers. Thank you for your time. It's precious and I'm so, so glad you spent some of it with me.

ABOUT THE AUTHOR

With a degree in international marketing and a varied career path that includes content management for a web firm, marketing direction for a high-profile sports agency, and a two-year stint with a renowned literary agency, Alexa Padgett has returned to her first love: writing fiction.

Alexa spent a good part of her youth traveling. From Budapest to Belize, Calgary to Coober Pedy, she soaked in the myriad smells, sounds, and feels of these gorgeous places, wishing she could live in them all—at least for a while. And she does in her books.

She lives in New Mexico with her husband, children, and ginormous, piano-hating Anatolian Shepherd, Mozart. When not writing, schlepping, or volunteering, she can be found in her tiny kitchen, channeling her inner Barefoot Contessa.

Write her at alexa@alexapadgett.com or sign up for her newsletter to receive notifications for upcoming books and exclusive excerpts. You can also find her on Facebook or follow her on Twitter (@AlexaPadgett).

CHAPTER ONE
Evie

The SUV's wide white bumper filled the entire windshield. Where did the monstrosity come from? My light was green—had been for long enough that I wasn't the first to go through the intersection.

I swerved, but there was nowhere to go, my reaction too slow.

Metal screamed as it hit, caught, tore. I screamed, too, as my car spun and I slammed forward in my seat. The belt held even as I was flung back, then across the small compartment, hitting my head on the passenger seat. The airbag shot forward, white powder spraying forth as the seat belt strained against my chest, but the spinning didn't stop. More crunching metal as my once-trusty Honda slammed into another—the same?—vehicle. I screamed again as something else slammed into my car. Horns blared.

All the lights inside my car flashed brightly before blinking out.

Ibeyi's soulful music muted, crackled, then poured too sharp from the speakers. Another smash of metal against metal. From the back, maybe. I wasn't sure. Bits of glass tinkled down, ripping at my hands and arms. A sharp sting settled at my hairline, joining the ache on the other side from where my head had slammed into the seat.

The powder from the airbag filled the small space, clogging my nose, my lungs. I wanted to cough, but my chest hurt. I was going to die in my car. Tonight, of all nights, when I'd just finally figured out my life.

Blackness, faster even than the huge white bumper, swallowed me. The faintest trickle of something slid into my ear.

I woke with a scream building in my throat. The one I wasn't sure I'd uttered then, in my car, during the last crash of vehicle-to-vehicle.

"You're okay. Hear me, Evie?"

Marilyn. I turned my head, my eyes struggling to focus. Not easy to do. The hit to the head—the first one against the passenger seat—probably caused my concussion. I'd hit my head at least one more time, but the first one…No wonder my stomach was gurgling with angry intent, and my head was pounding worse than a deep bass beat.

"What happened?" Not exactly what I meant to ask, but my mind rolled over like an otter at sea. Slow, balancing on the small waves. I moaned softly, closing my still unfocused eyes.

"Evangeline? Look at me, honey."

I forced my eyes to unglue and turned my head a little. There she was. My savior. Her dark skin was puckered between her thin, black brows. Her eyes were bloodshot, making the brown of her irises stand out even further. "You were in a car accident, honey."

"Bad one. Head-on," I said. I wanted to raise my hands to my ears to clamp out the sound, but I couldn't. I wouldn't be able to block the sound of metal being ripped from its chassis, the violent shove of my body into the seat belt, then the harder slam back of the airbag hitting me in the face.

I hurt everywhere.

"Yes. Real bad." Marilyn dropped her head and I stared at her thick black hair threaded with gray. "They pulled you out with those jaws things. Popped what little was left of your car open to get to you. The engine didn't blow because it was on the road ten feet behind the rest of your Civic."

"Guess it's good that you made me purchase such a safe car, huh?"

Marilyn shook her head, her mouth set in a firm line as the fear slowly leached from her dark eyes.

"I'm going to be fine, Mama M," I said. I wasn't sure, but she needed the reassurance.

Marilyn squeezed my fingers tightly. "You will be, honey. And thank the sweet Lord for that."

"I love you." I'd never actually told her that before. I should have, years ago. But the words were tricky. My birth mother had said them to her boyfriends, often. Never once to me. Not even when she was healthy, and I was safe.

She dipped her head. "Not as much as I love you, child," she rasped. Clearing her throat, she raised her head and met my gaze. "Rest up now, honey child. I need you well."

I sighed, wanting to nod but my head was too heavy, my eyelids pressed shut once again.

Marilyn had been in my life since high school, more now that I was in college. She was the one constant I could count on—the one person in my life who actually cared. Meeting her had been a fluke. Both the first and the second time. But Marilyn had acquired me, as she did all her little chicks, and I was forever grateful for whoever or whatever made us meet.

———◆———

I wasn't sure how long I'd slept, but the intensity of the pain woke me. My chest and ribs ached so much each breath was a study in willpower. Tears formed in my eyes and I couldn't stop their flow down my cheeks.

"Oh, honey. How long have you been awake?" Concern flowed through Marilyn's words.

The silence was shattered by my sharp, hissing breaths that fought cannula forcing oxygen into my nose. The smell was foreign, and I choked, causing my lungs to spasm and the pain to spike to another level of excruciating. Footsteps pattered across the floor and someone raised my wrist, taking my pulse.

"She been awake long?" the light, female voice asked.

"I don't think so, but she's definitely in pain."

Papers rustled. "The doctor said we could up the meds if she was in pain. I'll do that now to see if we can get her comfortable. Did you hear me, Evangeline? I'm going to increase your pain medication. You have two broken ribs and we've reinflated your lung. That's why you're in so much pain right now."

I tried to nod to let her know I'd hurt, but I think I just moaned and scrunched my eyes tighter.

"That should help," the nurse said.

"Any word on the family?" Marilyn asked, her voice low.

"You know I'm not supposed to answer that, Marilyn."

"Sue already told me the doctors had to remove the girl's spleen."

"Sue isn't supposed to talk to you either." This time, censure filled in the spaces between her words.

"She and I have been friends for nearly thirty years. Please, Marcy, I'm worried about that little girl. Evie will be, too, once she's able to think coherently."

"I don't know why I thought I could stand up to your manipulation."

"You can't. And before you tell me it's none of my business, I care a doggone lot about what happens."

"The girl has some internal bleeding we're monitoring," Marcy said. "The doctors are still in OR with the mom."

Marilyn's voice dropped even lower. "What's her chance?"

"From what I saw, not good."

Oh, God. The accident. That vehicle—the one with the big white bumper—must have carried a family. No one mentioned the father. Had he been in the car? The mother—chances not good. She was like me, that little girl with her broken arm and no spleen. Like me because my mom left me, too. First to drugs, then to the parade of men. Gone when I needed her most.

My thoughts fragmented and I couldn't hold them together anymore, but tears continued to leak from under my lashes.